epic katha

epic katha

Stories from the Vedas, Puranas, Upanishads, Ramayana, Mahabharata and Folklore

Deepam Chatterjee

EMBASSY BOOKS
www.embassybooks.in

First Indian Edition,
Published in 2025 by:
Embassy Book Distributors
120, Great Western Building, Maharashtra Chamber of
Commerce Lane, Fort, Mumbai 400 023, India
Tel: (+9122) -30967415, 22819546
Email: info@embassybooks.in
www.embassybooks.in

ISBN: 978-81-19727-31-5

Distribution Centres:
Mumbai, Ahmedabad, Bangalore, Kolkata, Chennai, Hyderabad,
New Delhi, Pune

Cover Design by Rishikumar Thakur for Embassy Book Distributors
Cover & Inside Illustrations by Onkar Fondekar

Printed & bound in India by Thomson Press India Ltd.

To My Parents

Manjushree and Varun

You give life to my stories
and
bring my stories to life

Table of Contents

Introduction **xi**

Preface **xv**

***Nāsadiya Sūkta*: The Hymn of Creation** **xix**

Part I: The Vedas **1**

1. *Indra* Slays *Vritra* 3
2. *Bhrigu's* Sacrifice: A Tale of Cosmic Renewal 9
3. The Birth of *Agni* 13
4. The *Āshwins* Rescue *Bhūjyu* 17
5. The Birth of *Purusha* 23
6. The Marriage of *Sūryā* and *Soma* 29
7. *Saramā*: Retriever of the Stolen Cows 33

Part II: The Upanishads **37**

8. *Svetaketū* and the Banyan Seed 39
9. The Dance of the Five Fires 47
10. *Janashruti* Encounters *Raikva* 53
11. *Satyakāma* Gains Wisdom 59
12. *Yama* Enlightens *Nachiketā* 67
13. The Five Awakenings of *Bhrigu* 73

Part III: The Bhāgavata Purāna 77

14. The Chastisement of Sage *Durvāsā* 79
15. The Trials of *Prahlāda* 87
16. *Krishna* Dances on the Hoods of *Kāliyā* 93
17. *Muchukunda* Incinerates *Kālayavana* 99
18. The Emancipation of *Gajendra* 103
19. *Krishna* Lifts *Govardhan* Hill 109

Part IV: The Devi Bhāgavatam 113

20. *Ādi Shakti* Creates the Trinity 115
21. The Slaying of *Madhu* and *Kaitabha* 121
22. *Devi* Humbles *Vindhya* 125
23. The Redemption of *Subāhu* 131
24. *Arjuna* Invokes *Devi* 134
25. *Devi* Triumphs over *Asura Durgam* 141

Part V: The Shiva Purāna 147

26. The Infinite Fire Pillar 149
27. The Ashes of Eternity 155
28. *Kāmadeva's* Supreme Sacrifice 159
29. The Lord of Beggars 165
30. The Eternal Dancer 171
31. The Lord of the Locks 175
32. The Blue-Throated Saviour 181

Part VI: Other Purānas 185

33. The Emergence of *Harihara* 187
34. The Princess Who Travelled across Time 191
35. *Shiva* Halts *Kāli's* Rampage 197

36. *Agastya* Drinks the Ocean 203
37. *Svāhā* and *Agni* Fall in Love 211
38. *Dhruva*: The Eternal Star 215
39. The Shadow Wife 221

Part VII: The Rāmāyana 227
40. *Chand Saudāgar* and *Hanumān* 229
41. The Wrath of *Sitā* 235
42. The Boatman Who Washed *Rāma's* Feet 241
43. *Varuna* Faces the Wrath of *Rāma* 247
44. *Rāma* Meets *Shiva* 253
45. The Squirrel's Stripes 259

Part VIII: The Mahābhārata 263
46. The Daughter of Fire 265
47. *Sudyumna* and the Enchanted Forest 271
48. The Demon Eater 277
49. The Lake-Dwelling *Yaksha* 283
50. The King Who Bore a Son 291
51. The First Bittersweet Romance 295
52. *Navagunjara*: The Many Within the One 303

Acknowledgements 312
Glossary 314

Introduction

Storytelling has been central to human civilisation since time immemorial. Across cultures and epochs, stories have served not only as entertainment but as repositories of wisdom, tools for teaching, and bridges to understanding the mysteries of life. Within the tradition of Hinduism, stories hold a specially exalted place. They are seen not merely as tales but as carriers of profound truths—truths that transcend the limits of reason and logic, truths that can be experienced only in the heart and soul of the listener.

The narratives contained in Hindu scriptures are unparalleled in their richness and depth. They are not confined to one text or genre but span a vast corpus of literature that includes the Vedas, Upanishads, Purānas, and the great epics—the Rāmāyana and the Mahābhārata. Together, these works constitute an ocean of wisdom that has been drawn upon for thousands of years by sages, poets, and common folk alike.

In the Hindu tradition, storytelling is seen as a sacred act. It is not merely the telling of events or the recounting of history but a way of transmitting knowledge, values, and spiritual insight. The stories are crafted to engage the listener on multiple levels—intellectually, emotionally, and spiritually. On the surface, they may appear to be simple tales of gods, kings, and sages. But as one delves deeper, the layers of meaning begin to unfold, revealing profound philosophical truths and pathways to self-realisation.

These stories, and countless others like them, are more than allegories or parables. They are vehicles for inner transformation. They challenge us to look beyond the surface of life, to question our assumptions, and to seek the deeper truths that lie hidden beneath the veil of appearances.

The power of Hindu storytelling lies in its universality. Although these tales are deeply rooted in the culture and philosophy of India, their themes resonate with people of all backgrounds and beliefs. The struggles of heroes, the dilemmas of kings, the wisdom of sages, and the mysteries of the cosmos are not confined to any one culture or era. They speak to the universal human experience, to the aspirations and challenges that define our lives. This book, *Epic Kathā: Stories from the Vedas, Puranas, Upanishads, Ramayana, Mahabharata and Folklore,* is a testament to the enduring relevance of these narratives.

One of the most remarkable aspects of Hindu storytelling is its integration of the cosmic and the personal. The tales of the gods, such as Indra slaying Vritra to release the waters, are metaphors for inner battles. Vritra, the demon-serpent who hoards the rivers, represents the forces of stagnation and ignorance that must be overcome to restore the flow of life and wisdom. Similarly,

Nachiketā's encounter with Yama, the god of death, is not just a story about mortality but a profound exploration of the nature of the self and the ultimate truth of existence.

In a world increasingly dominated by materialism and division, these ancient tales offer a counterbalance. They invite us to see the unity that underlies diversity, to recognise the sacred in the mundane, and to live with compassion and awareness. Each story is a microcosm of the larger philosophical and spiritual worldview of Hindu thought. The Vedic hymns, the Upanishadic dialogues, the myths of the Purānas, and the epic battles of the Rāmāyana and the Mahābhārata are not isolated texts but interconnected threads of a single, grand narrative. Together, they form a mosaic of human experience, divine wisdom, and cosmic truth.

As you turn the pages of this book, I encourage you to approach these stories with an open heart and a curious mind. Let them speak to you, not just as ancient texts but as living, breathing guides to life. Allow them to challenge your assumptions, ignite your imagination, and inspire your spirit.

The beauty of Hindu storytelling lies in its ability to grow with us. Each time we return to these tales, we discover new meanings and new connections. They are like rivers that change their course over time, yet always flow towards the same ocean of truth.

Preface

When I first set out to write *Epic Kathā: Stories from the Vedas, Puranas, Upanishads, Ramayana, Mahabharata and Folklore,* I did not fully comprehend the journey I was embarking on. The idea came to life during a series of vibrant discussions with my publisher, Sohin Lakhani of Embassy Books, whose enthusiasm for storytelling matched my own, and my editor, Aruna Joshi, whose insights helped shape this work into what it is today. Their encouragement and belief in the power of these tales made this book possible.

The seed for this project was planted in my constant fascination with the timeless stories of Hindu scriptures. I have always marvelled at their capacity to transcend time and space, to speak as much to a contemporary audience as they did to the ancients. These tales, with their layers of meaning and profound wisdom, are not just the inheritance of *Bhāratvarsha* but treasures of humanity itself.

I remember the joy and awe I experienced whilst recounting these stories to friends, family, and readers, including Sohin, who has become a close friend—mainly because of our regular story sessions. I often see my listeners' eyes light up, not just because of the narrative, but also on account of the deep truths these tales reveal about the human condition. It is this very response that has inspired me to compile these stories into this book, hoping to share the same wonder with a wider audience.

This collection is not exhaustive, nor does it claim to be. It is a humble attempt to retell some of the most poignant and powerful stories from the Hindu scriptures, to breathe life into the Vedas, Upanishads, Purānas, and epics like the Rāmāyana and the Mahābhārata. Whilst some of the tales may be familiar, others are less well-known, waiting to surprise and enlighten the reader.

Amongst my favourites is the hymn of creation, the *Nāsadiya Sūkta*, which dares to ask the ultimate questions about existence and offers no definitive answers. Its beauty lies in its openness, its humility in the face of the great unknown. Another tale, that of Svetaketū and the banyan seed, reveals the profound truth that the infinite resides within the finite, that the essence of all existence is within us.

Writing this book was as much a journey inward as it was a scholarly endeavour. These stories, whilst rooted in mythology and philosophy, also hold up a mirror to our lives. They speak of courage, humility, devotion, and the eternal search for truth. They remind us of the struggles and triumphs that define the human experience, urging us to look beyond the surface and seek the deeper essence of life.

Working on this project, I often thought of my own childhood, filled with wonder and questions. My parents, Manjushree and Varun, are the true inspirations behind this book, for they planted in me the love for storytelling and the wisdom of the ages.

To my readers, this book is my offering to you. It is a bridge to the ancient past, a way to reconnect with the wisdom of the sages and the enduring truths of our tradition. I hope that these stories inspire you to reflect, question, and discover your own connection to the eternal.

You will find in these pages not just tales of gods, sages, and cosmic events, but reflections of your own journey—the battles you fight, the wisdom you seek, and the truths you hold dear.

As you turn these pages, I invite you to lose yourself in the magic of these tales, and in doing so, discover yourself anew.

Nāsadiya Sūkta: The Hymn of Creation

The *Nāsadiya Sūkta* reflects the Vedic tradition's deep reverence for the unknown and the unknowable, honouring the questions as much as the answers. The hymn does not declare certainty. It leaves creation's origin open to interpretation, an eternal mystery that invites wonder.

In the beginning,
there was neither existence nor non-existence.
There was no air, no sky, no realm above,
nor was there anything below.
Darkness was wrapped in darkness,
an indistinct and formless void.

There was neither death nor immortality,
no light nor the absence of it.
The endless expanse was shrouded
in a profound stillness.
All that existed was an unfathomable,
deep abyss of potential,
hidden in unmanifested waters.

In that timeless moment,
a stirring arose—

a deep, inherent force within the void.
Desire was born,
the first seed of consciousness,
an impulse to bring forth creation.
The sages, reflecting upon this,
understood it as the primal cord
binding the unmanifest to the manifest.

Who knows how
this vast universe came into being?
Where did it emerge from, and why?
Did the gods themselves know?
They were born after creation,
arising from its mystery, not before it.

Perhaps it arose from nothingness,
or perhaps from some eternal principle.
The waters, formless and indistinct,
may have carried within them
the seed of all creation.
The truth of this remains veiled,
an enigma beyond mortal comprehension.

He who oversees all, the Supreme Being
beyond time and space—
Did He know how creation unfolded?
Or did He, too, watch the mystery unfold,
a witness to the self-becoming of the universe?

Even now, the question lingers:
Did creation emerge through an act of will,
or was it born of its own accord?
The answers remain elusive,
shrouded in the same profound silence
that preceded existence itself.

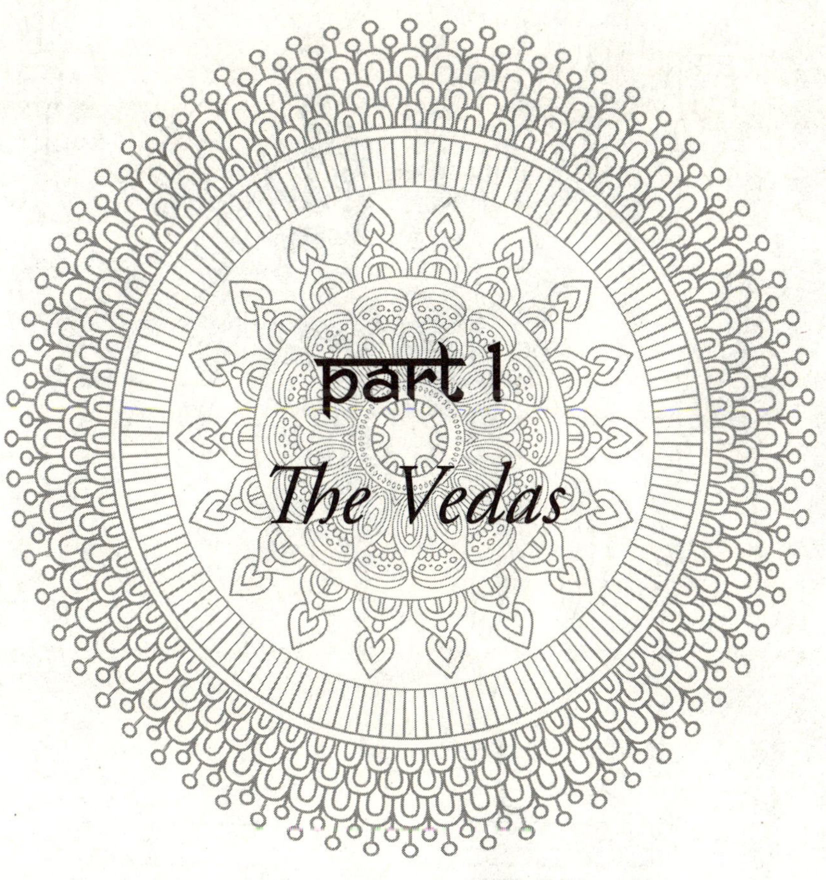

part 1

The Vedas

Indra Slays Vritra

From The Rig Veda

The earth lay still under a pall of silence. A silence so deep, it seemed as though time itself had stopped to mourn. Rivers that once danced and sparkled in the sunlight now lay dry, their beds cracked like the skin of ancient giants. The air, thick and oppressive, carried the scent of decay and despair. Across the lands, crops lay withered under the relentless sun, their golden hues turned to ashen grey. Forests stood lifeless, their leaves crumbling to dust, and even the wind, once vibrant with whispers, was now still.

At the heart of this desolation, atop a mountain shrouded in perpetual gloom, *Vritra*, the demon-serpent, was coiled. His body, a labyrinth of scales as black as the abyss, each scale gleaming with a faint, malevolent sheen. His eyes, twin embers of hatred, pierced the suffocating darkness. Around him lay the waters of the world, bound in chains of shadow and stone, their gentle murmurs silenced.

From the mortal plains below, the cries of the suffering rose like a dark hymn to the heavens. The people, frail and broken, knelt in fields turned to dust, their hands raised in desperate prayer. 'O Gods, hear us,' they pleaded. 'Deliver us from this deathly drought. Restore the waters and grant us life!'

In the celestial assembly, the Gods gathered under the luminous dome of the heavens. Their faces were grave, their eyes reflecting the anguish of the world below.

Agni, the fire god, his flames subdued to a sombre glow, spoke first. 'The people suffer. The rivers sleep in their stony graves. It is Vritra, the great hoarder, who holds the waters captive.' His voice, though calm, carried the weight of ages. 'Without the waters, the earth falters, and with it, all life. *Indra*! You alone possess the strength to shatter his bonds.'

At these words, all eyes turned to Indra, the warrior King of the Gods. He rose from his seat, his form resplendent with divine energy. The *Vajra*, his thunderbolt, rested at his side, its edges humming with dormant power. His gaze, fierce as the midday sun, swept across the assembly.

'I shall face him!' Indra declared, his voice ringing with unshakeable resolve.

Agni stepped forward, bearing a chalice of *Soma Rasa*, the drink of immortality and strength. The liquid within shimmered with hues of gold and crimson, as though it held the essence of fire and sunlight.

'Drink, Indra!' Agni said, his voice a low murmur. 'Let the

Soma Rasa fortify your spirit and amplify your might.'

Indra accepted the goblet, lifting it to his lips. As the first drop touched his tongue, a surge of power coursed through him. His veins burned with the heat of a thousand suns, and his muscles coiled with newfound strength. He drained the chalice, the glow of the Soma Rasa radiating from his skin, and rose to his full height.

'The time has come!' Indra said, his voice echoing through the hall like rolling thunder.

Grasping the Vajra, he mounted his celestial chariot, its wheels forged of fire and its steeds shimmering like clouds at dawn. As the chariot descended from the heavens, the skies grew dark, and the air vibrated with the promise of a coming storm.

Far below, Vritra stirred. The serpent uncoiled, his body stretching across the mountain, a river of shadow and malice. He sensed the approach of his adversary, and a low, guttural growl escaped his maw. 'So, the God-king comes,' Vritra hissed, his voice like the grinding of millstones. 'He seeks to challenge me? Let him try, and I shall show him the futility of his arrogance.'

The stage was set for a battle that would shake the heavens and the earth.

Indra's chariot approached, the Vajra blazing in his hand. The serpent's laughter rumbled across the land, but the God was undeterred. The clash of divine and demonic forces was imminent, and the fate of the world hung in the balance.

'Vritra!' Indra's voice boomed across the skies. 'Release the waters, or prepare to meet your doom!'

The chariot raced across the grey skies like a bolt of lightning, and the heavens trembled with anticipation of the coming storm. Indra's horses, shining like the dawn, tore through the sky with unrelenting speed, their hooves sparking as they raced toward the mountain where Vritra, the serpent, lay in wait. The air around them crackled with the energy of the impending battle.

At the foot of the mountain, Vritra's colossal form rose from the gloom. His immense, serpent-like body twisted and coiled around the peak, blocking the sky, the very air thick with his oppressive presence. His eyes, burning like two hellish embers, watched Indra's approach with cold malice.

'Foolish God,' Vritra hissed, his voice like a low rumble that shook the earth beneath Indra's feet. 'You think you can defeat me? Your weapons are but toys against my might! I have held these waters captive for ages, and I will never yield to you!'

Indra, unflinching, raised the Vajra high. The thunderbolt pulsed with radiant light, and the air shimmered with its divine power.

'The time for your tyranny is over, Vritra,' Indra proclaimed, his voice a rumble that echoed across the heavens. 'The waters will be freed, and the world will know the light of life once more.'

Vritra struck first, unleashing a torrent of dark, venomous flames that erupted from his gaping mouth, scorching the very air. The blast surged toward Indra like a wave of fire, consuming everything in its path. But Indra was swift. He raised the Vajra in a mighty arc, and with a deafening crack of thunder, the bolt cleaved through the flames, scattering them like ash in the wind.

Vritra roared in fury, his massive tail whipping through the air, smashing boulders and sending tremors through the ground. The serpent's body moved with terrifying speed, and yet, his coils seemed endless, his reach stretching across the horizon. With every lash, the earth trembled and the sky darkened further. But Indra, fuelled by the divine Soma Rasa, was undeterred.

He closed the distance, his chariot soaring between the strikes, and with a warrior's cry, he hurled the Vajra with all his might. The thunderbolt flew through the air like a comet, its golden light cutting through the darkness. Vritra raised his head, his jaws gaping wide, ready to swallow the bolt in an act of defiance.

But the Vajra struck true. With a resounding crash, the thunderbolt pierced Vritra's skull, shattering his armoured hide as if it were brittle clay, before returning to Indra's outstretched hand. A moment of stillness fell over the battlefield, as if the world itself held its breath. Then, with a deafening roar, the serpent's body fell to the ground in great, crumbling heaps, and with it, the darkness that had gripped the land for so long.

From the broken mountain, the imprisoned waters surged forth in a mighty flood, cascading down like rivers freed from their chains. The world, once parched and barren, was reborn.

Indra stood tall amidst the rushing waters, his Vajra glowing brightly in his hand. The rivers roared in triumph, filling the dry channels and nourishing the earth once more. The skies began to clear, their dark clouds dissipating as the sun's rays pierced through, casting golden light over the rejuvenated land.

As the waters flooded the plains, the Gods gathered in the heavens, their voices rising in joyous celebration. The people below, their faces upturned to the sky, raised their arms in gratitude, singing praises to Indra for his victory. 'Hail Indra, the liberator of the waters! Hail the mighty King of the Gods!'

Indra, his heart still burning with the energy of his divine triumph, turned his gaze to the heavens. His voice was steady and resolute as he spoke:

'Let this be a reminder to all. The forces of darkness may rise, but the light of truth will always prevail.'

The divine warriors returned to their celestial halls, their hearts lifted by the victory. Indra's name would echo through the ages, a symbol of strength and justice, and the waters—freed once again—would flow for eternity, bringing life and sustenance to all.

Bhrigu's Sacrifice: A Tale of Cosmic Renewal

From The Atharva Veda

In the vast, unbroken silence of the cosmos, a shadow began to grow over the mortal realms. The sacred fires on earth, once vibrant with offerings, began to dwindle. Mortals, distracted by worldly desires, had forgotten their sacred duties. Without their rituals, the divine bond between the heavens and the earth weakened. The Gods felt their strength ebb, and the balance of creation teetered dangerously.

In the celestial assembly, *Agni*, the ever-burning flame, spoke with urgency. 'The mortals' neglect has darkened our path. The cosmic wheel falters. A sacrifice of supreme purity must reignite the connection between realms.'

The Gods nodded in solemn agreement. 'Only *Bhrigu*, the sage of unwavering devotion, can perform such a *yajna*,' declared *Indra*, the King of the Gods.

Bhrigu, renowned for his wisdom and penance, lived in a forest of eternal serenity. When the Gods arrived, their luminous forms brightened his humble *āshram*. The sage, seated beneath a grand banyan tree, rose to greet them.

'Honoured Gods,' he said, his voice calm as a still river, 'to what do I owe this visit?'

Agni, his fiery form radiating intensity, stepped forward. 'O great seer, the worlds falter as mortals have turned away from the sacred rites. We beseech you to perform a sacrifice so pure and powerful that it renews the bond between mortals and Gods.'

Bhrigu's gaze turned inward. 'A sacrifice of such magnitude demands precision, purity, and the will of the cosmos itself. I shall prepare the yajna and invoke the divine forces.'

Bhrigu's preparations were meticulous. The sacrificial altar was constructed according to ancient Vedic geometry, its dimensions aligned with the cosmos. Golden *kusha* grass adorned its edges, and sacred *ghee* was brought forth in vessels carved with Vedic symbols.

As twilight descended, Bhrigu stood before the altar, his hands lifted to the heavens. He began the chant, his voice resonating with powerful *mantras*. The words seemed to echo beyond the physical realm, stirring the elements themselves.

'Agni, carrier of offerings, I call upon you to witness this yajna. Accept these gifts and restore the cycle of creation.'

The fire on the altar blazed to life. Flames rose, dancing in intricate patterns as if responding to the sage's incantations.

The wind, once still, swirled around the grove, carrying the sacred smoke skyward.

As the offering reached its zenith, the flames grew brighter, their light piercing the heavens. Agni himself appeared, his fiery form towering above the altar.

'Bhrigu!' he said, his voice resonating like a thunderclap, 'your devotion has kindled the cosmic fire. The Gods accept your sacrifice, but the final offering must transcend the material. What will you give?'

Without hesitation, Bhrigu responded, 'I offer the essence of my penance and devotion, the very core of my being.'

The fire surged, and a celestial energy emanated from the altar. The Gods in heaven felt their strength renewed as the yajna bridged the realms. Rivers flowed once more, crops sprouted across the lands, and mortals felt an awakening of their spiritual consciousness.

When the flames finally subsided, Bhrigu stood exhausted but serene. The grove was bathed in an otherworldly glow, a testament to the power of the yajna.

Indra descended from the heavens, his golden chariot gleaming. 'Bhrigu, your sacrifice has restored the order of creation. The bond between mortals and the divine is renewed. For your devotion, your name shall be remembered for all time.'

Bhrigu bowed. 'The yajna is but a reminder that balance is fragile and requires the effort of all—mortal and divine alike. Let this serve as a call for unity and devotion.'

Bhrigu's sacrifice became a cornerstone of Vedic tradition, inspiring future generations to uphold their sacred duties. The Atharva Veda immortalised his act, celebrating the power of pure intent and devotion in maintaining cosmic harmony.

The sacred fire continues to burn in the hearts of those who listen, a reminder that even in moments of despair, the divine bond can be rekindled through unwavering devotion.

The Birth of Agni

From the Rig Veda

The world lay cloaked in an ancient darkness, a primordial void where the spark of life struggled to take hold. The gods, restless in the stillness, convened in the ethereal realm, their radiant forms casting faint glimmers across the cosmic expanse. A solution was needed, for light and warmth were absent, and the realms shivered in the cold embrace of the void.

'Who shall be the light-bringer?' asked *Varuna*, his voice as deep and resonant as the oceans. His gaze turned to the assembly. 'Who among us will ignite the fire of existence and offer life its vital spark?'

The deities murmured, their celestial voices like the rustling of stars. It was then that *Agni*, the divine fire, stirred within the hidden folds of the universe. He had not yet taken form but lingered as a dormant energy, waiting to be called forth.

Aditi, the boundless mother of all, sensed the growing need.

She whispered her will to the heavens: 'The time has come for the birth of fire, the essence of life and the carrier of offerings.' She stretched her arms across the void, her hands shaping the unmanifest into being.

In the quiet stillness, the first spark of Agni emerged. It was faint at first—a glimmer of light no larger than a firefly. But it grew rapidly, glowing brighter, until the brilliance rivalled the sun. The gods stepped back in awe as the fiery child roared to life, his flames reaching upward like a lion unfurling its mane.

Agni's voice rang out, youthful and unyielding. 'I am born of this cosmos, from the womb of the waters and the embrace of the earth. I shall be the bridge between mortals and immortals, the bearer of offerings and the sustainer of life.'

Agni's birth was not without challenges. His flames surged wildly, threatening to consume everything in their path. The gods, awestruck, approached cautiously. Indra, the wielder of thunder, stepped forward.

'Agni,' Indra called, his voice firm yet gentle, 'thou art the spark that shall sustain us all. But thy power is great and must be tempered. Let us grant thee forms to serve every realm.'

Agni nodded, his flames pulsing in rhythm with his understanding. 'Give me my purpose, O gods, and I shall fulfil it with devotion.'

Varuna spoke next: 'Thou shalt dwell in the sacred altars,

carrying the offerings of mortals to the heavens. Thy flames shall be a bridge, uniting the worlds.'

Mitra added, 'Thy warmth shall nurture life, bringing light to the dark and heat to the cold. Thou shalt be the hearth-fire, a companion to all who seek shelter.'

Saraswati, the goddess of wisdom, smiled upon him. 'And thy knowledge, Agni, shall illuminate the minds of mortals. Thou shalt be the fire within—the inspiration, the vitality, the sacred spark of thought.'

Agni took on three forms to fulfil his purpose. First, he descended into the waters, where he became latent energy, hidden yet potent. His second form ignited upon the earth, where he burned brightly in altars, forests, and hearths. Finally, he rose into the heavens as the celestial fire, shining as the sun and the stars.

The *rishis*, ancient seers, beheld his divine form and sang in praise:

'Born of the waters, the earth, and the heavens,
Agni, the bearer of offerings, thou dost rise.
Thy flames dost consume, yet thou dost sustain,
O divine fire, the bridge to the skies.'

Having taken his forms, Agni addressed the assembly. His flames were steady now, controlled yet powerful. 'I accept my roles, O gods, for I am the essence of life itself. To mortals, I shall bring warmth, light, and the sacred connection to the divine. To the gods, I shall carry their offerings and their prayers.'

The gods rejoiced, their voices blending into a hymn of creation. The realms, once dark and cold, now glowed with the warmth of Agni's presence. Rivers sparkled, trees bore fruit, and mortals gathered around hearths, their songs of gratitude carried upward on wisps of smoke.

Thus, Agni, the eternal flame, was born—a symbol of life, sacrifice, and the eternal connection between mortals and the divine.

The Āshwins Rescue Bhūjyu

From The Rig Veda

In a time when gods walked the heavens and men sang their praises on earth, there ruled a king of wisdom and valour named *Tugra*. King Tugra was famous for his exploration of unclaimed territories. Tugra's son, *Bhūjyu*, was as fearless as the sea winds, a youth of fiery ambition who sought glory beyond the horizons. Tugra assigned his young son and naval commander Bhūjyu to a challenging mission—to sail across vast and uncharted oceans to secure wealth and expand the kingdom's influence.

Bhūjyu, eager to prove his valour, embarked on this daring voyage with a fleet of ships and loyal sailors. However, the expedition was fraught with danger. As the fleet ventured into deeper waters, the environment turned hostile. Dark omens appeared—clouds thickened unnaturally, winds shifted unpredictably, and the once-clear seas churned ominously.

The winds howled like a pack of ravenous wolves, and the waves rose like monstrous giants. Bhūjyu's crew fought valiantly to tame the raging tempest, but the sea showed no mercy. The ship was torn asunder, its mighty timbers splintering like dry twigs under the onslaught of the storm. Bhūjyu and his men were cast into the abyssal depths, their cries lost in the roar of the maelstrom.

Adrift amidst the wreckage of his ship, Bhūjyu struggled against the crushing embrace of the ocean as he clung to a fragment of his shattered vessel. Salt-laden winds whipped his face as the storm dragged him further into the abyssal expanse.

For days, he drifted aimlessly, battered by the waves and scorched by the sun. His strength waned, and despair crept into his heart. It was in this moment of utter helplessness that Bhūjyu cried out to the heavens, calling upon the gods to save him from certain death.

'O gods who dwell above!' he cried, his voice raw with desperation. 'If ever I have offered prayers or sacrifices worthy of your grace, I beg you now: deliver me from this watery grave!'

His words carried upon the winds, rising through the storm's fury, and reached the celestial realms. There, in the divine assembly, the gods listened. Among them were the *Āshwins*—the twin horsemen, celestial physicians, and bringers of swift salvation.

The Āshwins, always attuned to the suffering of mortals, heard Bhūjyu's plea. *Nāsatya* and *Dasra*, as they were also called, were radiant beings with golden chariots that blazed like the first light of dawn. Their steeds, swift as thought, carried them across the heavens faster than the blink of an eye.

'Brother,' said Nāsatya, his voice resolute yet gentle, 'a noble soul is in peril. We must act.'

'Indeed!' replied Dasra, his eyes shining with determination. 'Let us descend and rescue him from the clutches of the raging sea.'

They mounted their resplendent chariot, and with a flick of their reins, they descended towards the mortal plane. The storm seemed to falter at their approach, as if the elements themselves bowed before their divine might.

Bhūjyu, his strength waning, felt a warmth enveloping him. He looked up to see the Āshwins, their forms radiant and their chariot cutting through the storm like a blade of light.

'Fear not, Bhūjyu,' said Nāsatya, his voice a balm to the prince's despair. 'We have heard your plea and have come to deliver you.'

Dasra extended his hand, and with a firm yet gentle grip, he pulled Bhūjyu into their chariot. The celestial steeds neighed triumphantly as they soared above the waves, the storm receding in their wake.

'Rest now,' Dasra said, placing a comforting hand on Bhūjyu's shoulder. 'You are safe with us.'

The chariot climbed higher, the sea shrinking below until it was but a glimmer on the horizon. Bhūjyu, though exhausted, gazed in awe at the splendour around him. The Āshwins' chariot was adorned with golden filigree, and its interior shimmered with the light of a thousand suns.

As the chariot sped towards safety, the Āshwins spoke to Bhūjyu.

'You, son of Tugra, have been spared this day not by chance but by the merit of your devotion,' said Nāsatya.

Dasra added, 'The gods watch over those who honour them. You have faced the fury of the sea and survived. Now you shall be returned to your people, who await your triumphant return.'

Their words filled Bhūjyu with gratitude and humility. 'Great Āshwins,' he said, his voice trembling, 'you have saved me from certain death. How can I repay such divine kindness?'

'Live with honour and serve the world with justice,' Nāsatya replied. 'That is the only repayment the gods seek.'

The Āshwins guided their chariot back to Bhūjyu's homeland, the kingdom of Tugra. The skies parted in welcome as the celestial chariot descended upon the palace grounds. King Tugra, who had mourned his son as lost, rushed out to meet them. His eyes widened in disbelief and joy as he beheld Bhūjyu, alive and well, stepping from the chariot.

'My son!' Tugra exclaimed, embracing Bhūjyu. 'The gods have shown their mercy this day!'

Bhūjyu turned to the Āshwins, who stood radiant in the morning light. 'Father,' he said, his voice filled with reverence, 'it is the Āshwins who saved me from the depths of the ocean. To them, I owe my life.'

The king and his court fell to their knees, offering prayers and hymns of gratitude to the twin gods. The Āshwins, ever modest, simply nodded.

'Remember,' Dasra said, 'divine intervention is rare and precious. Live your life in a manner worthy of the grace you have received.'

With that, they mounted their chariot and ascended into the heavens.

The Birth of Purusha

From The Rig Veda

Before time began, before the Sun lit the heavens or the earth bore life, there was only the great void. Endless, formless, and immeasurable, it stretched beyond comprehension. In this vast emptiness, the seed of creation stirred—a presence, infinite and eternal, waiting to awaken.

This presence was *Purusha*, the cosmic being, encompassing all that was, is, and will ever be. His form spanned the Universe, reaching beyond the farthest stars, his essence encompassing the mortal and the divine, the seen and the unseen.

In the twilight of the void, the Gods convened. *Agni*, the flame eternal, flickered with restless energy. Indra, the lord of thunder, stood resolute, his gaze fixed on the endless darkness. *Varuna*, the keeper of cosmic order, spoke with a voice like the rolling sea.

'The time has come,' Varuna declared, his tone grave. 'The Universe must be born, and with it, the cycles of existence: creation, preservation, and dissolution.'

'How shall it be done?' asked Agni, his flames leaping higher. 'What force can shape the formless void?'

'The sacrifice,' whispered the Gods in unison. 'Purusha, the cosmic being, must give of himself so that the Universe may be woven from his essence.'

The Gods turned their gaze towards Purusha, who existed in serene radiance, his form stretching across all realms. A voice resonated from his being, deep and all-encompassing, 'I am the seed and the soil, the beginning and the end. If the Universe must be born, let it rise from my sacrifice.'

With solemn reverence, the Gods prepared for the great *yajna*—the first and greatest sacrifice. They assembled sacred tools crafted from the primordial elements: wind wove the altar, fire lit the space, and water consecrated it. The chants of the *Purusha Sūkta* reverberated across the void, their vibrations igniting the fires of creation.

'Agni,' *Indra* commanded, 'let the flame carry this offering across realms.'

Agni surged forward, his brilliance illuminating the void. Purusha, in his infinite grace, allowed himself to be divided. His head became the heavens, his feet the earth, and his breath the wind. From his eyes emerged the Sun, and from his mind, the Moon. His blood flowed as the rivers, and his flesh became the fertile soil.

As the Gods chanted, the pieces of Purusha's essence wove together the fabric of existence. The heavens unfurled like a vast canopy, adorned with the stars born from his luminous soul. The earth took form, its mountains rising from his bones, its forests sprouting from his hair.

From Purusha's sacrifice emerged the four *varnas*, the divisions of human society. His mouth gave birth to the *Brahmins*, the keepers of knowledge and sacred rituals. His arms became the *Kshatriyas*, warriors and rulers who would protect and govern. His thighs formed the *Vaishyas*, who would till the land and trade. From his feet arose the *Shudras*, who would labour and support the great foundation of society.

Time began its endless march as the sacrifice reached its zenith. Day and night emerged, weaving the rhythm of existence. The Gods, their purpose fulfilled, gazed upon the newly formed Cosmos with awe.

Varuna spoke, his voice resonant, 'From this sacrifice, the cycle of life and death is born. The yajna is eternal; its echoes will sustain the Cosmos until the end of time.'

Indra raised his thunderbolt, his voice triumphant. 'Let mortals and Gods alike honour this sacrifice, for it is the foundation of all that is.'

Though Purusha had given of himself, he was not diminished. His essence, infinite and indestructible, remained woven into the fabric of creation. In every breath of wind, in every ray of light, in every beat of a mortal heart, Purusha lived on.

The Gods bowed in reverence. 'You are the source, Purusha,' they said, their voices echoing through the Cosmos. 'Your sacrifice is eternal, your presence undying.'

Purusha's voice resounded, gentle yet powerful. 'I am the witness and the participant. Honour the yajna, for it binds all realms. Through its fire, the Universe is born anew.'

The Gods sang praises to Purusha, the eternal being. Their voices carried the sacred verses of the Purusha Sūkta, an eternal testament to the sacrifice that birthed creation:

'A thousand heads hath Purusha,
a thousand eyes, a thousand feet.
He, pervading the earth on every side,
still extends beyond it.
With three-fourths Purusha ascended;
one-fourth of him remains here.
From him was born Viraj,
and Purusha took form thereafter.
From his navel arose the air,
from his head the heavens.
His feet became the earth,
and the regions of space his ears.'

The hymn echoed through the Cosmos, a timeless ode to the infinite being who had given of himself to create all.

The tale of Purusha's sacrifice became the foundation of Vedic thought, encapsulating the interconnectedness of all existence. Every yajna performed by mortals echoes that first cosmic act, reminding humanity of its role within the divine order.

Purusha remains eternal, his essence present in every atom of creation. His sacrifice is celebrated, not as a loss, but as the ultimate act of creation—an undying testament to the unity of all things.

The Marriage of Sūryā and Soma

From The Rig Veda

The heavens buzzed with energy, each divine realm preparing for a momentous occasion: the marriage of *Sūryā*, the radiant daughter of *Sūrya*, with *Soma*, the Moon God. A union ordained by the Gods themselves, it would symbolise the eternal balance of light and shadow.

In the grand halls of the Solar Palace, where rays of light danced upon golden spires, Sūryā stood in quiet anticipation. Her flowing robe shimmered like the first blush of dawn, her eyes like molten amber. She was not merely the daughter of the Sun; she was a Goddess whose destiny was to unite the celestial cycles.

Her father, Sūrya, the Sun God, radiated pride as he addressed the gathered deities. 'Today, my daughter shall wed Soma, the lord of the silvery glow. This union shall bind the heavens and bring balance to all realms. Let all who are gathered here bear witness!'

The Gods, seated upon their jewelled thrones, nodded in solemn agreement. *Savitr*, the divine inspirer, prepared the bridal chariot, a magnificent vessel crafted of thought itself—swift and unyielding. Its steeds, white as starlight, snorted impatiently, eager to traverse the celestial realms.

The time had come. Sūryā stepped into the chariot, her golden form bathing the heavens in brilliance. The *Rishis* and *Devas* sang hymns to guide her journey:

'Swift doth her chariot take flight,
Guided by thought and filled with light.
The Gods do sing with blessings bestowed,
For bride and groom, their fates unfold.'

The *Āshwins*, twin Gods of healing and speed, rode ahead, their celestial steeds blazing a trail across the empyrean. They called out, their voices echoing across the heavens: 'Make way for Sūryā, daughter of the Sun! The bride cometh in all her splendour!'

Below, mortals looked up at the radiant procession, their prayers rising like incense. 'Bless us, O Gods, as light and calm unite,' they murmured, their words carried to the heavens by the wind.

At the end of her journey, Sūryā's chariot slowed. Before her stood Soma, his silvered form glowing with a calm, serene light. The Moon God awaited her in the heart of his palace, where rivers of silver flowed and trees of pearl lined the paths.

Savitr stepped forward, carrying sacred water to bless the

couple. His voice rang out like a hymn: 'From this union shall come the eternal cycles of time—day and night, waxing and waning, the pulse of existence itself.'

The *Rishis* began their invocations, and the Cosmos resonated with their chants:

'As Sun doth greet Moon in the heavenly sphere,
Their union bringeth balance near.
Day and Night in turn dost blend,
The harmony of time shall never end.'

Sūryā and Soma stood before the gathered Gods. With voices steady and resolute, they exchanged vows.

Sūryā: 'I bring light to your calm, strength to your stillness.'

Soma: 'And I temper your blaze with serenity, your brilliance with peace.'

The rishis blessed the couple, their hymns weaving the fabric of the Cosmos:

'May she, fair maiden, with golden glow,
Bringeth prosperity where'er she go.
From their bond the seasons doth arise,
And life doth flourish 'neath sunlit skies.'

As the ceremony concluded, the heavens erupted in jubilation. Stars danced in rhythm, comets streaked across the skies, and the Earth bloomed in response. From this union, the cycles of day and night were set in motion.

The Gods declared: 'Let this union forever guide the world. May their harmony never waver, and may the Cosmos thrive under their eternal rhythm.'

And so, the marriage of Sūryā and Soma became immortalised in the hymns of the *Vedas*, a tale of light and shadow, balance and unity, celebrated by Gods and mortals alike. The Hindu rites of marriage emulate their union to this day.

Saramā: Retriever of The Stolen Cows

From The Rig Veda

In the golden age, the cows of light grazed freely in the heavenly pastures. Their milk nourished the Gods; their presence dispelled darkness across the world. But the malevolent *Panis*, the demonic hoarders of wealth, coveted the divine herd. Under the cover of night, they stole the cows, locking them deep within a stone cave, guarded by walls of gloom.

In the celestial court, the Gods gathered, their faces shadowed with concern. *Indra*, the thunder-wielding King, rose. 'These cows sustain the world,' he declared. 'Without them, life falters. Who among us will find their hiding place?'

All eyes turned to *Saramā*, or *Deva-shuni*, the swift-footed hound of the Gods. Her golden fur glistened as she stepped forward, her gaze unwavering. 'I shall go,' she said, her voice a blend of resolve and reverence.

The journey was arduous. Saramā traversed rugged mountains and endless deserts, guided by an inner light that pierced the darkness. At last, she reached the cave where the Panis jealously guarded their spoils.

'Who comes to disturb us?' the Panis hissed, stepping forward from the shadows. Their eyes glinted like coals.

'I am Saramā, sent by the great Indra,' she replied. 'Return the cows to their rightful place.'

The Panis laughed, their voices echoing through the cavern. 'Why take the risk, Saramā? Join us. We shall share these treasures with you. Gold, food, all will be yours.'

But Saramā stood firm, her eyes flashing in anger. 'I am bound by duty, not greed. Your offers are as empty as your hearts.'

The Panis growled but dared not strike. Saramā turned and raced back to Indra, her feet swift as the wind. 'The cows are hidden in the cave of shadows,' she reported.

Indra rose from his golden throne, his eyes blazing with resolve. The *Vajra*, his thunderbolt forged by the divine artisan *Tvastr*, crackled with power in his grasp. Beside him stood the *Angirasas*, the priest-warriors of celestial wisdom, their chants rising in unison to summon the energies of the Cosmos.

'Today,' Indra declared, his voice reverberating through the heavens, 'we shall reclaim the light and the truth stolen by these wretches. The Panis will know the fury of the Gods!'

With a mighty roar, the assembly of divine forces surged

forward, led by Indra. They crossed vast fields of stars, their celestial chariots streaking across the sky like lightning. As they approached the cave, the air grew heavy with the stench of deceit and hoarded wealth.

The Panis, their dark eyes narrowed, sensed their approach. 'Indra comes,' one of them growled, his voice trembling. 'Fortify the gates! Let the cows remain buried in darkness!'

Indra and his companions reached the mouth of the cave. Shadows curled around them, hissing and snapping like serpents. Indra raised his Vajra high, and a blinding flash of light pierced the gloom. The gates of the cave trembled under its force but did not yield.

The Panis taunted him from within. 'Is this the might of the so-called King of the Gods?' they jeered. 'Your thunderbolt cannot breach our stronghold. Turn back, for this darkness will consume even you!'

But Indra was undeterred. 'Angirasas!' he commanded, 'Invoke the sacred hymns! Let the sound of truth dismantle their lies!'

The priests stepped forward, their voices rising in harmonious chants. Each syllable carried the weight of ancient knowledge, vibrating through the stones. The cave began to quake. Cracks spread across its walls, releasing faint glimmers of the light imprisoned within.

The Panis, now panicking, summoned their own dark forces. Shadows writhed and took shape, lunging at the intruders. Indra met them head-on, the Vajra spinning in his hand like a wheel of fire. Each strike shattered the shadow-beasts, their howls dissolving into the void.

With a deafening roar, Indra unleashed the full power of the Vajra. The thunderbolt tore through the gates, shattering the stone barriers into shards. The cave exploded with light as the imprisoned cows surged forward, their golden forms glowing brighter with each step.

The Panis, now exposed, scrambled to flee, their mocking arrogance replaced by desperate cries. But the Angirasas stood firm, chanting hymns that bound the cowards in place.

One by one, the radiant cows emerged, their presence banishing the last traces of darkness from the land. The earth seemed to exhale, revitalised by their return. Indra stood amidst the luminous herd, his eyes calm but unyielding.

'Let this be a lesson!' he declared, his voice cutting through the silence, 'that the forces of light and truth shall never be chained by greed or deceit.'

The *Angirasas* bowed, their hymns shifting into songs of victory. The divine forces began their triumphant return, the radiant cows leading the procession as beacons of hope.

part 2

The Upanishads

Svetaketū and The Banyan Seed

From The Chhāndogya Upanishad

The sun cast long fingers of golden light over the *āshram* as *Uddālaka Aruni* sat beneath the shade of an ancient banyan tree. The branches stretched outward, their roots descending to the earth in graceful arcs, creating a vast canopy of life. It was a tree as old as memory itself, standing as witness to countless seasons, stories, and souls that had passed beneath its shade. Uddālaka, a sage of gentle demeanour but keen insight, observed the tree with the quiet reverence of one who saw the infinite in the ordinary.

Uddālaka had a son, *Svetaketū*, whom he cherished dearly. Svetaketū was bright and eager, and his father knew that, in time, he would become a worthy bearer of sacred knowledge.

As Svetaketū grew, Uddālaka sensed the time was right for him to begin his journey of formal study. With care and ceremony, he performed the rites to invest his son with the sacred thread, marking his initiation into the pursuit of wisdom.

One day, after the morning rituals, Uddālaka called his son to his side.

'Svetaketū, my son,' he began with a voice both gentle and firm, 'it is time for you to seek knowledge beyond this āshram. You must go to a *gurukula* and live as a student, studying the Vedas under a worthy *guru*. For in our family, none remain unlearnt in these sacred texts.'

Svetaketū bowed respectfully. 'I will go, Father,' he replied, his heart stirred with a mix of eagerness and duty. He left soon after to live in a gurukula, where he spent many years devoted to study, immersing himself in the teachings of the Vedas and the philosophies of the ancients. Under the watchful eye of his guru, he learnt rituals, chants, and the deeper mysteries of the cosmos, and he returned home at the age of twenty-four, confident in his knowledge.

Twelve years went by.

Svetaketū walked into the āshram with his head held high, his demeanour subtly marked by pride. His mastery of the scriptures and the recognition he had earned amongst his peers had given him a new sense of self-importance—perhaps, his father noticed, too much so.

After some days of observing his son's newly acquired proud

bearing, Uddālaka decided it was time to impart a lesson beyond any that Svetaketū had yet encountered. Calling his son to sit with him beneath the shade of the great banyan tree, he regarded him with thoughtful eyes.

'My son,' Uddālaka began, his voice calm but laced with a subtle firmness, 'I see you have returned with great knowledge. You believe you have mastered all that is to be known, do you not?'

Svetaketū nodded, a trace of pride in his expression. 'Indeed, Father. I have studied under wise teachers, and I have learnt well. I do not think there is anything in the Vedas or the teachings of the sages that I have not grasped.'

Uddālaka smiled inwardly, for he saw the pride swelling within his son. 'Then tell me, Svetaketū,' he said, his tone sharpening slightly, 'have you learnt of that knowledge which allows one to hear what cannot be heard, perceive what cannot be perceived, and know what cannot be known?'

Svetaketū blinked, caught off guard. For all his years of study, no teacher had ever posed such a question to him. He faltered, searching for words, and finally answered, 'No, Father. I do not know of such knowledge. Is there truly a knowledge so profound?'

Uddālaka's gaze softened, seeing the curiosity awaken in his son's eyes. 'Indeed, my son,' he replied. 'There exists a wisdom by which one can see beyond the forms of this world, to the very essence of all things. When you know a single clod of clay, you can know all that is made from clay. When you understand a nugget of gold, you understand all ornaments made of gold, for it is the same gold within them all.'

Svetaketū's brow furrowed, his pride melting into wonder. 'Then, Father,' he asked humbly, 'will you teach me this knowledge?'

'Yes, my son,' Uddālaka said, pleased. 'But know that this teaching is not like any you have heard before. You must listen closely, for this wisdom dwells within every part of existence itself.'

He spoke with gentle clarity, his words flowing like a steady river of insight. 'In the beginning of creation, my child, there was only the True Being—the *Sat*. This Sat was without equal, alone and unchanging. In its pure thought, the Sat desired to multiply, to bring forth beings into creation. From this desire, it first created *Tejas*, the fire. Fire, in its turn, sought to multiply, and from it came *Apas*, water. Water, too, desired to create, and from it arose *Anna*—food, the sustenance of all life.'

Svetaketū listened, eyes wide with awe as Uddālaka's words unfurled a vision of creation as though he were witnessing it himself.

'But, Father,' Svetaketū said hesitantly, 'how can this Sat become so many things and yet remain unchanged?'

Uddālaka smiled faintly, as if the question were a spark that had ignited his son's true journey. 'Do you see this great banyan tree above us?' he asked, gesturing to the towering branches.

'Of course,' Svetaketū replied.

'Bring me a fruit from it,' Uddālaka said.

Svetaketū rose, plucked a small, fig-like fruit, and returned, handing it to his father.

'Now, break it open.'

Svetaketū did as instructed, splitting the fruit to reveal its soft pulp and countless tiny seeds.

'What do you see?'

'Seeds, Father. Many, many seeds.'

'Take one seed. Break it open.'

Svetaketū obeyed, though it took effort to split something so infinitesimal. 'It is done,' he said, showing the tiny fragment on his fingertip.

'What do you see now?'

'Nothing, Father,' Svetaketū admitted, squinting at the speck of a seed. 'It is too small to see anything more.'

Uddālaka leaned closer, his gaze both tender and piercing. 'From this 'nothing', Svetaketū, this great banyan tree arises. The essence of that seed, invisible to your eye, is the subtle essence that pervades all things. It is that essence, Svetaketū, which is the truth. And you, my son, are that essence. You are *Tat Tvam Asi*—that thou art.'

The words hung in the air, weaving themselves into the fabric of Svetaketū's understanding. His arrogance faltered, replaced by wonder and humility.

'But how can that be, Father?' he asked, his voice tinged with awe. 'How can something so vast emerge from something so small, so... unseen?'

Uddālaka leaned back, letting his gaze wander to the sky beyond the canopy. 'Consider the rivers, Svetaketū. They may flow from the mountains, twist through forests, and spread across the plains. But when they reach the ocean, do they not become one with it? The water you see here, and the water in the sea, are not different. It is the same with the essence of the world. You and I, this tree, the stars, all arise from that same subtle truth.'

Svetaketū sat in silence, his youthful certainty unravelling like a tightly bound rope loosened by wisdom. He looked up at the banyan tree again, seeing it not as a mere tree, but as a living testament to a truth far greater than he had ever imagined. The young man felt his mind open like a new dawn breaking. He listened with rapt attention as his father continued.

'Now, my son,' Uddālaka instructed, 'bring me a cup of water and a handful of salt.'

Svetaketū returned with the items, and Uddālaka asked him to dissolve the salt in the water. After some moments, he asked, 'Can you take the salt back out of the water?'

Svetaketū shook his head, puzzled. 'No, Father. It has dissolved completely.'

'Yet,' Uddālaka replied, 'taste a drop from the top of the water.'

Svetaketū did so. 'It is salty, Father.'

'Now taste from the middle and the bottom.'

Svetaketū tasted again, finding saltiness throughout. Uddālaka nodded, his eyes filled with the wisdom he hoped to pass on. 'The salt is everywhere in the water, though unseen. In the same way, the True Being, the Sat, pervades everything in this universe, though invisible to our ordinary senses. This essence is present in all, yet beyond all forms. It is the desire of all beings and the subtle essence of all creation.'

Humbled and enlightened, Svetaketū realised that all he had learnt until now was but a small fragment of the vastness of truth. The pride that once filled him had dissolved, replaced with reverence and a quiet longing to know more of this boundless essence.

And in that moment, beneath the timeless shade of the banyan, Svetaketū began to grasp the infinite.

'Father,' he said softly, 'teach me still more.'

The Dance of The Five Fires

From The Chhāndogya Upanishad

The sun was high in the sky, upon the western hills, gilding the palace of the *Pānchālas* in molten fire. Its towers rose like spears into the midday sky, their marble facades veined with gold and silver. Pennants drifted on the wind, their colours faded with age, bearing the ancient sigils of kings who had long turned to dust.

Into this realm of stone and silence came *Svetaketū*, son of *Uddālaka Aruni*, his heart brimming with the conceit of youth. His robe was simple, his brow proud, his eyes bright with the restless flame of one who believes he has mastered the lore of the ancients.

Had he not studied beside his father, a sage among sages? Had he not recited the hymns, learnt the *brahmavidyā*, heard the whispers of the forest where the *Rishis* walked unseen? Yet knowledge is but the skin of understanding, thin and fragile as a serpent's cast-off shell.

The scent of sandalwood drifted faintly through the stone-pillared corridor, as Svetaketū waited, seated cross-legged upon a woven mat. The mid-morning sun filtered through latticework windows, casting patterns of light and shadow along the ground. Beyond the carved doors, faint echoes of voices rose and fell—the hum of King *Pravahana Jaivali's* court.

An attendant arrived, and respectfully indicated that the King was ready to see him.

Svetaketū got up, patted down his hair, straightened his robe and quickly followed the attendant. As he entered the court, he slowed down his pace to a dignified stroll. The court of King Pravahana Jaivali awaited him—a hall of granite columns and vaulted shadows, its walls adorned with carvings of lions, elephants, and birds whose wings stretched toward eternity. The court of King Pravahana Jaivali was unlike the hermitages of the sages. Pravahana himself, tall and grave, bore the air of a man who had walked beside mysteries no mortal tongue could easily reveal. His dark eyes, like still pools, saw through the illusions that men wore like cloaks.

Svetaketū had come to impress him. Instead, he stood exposed—stripped of certainty, his clever words turned to ash.

'Tell me, son of Aruni,' the king's voice rose, measured as the wind upon ancient seas, 'do you know where a man journeys when the breath leaves his bones? Where the soul treads when the fire of life is quenched?'

Svetaketū faltered. His words, once so sure, turned brittle as dry leaves in the autumn wind. The verses he had memorised crumbled like old parchment in the face of the king's quiet knowing.

Ashamed, he returned to his father, and beneath the spreading boughs of the fig tree, amid the crackling of sacred fires, he confessed his ignorance.

Uddālaka, grey of beard and grave of countenance, laid a hand upon his son's shoulder. 'Even the deepest river begins as a hidden spring,' he said. 'Go, seek the hidden currents. Listen, and let pride fall away like chaff upon the wind.'

Thus, Svetaketū returned to the palace, no longer as one who would boast, but as one who would listen.

King Pravahana awaited him with neither fanfare nor reproach. His eyes, deep as forgotten wells, measured the young seeker in silence. 'You have come humbly,' the king observed, his voice woven with the hush of ancient years. 'Then listen well, for I shall reveal to you the knowledge of the *Panchāgni Vidyā*—the sacred wisdom of the five fires, a song the stars have whispered since the first flame was kindled.'

And the king spoke, his words winding through the air like smoke upon still waters.

First was the fire of the heavens, where the sun burns upon the altar of the sky. From this flame, unseen hands offer prayers, hopes, dreams—the flickering sparks of mortal longing. From that sacrifice, the moon is born, a pale wanderer bearing the echoes of forgotten lives.

Second burns the fire among the clouds, where the moon, gathered as an offering, weeps upon the earth in silver streams—the rain that stirs the sleeping seed.

Third smoulders the fire within the earth, where rain kisses root and stone, and from that union, life awakens—the grain, the fruit, the sustenance of all beings.

Fourth burns the fire within man, where that which is consumed transforms, where the seed stirs, carrying the memory of earth and rain and fire.

Fifth and final is the fire within woman, the sacred hearth where the seed is received, and from its embers, a child is shaped—a vessel of all that has come before, woven of sun, moon, rain, earth, and flesh.

Thus spoke Pravahana, and as he spoke, it seemed to Svetaketū that the torches lining the hall flickered brighter, as though stirred by ancient breath.

In the hush that followed, the king lifted his voice, and it rang with the cadence of olden songs, as though the stones themselves remembered.

'In fire was born the seed of stars,
In rain the rivers run,
From earth the fruits of life arise,
The dance of all begun.'

'The sun, the moon, the silver streams,
The child upon the shore,
All weave the endless, ancient threads,
One circle, evermore.'

The hall fell silent, save for the crackle of distant flame.

But the king's eyes held shadows still, and his voice, low as wind in forgotten tombs, continued:

'There are two roads, O son of Aruni,' he said, 'and each man walks by his choosing.'

The *devayāna*, the way of the gods, lifts those of wisdom and sacrifice beyond the veils of night, past the sun's golden gate, into realms untouched by death, where rivers run clear and sorrow holds no dominion.

The *pitriyāna*, the way of the ancestors, draws others back upon the wheel—through shadowed realms of dream and memory, into the ever-turning dance of birth and toil and mortal striving.

Again the king's voice rose in song, like a bard recalling the lay of forgotten heroes:

'Two roads the soul must tread in time,
Two gates, both veiled and wide,
One path ascends beyond the stars,
One circles by death's side.'

'Yet fire remains in every heart,
And stars within the sea,
The soul that learns the ancient dance,
Shall one day wander free.'

Svetaketū bowed his head, the pride within him crumbling like old stone before the river's patient hand.

In that twilight, beneath the gaze of the king, amid the

flickering of flames older than kingdoms, the young sage understood—wisdom is not seized, but sought; not shouted, but whispered through fire, rain, earth, and time.

And so the tale of the five fires was woven into his soul, a song of sacrifice, of worlds reborn, of endless roads winding beneath the stars.

Janashruti Encounters Raikva

From The Chhāndogya Upanishad

King *Janashruti* was a noble and generous ruler, renowned throughout his land for his charity and righteousness. His fame spread far and wide, and his heart brimmed with pride, for he believed there was no one greater than him in benevolence and piety.

One serene evening, Janashruti sat on the terrace of his grand palace, under the star-lit sky. The air was cool, and the gentle rustle of leaves whispered calming lullabies. Just then, two swans flew over his palace. Unknown to the king, these were no ordinary swans but celestial beings who often conversed about the truths of the universe.

As they glided over the palace, one swan remarked to the other, 'See how brightly the light of King Janashruti shines, illuminating the earth below. His fame is unmatched amongst men.'

The second swan chuckled. 'Indeed, his light shines far, but can it rival the wisdom of *Raikva*, the humble cart-puller? The radiance of Raikva's knowledge far surpasses anything Janashruti has achieved.'

Hearing this, King Janashruti's heart sank. The swans' words unsettled him. Was it possible that a mere cart-puller could be greater than him, a king renowned for his virtue and generosity? That night, sleep eluded him, and his thoughts were consumed by the mysterious Raikva.

Determined to find this man of wisdom, Janashruti summoned his most trusted servants the following morning. 'Go forth,' he commanded, 'and search every corner of my kingdom. Find this extraordinary sage Raikva, the cart-puller, whose knowledge surpasses even the deeds of kings.'

The king's servants roamed the land, seeking a man unknown to the court but hailed as the wisest. Their journey took them to a remote, dusty settlement where they finally encountered Raikva.

Raikva was sitting under a broken-down cart, his appearance utterly unlike the image of a sage the servants had expected. His clothes were torn and soiled, his hair matted with grime, and his skin was caked in the dirt of long days spent in manual labour. His fingernails were cracked and darkened, and he sat scratching himself absentmindedly. The cart he rested under was equally battered, its wooden frame riddled with cracks, wheels barely attached.

When the king's servants approached, they hesitated, wondering if this dishevelled figure could truly be the man their master sought. Summoning their courage, they asked, 'Are you Raikva, the one praised by the gods for his wisdom?'

Raikva glanced at them, his face lined with years of toil but his eyes radiating a profound calm. 'Yes, I am Raikva,' he replied simply, his voice steady.

King Janashruti wasted no time upon hearing the news. He travelled to the settlement with an opulent caravan, bearing rich gifts: six hundred well-fed cows, a golden necklace that gleamed like the sun, and a luxurious mule-drawn chariot. The king approached Raikva and bowed low.

'Revered one,' Janashruti began, 'I have heard of your wisdom, which surpasses the deeds of kings and the wealth of empires. Please accept these humble offerings and teach me the path of ultimate truth.'

Raikva looked at the king's gifts with disdain. 'Do you think knowledge is a commodity that can be bought with gold and cattle? Take back your wealth. I have no use for these trinkets.'

The king, though humiliated, remained resolute. He withdrew, realising that Raikva's rejection stemmed from his perception of the king's pride.

Determined to prove his sincerity, Janashruti returned to Raikva. This time, he brought even more generous offerings: a thousand cows, the finest golden ornaments, another chariot, and his own daughter, promising her hand in marriage.

'Raikva,' the king said, bowing deeply, 'I come to you not as a king but as a seeker. I have nothing to offer except my sincere desire to learn. Please grant me your wisdom.'

Raikva, seeing the transformation in Janashruti's demeanour, was moved. He rose from under his cart, brushing dust from his tattered garments. 'Now,' he said, 'you are ready to listen.'

Seated on the ground, Raikva began to speak, his voice resonating with authority. 'O King, you believe yourself to be a great benefactor, but tell me, what drives your actions? What is the source of your charity and power?'

Janashruti remained silent, eager to hear more.

Raikva continued, 'Everything you see—the wind that blows, the fire that burns, the sun that shines, and the waters that flow—is animated by *Prāna,* the vital breath. This Prāna is the essence of all existence. Without it, there is no life, no movement, no creation.'

The king listened intently as Raikva elaborated. 'This Prāna is not separate from the self. It flows through you, through me, and through every living being. To understand Prāna is to understand the unity of all existence. And to live in harmony with this truth is the path to liberation.'

Raikva's eyes gleamed with intensity as he added, 'You must also learn the art of giving. True charity is not born of pride or a desire for recognition. Give as a river gives its waters—freely and without attachment. When you give, remember that you are merely a vessel of the divine. Nothing truly belongs to you.'

Janashruti's pride dissolved as he grasped the profound nature of Raikva's words. For the first time, he saw himself not as a king but as a part of the greater whole, connected to all beings through the vital breath of life.

Raikva's teachings culminated in a profound declaration. 'Know this, Janashruti: the self and the infinite are one and the same. To see this unity is the highest wisdom. When you act with this knowledge, you transcend fear, desire, and suffering. You become one with the eternal.'

Humbled and enlightened, King Janashruti bowed deeply before Raikva. 'You have given me a treasure far greater than all the wealth in my kingdom, O master. I now see the unity that binds all creation.'

Raikva nodded. 'Go forth, Janashruti, and let this wisdom guide your rule. Lead your people with humility and compassion, for a king's greatness lies not in his wealth but in his understanding of the eternal truth.'

The king, now transformed, returned to his palace. He continued his acts of charity, but now with a spirit of selflessness and devotion. The village where Raikva lived came to be known as *Raikvaparna*, in honour of the humble cart-puller whose wisdom rivalled that of the greatest sages.

Satyakāma Gains Wisdom

From the Chhāndogya Upanishad

Long ago, in a quiet village surrounded by forests, lived a boy named *Satyakāma*. His mother, *Jābāla*, was a humble and hard-working woman who had raised him alone. Satyakāma, from a young age, displayed an unshakeable curiosity and a deep longing for knowledge. He often sat under the banyan tree near their simple hut, watching the world around him, and dreamt of learning the mysteries of the Vedas.

One evening, as Jābāla was returning from the fields, carrying firewood on her back, Satyakāma approached her with a question that had been burning within him.

'Mother,' he said, 'I wish to become a disciple of a *guru* and learn the Vedas. But they will ask me about my lineage. Tell me, to which family do I belong? Who is my father?'

Jābāla paused, her face shadowed by a mixture of pain and resolve. She placed the firewood down and looked at her son with tear-filled eyes. 'My son,' she began, 'I do not know your lineage. In my youth, I served many households and lived a wandering life. You were born during that time, and I do not know who your father is.'

Satyakāma listened quietly. Though her words revealed a painful truth, they carried an air of dignity and honesty. Jābāla reached out and placed her hand on his shoulder.

'My child,' she continued, 'you are Satyakāma, the son of Jābāla. Go to the gurus and tell them this truth. Do not be ashamed of who you are, for truth is the highest virtue. Let your sincerity and honesty be your lineage.'

Hearing his mother's words, Satyakāma felt a surge of inner strength. He bowed deeply to her and said, 'I will do as you say, Mother. I shall declare myself truthfully, as Satyakāma, the son of Jābāla.'

Determined to pursue his dream, Satyakāma set out the next morning. He walked barefoot across the dusty paths of his village, carrying nothing but his resolve. He approached several hermitages, seeking admission as a student, but each time, the answer was the same.

'Who is your father?' the sages would ask.

'I do not know,' Satyakāma would reply honestly. 'I am Satyakāma, the son of Jābāla.'

Many sages turned him away, sceptical of his origins. 'Without a lineage, how can you claim the right to study the sacred Vedas?' they would say. 'A disciple must come from a noble family.'

Each rejection stung Satyakāma, but his mother's words echoed in his heart: *Truth is the highest virtue.*

At last, he reached the hermitage of the renowned sage *Gautama Haridrumata*. Gautama was a man of great wisdom, known for his ability to see beyond outward appearances. As Satyakāma approached him, the sage was seated under a tree, surrounded by other students.

Satyakāma bowed respectfully. 'O revered master,' he said, 'I have come to seek your guidance. I wish to become your disciple and learn the knowledge of *Brahman*.'

Gautama studied the boy carefully, sensing the earnestness in his eyes. 'Tell me, young one,' he said, 'to which family do you belong? What is your lineage?'

Satyakāma took a deep breath and replied, 'O master, I do not know my lineage. My mother, Jābāla, has told me that she served many households in her youth and does not know who my father is. She instructed me to speak the truth and declare myself as Satyakāma, the son of Jābāla.'

Hearing these words, Gautama's face softened, and his lips curved into a smile. 'Your honesty is your lineage,' he said. 'Only one who speaks the truth with such clarity and fearlessness can aspire to know Brahman. I accept you as my disciple.'

At these words, Satyakāma felt a wave of relief and joy. He bowed deeply before Gautama, his heart filled with gratitude.

As was the tradition in the ancient *gurukulas*, a new disciple was required to perform a task to symbolise humility and readiness to learn. Gautama handed Satyakāma a bundle of firewood and said, 'Take this and tend to the sacred fire. This fire represents the light of knowledge, and it must be kept burning always. Through this simple task, you will begin your journey towards understanding the eternal truth.'

Satyakāma accepted the firewood with reverence. He walked towards the sacrificial altar and carefully fed the fire with the dry wood, watching as the flames leapt and danced. For days and nights, he devoted himself to this task, silently meditating on its deeper significance.

One day, Gautama summoned Satyakāma and entrusted him with a unique task.

'Satyakāma,' the sage said, 'I see within you the potential to grasp the highest truths. However, this knowledge must be earned through discipline and service. Take these four hundred frail cattle into the forest, care for them, and return only when their number has grown to a thousand.'

Satyakāma bowed respectfully. 'I will fulfil your command, O master.'

Without hesitation, Satyakāma led the herd deep into the forest. The task seemed daunting at first—the cattle were weak, and the wilderness was vast and untamed. Yet, Satyakāma approached his duty with unwavering patience and care. He tended to the herd day and night, ensuring they grazed in fertile pastures and had clean water to drink. He protected them from wild animals, standing fearlessly with his staff in hand.

Years passed, and the frail herd blossomed into a thriving multitude. The once-weak cattle now grazed proudly, their numbers growing steadily. Satyakāma lived in harmony with nature, his heart filled with peace and devotion.

One evening, as Satyakāma sat under a starlit sky, the leader of the herd approached him. To his astonishment, the bull spoke in a deep, resonant voice.

'Satyakāma,' it said, 'the time has come for you to return to your guru. But before you go, I shall teach you a part of the knowledge of Brahman. Listen carefully.'

Satyakāma sat upright, his hands folded in reverence.

'Brahman,' the bull continued, 'is infinite and manifests in four quarters. The east, the west, the north, and the south are aspects of Brahman. Meditate on these directions as representations of eternal reality.'

The bull paused, its eyes gleaming with wisdom. 'This is only one quarter of the truth. There will be others who will reveal the rest. Now, gather the herd and begin your journey back.'

Satyakāma bowed deeply. 'Thank you, wise one. I will meditate on your teaching.'

As Satyakāma led the vast herd back towards Gautama's hermitage, he stopped by a serene lake to let the cattle drink. As he rested by the water's edge, a swan glided gracefully across the surface and spoke to him.

'Satyakāma,' said the swan, 'I shall teach you the second quarter of Brahman. Fire, the Sun, the Moon, and Lightning are manifestations of Brahman. Contemplate these as symbols of the divine.'

Satyakāma listened intently, his mind absorbing the profound truth. 'Thank you, noble swan,' he said. 'Your words will guide my meditation.'

Reaching the outskirts of a dense forest, he paused under the shade of a great banyan tree. There, perched on a branch, was a waterfowl. The bird, glowing with an otherworldly light, called out to him.

'Satyakāma,' it said, 'I shall teach you the third quarter of Brahman. The Breath (*Prāna*), the Eye (*chakshu*), the Ear (*shrotra*), and the Mind (*manas*) are manifestations of Brahman. These are the instruments through which the ultimate reality is perceived.'

Satyakāma folded his hands in gratitude. 'Your teachings are a gift, O divine one. I will meditate upon them.'

As Satyakāma neared Gautama's hermitage, he lit a sacred fire to mark his journey's end. Sitting before the flames, he offered his prayers. To his astonishment, the fire itself began to speak.

'Satyakāma,' it said, 'I shall teach you the fourth and final quarter of Brahman. The Earth, the Sky, the Heavens, and the Ocean are manifestations of infinite reality. These represent the boundless, unchanging truth. Yet know this: Brahman is beyond all divisions. It cannot be fully comprehended by the mind or senses. True realisation comes through experience and meditation.'

Satyakāma listened with awe, the light of understanding illuminating his heart. 'Thank you, O Sacred Fire,' he said. 'Your wisdom completes my journey.'

At last, Satyakāma reached Gautama's hermitage, the herd of a thousand cattle following him like a sea of white clouds. As he entered, Gautama rose to greet him, his face shining with pride.

'Satyakāma,' the sage said, 'you have returned, and I see the radiance of Brahman in you. Tell me, who has taught you this sacred knowledge?'

Satyakāma bowed and replied, 'O revered master, I was taught by the Bull, the Swan, the Waterfowl, and the Sacred Fire. Each revealed to me a part of the truth.'

Gautama smiled, his eyes gleaming with wisdom. 'Indeed, Satyakāma, the divine beings themselves have chosen you as their student. You are now a knower of Brahman. Your truthfulness, devotion, and humility have led you to the ultimate knowledge.'

Thus, Satyakāma Jābāla became one of the most revered sages, celebrated for his unwavering honesty and his journey towards self realisation.

Yama Enlightens Nachiketā

From the Katha Upanishad

Sage *Vājashrava*, also known as *Gautama*, desired to gain divine favour by performing a great *yajna*. As part of this ritual, he resolved to give away all his possessions. The sacrifice demanded that he donate cows to Brahmins and ascetics, as was customary. However, blinded by his desire for heavenly rewards, Vājashrava offered only old, feeble cows, incapable of providing milk or producing calves—cows that were of no value.

Observing this, *Nachiketā*, his young and inquisitive son, was struck by a sense of righteousness. He was a boy of unshaken truthfulness and a seeker of wisdom. Troubled by his father's actions, he approached Vājashrava and said, 'Father, to whom will you give me as part of your donation?' His question arose from the belief that a son, too, could be considered a gift in a sacrificial offering. Vājashrava ignored him, but Nachiketā repeated his question several times, each time more resolute.

Annoyed by his persistence, Vājashrava finally snapped, saying, 'I give you to *Yama* (Death)!' Though spoken in anger, these words were uttered during the sacred ritual and, therefore, carried the weight of a vow.

Nachiketā, hearing his father's words, calmly accepted his fate. Determined to honour his father's declaration, he prepared to journey to the realm of Yama, the God of death. Before leaving, he approached Vājashrava and said, 'Father, consider this: the deeds of a man determine his destiny. A father's duty is to guide his son towards virtue. Do you regret your words, or shall I carry out your command?'

Vājashrava, consumed by pride and unable to retract his words, remained silent. Nachiketā, firm in his resolve, departed to the abode of Yama.

Nachiketā travelled to the distant and mysterious realm of Yama. Upon arrival, he found the God of death absent, as Yama had gone to perform his duties in the mortal world. For three days and nights, Nachiketā waited patiently at the gates of Yama's home, without food or water, maintaining his composure and steadfastness.

When Yama returned and learnt of Nachiketā's presence, he was deeply remorseful. 'A Brahmin guest is like a sacred fire,' he said to himself. 'Neglecting such a guest brings great misfortune.' Seeking to atone for this lapse, Yama approached Nachiketā and greeted him with reverence.

'O noble child,' Yama said, 'I offer you my apologies for making you wait. To atone for this, I grant you three boons. Ask for anything your heart desires, and I shall fulfil your wishes.'

Nachiketā bowed respectfully and said, 'O Lord Yama, my first wish is that my father's anger towards me may be pacified. Let him welcome me back without resentment and acknowledge me with the same affection as before. This is my first boon.'

Yama smiled and said, 'So be it. Your father shall recognise you and be free of anger. When you return to him, his heart will be filled with joy and love. This boon is granted.'

Nachiketā's heart was gladdened by these words, for his foremost concern had been to restore harmony with his father.

For his second boon, Nachiketā sought to learn the sacred knowledge of the *Agni Vidyā* (fire sacrifice), which was believed to lead to the highest realms of heaven. Addressing Yama, he said, 'Teach me, O Lord, the sacred fire sacrifice that leads to heaven, so that those who perform it may achieve immortality in the heavenly realm. I desire to learn this ancient wisdom as my second boon.'

Pleased by Nachiketā's sincerity and thirst for knowledge, Yama replied, 'I shall teach you. Pay close attention.' Yama then described in detail the construction of the fire altar, the arrangement of the firewood, and the precise rituals to be performed. He spoke of the mantras, the offerings, and the symbolism of each element in the sacrifice.

'Nachiketā,' Yama said, 'this fire is the foundation of all worlds and the means by which mortals attain immortality. I name it after you, for you have asked with such pure intent.'

Yama then gave Nachiketā an additional blessing: 'This fire shall now be called *Nachiketa Agni*. Those who perform this ritual three times with faith and understanding shall overcome the cycle of birth and death.'

Nachiketā, having absorbed this profound knowledge, expressed his gratitude. 'O Lord Yama, what you have bestowed upon me is great wisdom. I am forever indebted to you.'

For his third boon, Nachiketā posed the ultimate question. 'O Yama, what happens after death? Some say the soul exists beyond death, while others deny it. Teach me, O Lord, the truth about this great mystery.'

Yama hesitated, for this question touched upon the most profound and guarded secrets of existence. 'Even the Gods have debated this question,' Yama said. 'It is subtle and difficult to comprehend. Ask me for another boon, Nachiketā—wealth, long life, power, or anything else you desire. But do not insist on this.'

Nachiketā remained steadfast. 'O Lord, no boon can compare to the knowledge of the eternal truth. Grant me this understanding, for it is the ultimate wisdom. All worldly pleasures are fleeting; I seek only that which is eternal.'

Yama tested him further. 'I can give you vast kingdoms, unending wealth, the longest life imaginable, and pleasures beyond your wildest dreams. Turn away from this question and choose these instead.'

But Nachiketā was resolute. 'O Lord Yama, all these are

transient. They wither with time. I do not seek pleasures that perish. Teach me that which endures beyond death—the truth of the immortal soul.'

Seeing Nachiketā's unwavering determination, Yama was deeply impressed. 'Very well,' he said. 'You are indeed worthy of this knowledge. Listen carefully, for I shall now reveal the supreme truth.'

Yama began, 'The *Ātman*, the self, is eternal. It is neither born nor does it die. It is unborn, eternal, unchanging, and ancient. When the body dies, the Ātman does not perish. Fools, attached to the material world, do not perceive this truth, but the wise who seek the self within attain liberation.

'Know that the self is like a rider, and the body is the chariot. The intellect is the charioteer, and the mind is the reins. The senses are the horses, and the objects of the senses are the paths they tread. Those who lack understanding allow their minds and senses to lead them astray, but the wise, with disciplined intellect, reach the ultimate goal.

'The Ātman is beyond the senses, beyond the mind, and beyond the intellect. It is the ultimate reality, the unchanging truth that pervades all existence. Those who realise the self become free from the cycle of birth and death and attain eternal bliss.'

Nachiketā listened intently, absorbing every word. Through Yama's teachings, he attained the supreme knowledge of the self and realised the ultimate truth.

After imparting this wisdom, Yama blessed Nachiketā and allowed him to return to the mortal world. When Nachiketā reunited with his father, Vājashrava, he was welcomed with great joy and affection, just as Yama had promised. Nachiketā lived the rest of his life guiding others towards the path of self-realisation.

The Five Awakenings of Bhrigu

From the Taittiriya Upanishad

In the ancient pristine age of awe and wonder, when sacred groves whispered the secrets of the cosmos, there dwelt a sage named *Bhrigu*, the son of *Varuna*, Lord of Waters. Bhrigu was a seeker of the deepest wisdom, yearning to pierce the veils of existence and behold the essence of *Brahman*, the eternal and all-encompassing truth.

One day, with the weight of this yearning heavy in his heart, Bhrigu approached his father. The air was thick with the incense of wisdom, and the river nearby glimmered like molten silver under the gaze of the midday sun. Varuna regarded his son with eyes that gleamed like the unfathomable depths of the ocean.

Bhrigu knelt before him, his voice steady yet imbued with the trembling eagerness of a seeker. 'Father,' he said, 'teach me of Brahman. What is it that pervades all, that sustains this vast creation, and in which all rests?'

Varuna, the sage-lord, smiled, a smile that held galaxies within its curve. 'Bhrigu,' he said, his voice a deep, resonant tide, 'Brahman is that from which all beings are born, that by which they are sustained, and that into which they merge at the end of their journey. Seek it, my son, not through my words but through meditation and *Tapasyā* (austerity). Contemplate deeply, and Brahman shall reveal itself to you.'

With these words, Varuna closed his eyes, retreating into his own communion with the infinite, leaving Bhrigu to embark on his quest.

Bhrigu retreated to a grove where silence reigned, broken only by the rustle of leaves and the distant murmur of a sacred river. There, he sat cross-legged, his form still as a mountain, his mind delving into the mysteries of existence. Days turned to nights and back again, the cycles of the sun and the moon unnoticed by the meditating sage.

When at last his mind settled, like a lake undisturbed by wind, the first vision dawned upon him. He saw the world teeming with life—creatures that walked, flew, and swam, all nourished by the bounty of the earth. Grains, fruits, and sustenance of every kind flowed through the hands of men, the beaks of birds, and the jaws of beasts. He understood: *Anna* (food) is Brahman, for it is food that sustains all life.

Elated by his revelation, he returned to Varuna, his steps light but purposeful. 'Father,' he said, 'I have seen that food is Brahman. Is this the ultimate truth?'

Varuna regarded him with the patience of eternity. 'You have glimpsed but a fragment of Brahman's vastness. Meditate further, my son. Seek deeper.'

Bhrigu returned to his grove, where the winds whispered through the trees, carrying the breath of the world. Once more, he immersed himself in meditation, diving deeper into the ocean of truth. As his consciousness expanded, he perceived the dance of life: the rise and fall of chests, the rhythmic pulse of breath in all living beings. He understood that it was *Prāna* (life-force) that animated all, that which sustained even the consumption of food.

When he returned to his father and shared his insight, Varuna nodded, but his gaze remained serene and unwavering. 'You have seen further, my son, but Brahman's essence lies yet deeper. Contemplate anew.'

Now, the grove seemed to shimmer with an unseen energy as Bhrigu meditated once more, his heart burning with the fervour of his quest. This time, his mind turned inward, and he beheld the thoughts and emotions that moved within him and all beings. He saw how the mind orchestrated action, how it desired, feared, and reasoned. *Manas*, the mind, he realised, was the architect of experience. He returned to Varuna with his revelation: 'Brahman is the mind.'

But again, Varuna sent him back, urging him to seek the depths beyond even the mind.

The stars wheeled overhead as Bhrigu entered the next stage

of his contemplation. He now perceived the guiding light behind the mind—the radiant force of *Vijnāna* (intelligence), which discerns truth from falsehood, light from shadow. It was intelligence that gave purpose to the mind's wanderings and meaning to existence. Once again, Bhrigu shared his realisation with Varuna, only to be told: 'You approach the truth, but the heart of Brahman eludes you still.'

By now, Bhrigu's austerities had grown so intense that the very earth seemed to hum with the force of his meditation. His body, once frail, now glowed with an otherworldly light, his presence radiating peace and power. In this final meditation, Bhrigu reached beyond the layers of food, life-force, mind, and intelligence. He touched the core of existence, where all dualities dissolved. There, he found *Ānanda* (bliss)—not the fleeting joy of the senses, but the boundless, eternal bliss of union with Brahman.

Bhrigu rose from his meditation transformed. He was no longer merely a seeker; he had become one with the truth he sought. He remained in his grove—totally content, joyous and completely at peace.

Much later, one day he encountered Varuna. His father's gaze softened with pride and love. 'Now, my son, you have truly seen. Brahman is bliss—the source, sustainer, and culmination of all that is.'

part 3

The Bhāgavata Purāṇa

The Chastisement of Sage Durvāsā

From The Bhāgavata Purāna

In the *Satya Yuga*, where truth and virtue reigned supreme, King *Ambarīsh* ruled his kingdom with unmatched devotion and justice. Known for his boundless faith in Lord *Vishnu* and his unwavering commitment to his people, Ambarīsh was beloved by his subjects. One year, to honour Vishnu and seek blessings for his kingdom, the king organised a grand *yajna*—a sacred fire ritual of immense magnitude, drawing sages and seekers from across the lands. The air buzzed with divine energy as sacred chants filled the sky, invoking blessings of prosperity and peace.

Moved by the sincerity and magnitude of Ambarīsh's yajna, Lord Vishnu appeared before him, radiant and resplendent. 'Your devotion and sacrifice have pleased me greatly, noble king,' said Vishnu with a voice that seemed to echo across the heavens. 'As a token of my blessing, I bestow upon you the *Sudarshana Chakra.*'

The Sudarshana Chakra, Lord Vishnu's mighty discus, was no ordinary gift. It was a divine weapon that held the power to protect its bearer from all harm, a symbol of Lord Vishnu's eternal guardianship. Its presence was awe-inspiring, its whirling edges gleaming with unearthly light. With the Chakra bestowed upon him, Ambarīsh's kingdom flourished like never before. The fields yielded bountiful harvests, the skies brought timely rains, and peace reigned within the realm.

However, the power of the Sudarshana Chakra did not stir arrogance in Ambarīsh's heart. Instead, he grew only more devoted and humble, ever mindful of the responsibilities it brought. To honour Lord Vishnu further, Ambarīsh undertook a strict *vrata* (vow) of fasting on *Ekadashi*, the eleventh day of every lunar month. For a full year, he observed this fast with unwavering sincerity, breaking it only during the auspicious moment the following morning with a sip of water. As the year-long fast began, little did the king know that this act of devotion would soon stir a series of celestial events that would test his faith and reveal the true strength of his heart.

This dedication soon caught the eye of *Indra*, the king of the heavens. Indra, ever wary of the strength and influence of others, began to feel a prickling unease. 'If Ambarīsh completes this fast,' Indra muttered to himself, 'his spiritual power may eclipse even my own.' Determined to prevent this from happening, he pondered a way to disrupt Ambarīsh's vow without invoking Vishnu's wrath directly.

As he sat contemplating, he remembered Sage *Durvāsā*—a figure whose temper was as legendary as his wisdom. Sage Durvāsā, an incarnation of Lord *Shiva*, was both revered and feared, for his anger was swift, fierce, and often accompanied by terrible curses. A plan began to form in Indra's mind, and with a wily smile, he summoned Durvāsā to his court.

'Ah, Sage Durvāsā! What an honour!' Indra said, bowing deeply and touching his forehead to the ground.

Sage Durvāsā's eyes sparkled with rare pleasure. Used to seeing others shy away or tread lightly around his wrath, he was surprised to find Indra so hospitable. 'It is rare to see such reverence, Indra,' the sage replied, stroking his beard. 'Tell me, what is it you seek?'

Indra smiled disarmingly. 'Oh, wise sage, I need neither boon nor blessing, but merely your company. I hoped to share with you a tale of devotion and virtue.'

Durvāsā leaned in, intrigued. 'Speak on.'

'There is a mortal king,' Indra continued, 'a mere human, yet he has captured even the attention of Lord Vishnu. Ambarīsh is his name, and his devotion is without equal. He has kept the Ekadashi fasts for an entire year and intends to break the final one tomorrow at the auspicious hour.' Indra's eyes gleamed as he went on. 'Imagine, a king powerful enough to wield Vishnu's Sudarshana Chakra. It would be an honour indeed to witness the moment he breaks his fast. Don't you agree, great sage?'

Durvāsā considered this, intrigued. 'Perhaps I shall visit this King Ambarīsh and witness his piety for myself. I shall test the devotion of this so-called paragon.'

Indra concealed his satisfaction, thinking, Durvāsā will surely find something amiss. And when he does, Ambarīsh's fast will be ruined.

The following morning, as the appointed hour of breaking the fast approached, King Ambarīsh stood with eyes closed, his mind absorbed in Lord Vishnu. His ministers and subjects gathered around, each eager to witness the culmination of the king's year-long penance. Yet, as the final minutes ticked by, a regal figure emerged at the palace gates.

'Sage Durvāsā has arrived!' a guard announced, and the assembly parted reverently as Durvāsā entered, his robes billowing and his expression inscrutable.

King Ambarīsh rose and bowed deeply. 'Welcome, revered sage,' he said, his tone filled with respect. 'I am honoured by your presence.'

Durvāsā inclined his head. 'You are about to break your fast, I hear?'

'Yes, esteemed one. In a short while, I will partake of water to complete my vow.'

'Ah,' Durvāsā replied thoughtfully. 'But first, allow me to bathe and perform my own prayers. Let us break your fast together once I return.'

Ambarīsh nodded. 'As you wish, great sage. I will await your return.'

However, as time wore on, Durvāsā did not reappear. The ministers glanced nervously at the sky. The auspicious moment was slipping away. 'My king,' one of the advisors whispered, 'the hour is passing. If you do not break the fast now, the entire year's vow will be in vain.'

King Ambarīsh hesitated, glancing towards the doors. 'But Sage Durvāsā has yet to return. I cannot proceed without him.'

'Even a mere sip of water would suffice to fulfil the vow,' the minister insisted. 'This way, you honour both your fast and the sage's wishes.'

After a moment's contemplation, Ambarīsh agreed. With a prayer to Lord Vishnu, he lifted a cup of water and took a single sip.

Just then, the doors flew open, and Durvāsā re-entered, his face flushed with anger. His eyes blazed as he stormed towards the king. 'Ambarīsh!' he thundered. 'Is this how you honour your guest? You could not wait for me before breaking your fast?'

Ambarīsh immediately bowed his head. 'Forgive me, sage. The auspicious time was passing, and I took only a sip of water to honour the vow. I meant no disrespect.'

'Auspicious time?' Durvāsā scoffed, his voice rising. 'You place your fasting ritual above your respect for a guest! How dare you!'

Durvāsā's fury was swift and unrelenting. With a fierce glare, he reached up and plucked a single hair from his head. With a surge of power, he cast it to the ground, and from the strand emerged a towering, fearsome demon, cloaked in smoke and fire. The creature bowed before Durvāsā, awaiting his command.

Durvāsā pointed at Ambarīsh. 'Destroy him!'

The demon roared, surging forward. King Ambarīsh's ministers gasped and stumbled back, weapons raised but trembling. Ambarīsh, however, remained calm. With a serene expression, he lifted his eyes and offered a prayer to Lord Vishnu, placing his faith entirely in the Lord's hands.

As the demon closed in, a whirring sound filled the air. From above, the Sudarshana Chakra appeared, blazing like a second sun. In a flash, it struck the demon, obliterating it instantly. But the Chakra did not vanish; it hovered in the air, spinning faster, its sharp edges glinting as it turned towards Durvāsā.

The sage's eyes widened in shock. Realising the divine weapon intended to strike him, he turned and fled. The Sudarshana Chakra followed relentlessly, cutting through air and sky, its speed unmatched.

Durvāsā ran across the earth, up mountains, through rivers, into caves, and even beneath the oceans, but the Chakra pursued him unceasingly. Desperate, he fled to Satyaloka, the abode of Brahmā, and fell at Brahmā's feet. 'Lord Brahmā, please, protect me! The Sudarshana Chakra seeks my life!'

Brahmā looked upon the sage with compassion but shook his head. 'The Sudarshana Chakra is the weapon of Vishnu himself. I am powerless to intervene. Seek aid from Lord Shiva.'

Durvāsā hurried next to Kailāsh, where Lord Shiva resided. He knelt before the god, pleading, 'Lord Shiva, help me! The Sudarshana Chakra is relentless!'

Lord Shiva regarded him with pity. 'The Chakra is bound to Lord Vishnu's will. Only he can call it off. Go to him.'

At last, Durvāsā arrived at *Vaikuntha*, Lord Vishnu's celestial realm. Exhausted and terrified, he collapsed at Vishnu's feet, gasping, 'My Lord, forgive me! Spare me from the Sudarshana Chakra!'

Vishnu looked down kindly, yet with an air of gentle reproof. 'Durvāsā, the Chakra is indeed mine, but it now protects Ambarīsh. Only he, with his compassionate heart, can pardon you.'

Durvāsā, his pride shattered, returned to King Ambarīsh. Haggard and trembling, he approached the king with deep shame. 'Ambarīsh,' he whispered, his voice broken, 'please... please call off the Chakra. I wronged you. Only you can save me.'

Ambarīsh's face softened with empathy. Without hesitation, he closed his eyes and prayed, 'Lord Vishnu, please withdraw your Chakra. The sage has repented; let this conflict end.'

The Sudarshana Chakra wavered, then vanished in a flicker of light. Durvāsā looked up, relief washing over him, and he fell at Ambarīsh's feet.

'You are a true devotee, Ambarīsh. Despite my wrath, you saved me. You are truly blessed by Vishnu.'

With a humble smile, Ambarīsh bowed to the sage, saying, 'Let us complete this fast together, honoured sage.'

And so, King Ambarīsh and Sage Durvāsā sat together, consuming *Prasāda* in peace, their hearts reconciled. The king's unwavering devotion and humility remained a legend, inspiring generations to uphold virtue and forgiveness, even in the face of injustice.

The Trials of Prahlāda

From The Bhāgavata Purāna

The kingdom of the *Daityas* was shrouded in darkness under the rule of *Hiranyakashipu*, the most fearsome of *Asuras*. His hatred for *Vishnu*, the preserver of the universe, burned with the intensity of a thousand suns. The reason for this enmity was rooted in tragedy. Hiranyakashipu's brother, Hiranyaksha, had been slain by Vishnu in the form of the divine boar, *Varāha*. Swearing vengeance, Hiranyakashipu embarked on a campaign to dominate all three worlds and to defy the gods and their protector.

Hiranyakashipu's asceticism was legendary. For thousands of years, he meditated, enduring unimaginable austerities to gain favour from *Brahmā*, the creator. His *Tapasyā* was so intense that the flames of his penance disturbed the balance of the universe. Finally, Brahmā appeared and offered him a boon.

'Ask what you will, O king,' said Brahmā, 'for your dedication has moved even the immutable heavens.'

Hiranyakashipu, ever cunning, sought a boon that would make him seemingly invincible. 'Grant me, O Lord,' he said, 'that I may not be killed by any creature born of your creation—neither man nor beast, neither god nor demon, neither during the day nor at night, neither indoors nor outdoors, neither on the ground nor in the sky. Let no weapon wielded by any hand strike me down.' Brahmā, bound by his promise, granted the boon.

Armed with this divine protection, Hiranyakashipu unleashed terror upon the worlds. The gods were subdued, temples of Vishnu were desecrated, and the very name of Vishnu became forbidden in his realm.

Yet amidst this reign of tyranny, a child was born to Hiranyakashipu and his queen, *Kayādhū*. This child, *Prahlāda*, was destined to defy his father in ways unimaginable.

From the moment of his birth, Prahlāda's soul resonated with divine grace. Even as a young boy, he displayed wisdom and equanimity far beyond his years. Unknown to Hiranyakashipu, Prahlāda had been blessed by Vishnu while still in his mother's womb. The sage *Narada*, who had sheltered Kayādhū during her pregnancy, had sung the glories of Vishnu to her. These hymns, imbued with the essence of dharma, had imprinted themselves on Prahlāda's heart.

As he grew, Prahlāda's devotion to Vishnu became evident. While his peers played or studied the teachings of the Asuras, Prahlāda would meditate on the name of Narayana. His unwavering faith and love for Vishnu were a direct affront to

Hiranyakashipu, who prided himself on being the supreme ruler of creation.

One day, Hiranyakashipu summoned his son to court. The throne room, adorned with the riches of conquest, was filled with the Asura king's ministers and soldiers. Hiranyakashipu, towering and intimidating, looked down at the young boy.

'Prahlāda,' he began, his voice a rumble of thunder, 'tell me, my son, what is the greatest knowledge you have learnt?'

Without hesitation, Prahlāda replied, his voice clear and unwavering, 'The greatest knowledge, O Father, is devotion to Vishnu, the eternal Lord of all creation.'

A stunned silence fell over the court. The ministers exchanged nervous glances, for to speak Vishnu's name in Hiranyakashipu's presence was to invite death. The demon king's face darkened with rage.

'Foolish boy!' he thundered. 'Who has filled your mind with such poison? Do you not know that I am the supreme Lord of all the worlds? There is no god but me!'

But Prahlāda stood firm. 'You may be powerful, Father, but Vishnu is beyond power and beyond death. He is the true protector of all beings.'

Hiranyakashipu's fury was boundless. He ordered his guards to take the boy away and have him re-educated by the Asura teachers, *Shanda* and *Amarka*, sons of the sage *Shukracharya*.

In the teachers' care, Prahlāda was instructed in the ways of the Asuras: warfare, deceit, and the rejection of the gods. But despite their best efforts, Prahlāda's devotion to Vishnu only deepened. When questioned, he would speak of Vishnu's glories, much to the horror of his instructors.

When word of Prahlāda's continued defiance reached Hiranyakashipu, the king's patience wore thin. He summoned Prahlāda once more and demanded, 'You are my own flesh and blood! How dare you defy me? Renounce Vishnu, or face the consequences!'

But Prahlāda, though just a child, displayed unyielding courage. 'Father,' he said calmly, 'you may kill this body, but the soul is eternal and belongs to Vishnu. Your power cannot harm the truth.'

The court was tense as Hiranyakashipu declared, 'If my own son defies me, let him face the consequences. Let him learn what becomes of those who challenge my will.' Thus began the ordeal of Prahlāda, through a series of punishments designed to break his spirit and force him into submission.

Hiranyakashipu ordered his soldiers to kill the boy. They tried to stab him with spears, but their weapons broke upon touching him. They threw him into a pit of venomous serpents, but the snakes refused to harm him. They hurled him into the ocean and threw him off cliffs. Despite these tortures, Prahlāda's unwavering courage and faith allowed him to emerge unharmed every time.

Hiranyakashipu ordered his guards to crush Prahlāda beneath massive boulders. They placed him beneath a mountain of stone and heaped the rocks atop him until the pile resembled a small hill. When they removed the stones, they found the boy sitting cross-legged, unhurt, his face serene as though he had been meditating.

At every turn, Hiranyakashipu's efforts to destroy Prahlāda failed. The king's rage grew, but so did his fear. How could this child, no more than a boy, withstand the fury of nature, beasts, fire, and stone?

Desperate to break his son's spirit, Hiranyakashipu devised a final test. He summoned his sister, *Holika*, who had been granted a boon that made her immune to fire. Together, they devised a cruel plan. Holika would sit in a blazing pyre with Prahlāda on her lap, intending to burn him alive while she remained unharmed.

The fire roared to life, its flames licking the heavens. Holika sat confidently, holding the child in her arms. But as the fire raged, her boon failed her, and she was consumed by the flames. Prahlāda, seated amidst the inferno, emerged untouched, his serene face glowing with divine grace.

Hiranyakashipu's fury reached its zenith. He decided to kill Prahlāda himself. Dragging the boy to the palace courtyard, he bellowed, 'If your Vishnu is everywhere, as you claim, let him save you now!'

Pointing to a pillar in the hall, Hiranyakashipu sneered, 'Is your Vishnu in this pillar too?'

'Yes,' replied Prahlāda, his voice steady. 'He is in the pillar, just as he is in every grain of sand and drop of water.'

Hiranyakashipu struck the pillar with his mace, and the air trembled with a deafening roar. From the shattered stone emerged *Narasimha*, the lion-headed incarnation of Vishnu. Neither man nor beast, Narasimha embodied the loophole in Hiranyakashipu's boon. It was twilight—not day nor night. Narasimha dragged Hiranyakashipu to the threshold of the courtyard—neither indoors nor outdoors—and tore him apart with his claws, needing no weapon.

Prahlāda knelt before Narasimha, who, still raging, appeared unstoppable. It was only the boy's gentle prayers that calmed the divine being. Vishnu, pleased with Prahlāda's unwavering faith, blessed him, promising that his lineage would prosper and his soul would always dwell in divine love.

Krishna Dances on The Hoods of Kāliyā

From The Bhāgavata Purāna

On the lush plains of Vrindavan, where the Yamuna River wound like a silver thread through emerald forests and blooming meadows, life was vibrant and bountiful. The village thrived under the guidance of *Nanda*, a wise and kind leader, and the community was filled with joy. However, this prosperity was shadowed by a lurking menace—a portion of the Yamuna had turned dark and toxic, its waters lifeless and poisoned.

The villagers spoke of a great serpent, *Kāliyā*, who had taken refuge in the river. This serpent's venom seeped into the Yamuna, killing fish, withering plants, and spreading a toxic miasma that drove away wildlife. The villagers, terrified, avoided the poisoned stretch of the river, but their lives were deeply affected, as the bountiful Yamuna was essential for their daily sustenance.

Among the villagers was *Krishna*, a young boy with a mischievous smile and an aura that seemed larger than life. Krishna was no ordinary child—his dark skin gleamed like a raincloud, and his eyes sparkled with the mysteries of the cosmos. Though young, his courage and wisdom often left the elders astonished. Krishna was always surrounded by his elder brother, the loyal and brave *Balarama*, his close friends and a host of playful cowherd boys who looked to him as their leader. Together, they roamed the forests, their laughter echoing through Vrindavan.

One day, while tending to their cows, Krishna and his friends approached the banks of the Yamuna. The poisoned waters reflected a haunting green hue, and the air was thick with a pungent smell. Some of the boys threw stones into the river, their curiosity mingled with fear. 'This is where the serpent lives,' said one, his voice trembling. 'Our parents warned us not to come close.'

Krishna stood at the edge of the river, his gaze fixed on the turbulent waters. His friends pleaded with him to stay away. 'Krishna, don't!' cried *Subala*, one of the cowherds. 'Kāliyā will devour you!'

But Krishna smiled, a serene expression that belied his youth. 'The Yamuna belongs to all of us,' he said. 'We cannot live in fear while this creature poisons our lands.'

Meanwhile, deep beneath the river's surface, Kāliyā stirred. The serpent was massive, his body covered in black scales that shimmered like polished onyx. His numerous hoods, each adorned with a gleaming gem, swayed ominously as he sensed a disturbance above. Kāliyā's lair was a cavernous hollow in the riverbed, and the venom he exhaled created an impenetrable barrier around him. His red eyes glowed with malice as he prepared to face the intruder who dared to challenge his reign.

The villagers gathered at a safe distance, drawn by Krishna's fearless proclamation. Nanda and *Yashoda*, Krishna's parents, watched with growing concern. The air was heavy with tension as Krishna stepped into the river, the cool waters rising around his ankles. With each step, the poison seemed to retreat, as if unwilling to touch him. Krishna's friends and the villagers called out to him, their voices filled with a mixture of admiration and dread. 'Krishna, come back!' they shouted. But Krishna did not falter.

The serpent Kāliyā rose from the depths with a thunderous roar, his many heads swaying like a forest of cobras. The sight was terrifying—a creature born of nightmares, exuding power and malice. The river churned violently as Kāliyā towered above Krishna, his venomous breath darkening the air.

Kāliyā struck first, his fanged maw snapping at Krishna with a speed that belied his massive size. But Krishna, swift as the wind, evaded the attack effortlessly. He darted through the water, his movements a dance of divine grace. Furious, Kāliyā coiled his massive body around Krishna, intending to crush the boy within his serpentine embrace. The villagers on the riverbank gasped in horror, some falling to their knees in prayer.

For a moment, all seemed lost as Kāliyā tightened his grip. But then, with a surge of power, Krishna expanded his form, radiating a light that forced the serpent to loosen his hold. Seizing the moment, Krishna leapt onto Kāliyā's head.

What followed was a spectacle that defied mortal comprehension. Krishna, standing atop Kāliyā's largest hood, began to dance. Each step was a rhythmic beat of divine power, his anklets ringing like celestial chimes. Kāliyā thrashed, his hoods rising and falling in a desperate attempt to dislodge the boy. The river erupted in waves, and venom spewed into the air, but Krishna remained unshaken. With each step, Krishna's feet struck Kāliyā's hood, subduing the serpent's immense power. The marks of Krishna's divine footprints began to etch themselves into Kāliyā's scales, symbols of the cosmos imprinted onto the beast's very being. The serpent's thrashing slowed, his resistance waning as he realised the futility of his rage.

The serpent's wives emerged from the depths, their forms delicate and shimmering, like pearls drawn from the ocean's deepest vaults. They prostrated themselves before Krishna, their hands folded in supplication. 'O Lord,' they pleaded, their voices trembling with reverence, 'spare our husband. His arrogance blinded him, but he now sees your power and grace. Grant him mercy, and we vow he shall trouble the Yamuna no more.'

Hearing their plea, Krishna paused. His gaze fell upon Kāliyā, who now lay subdued, his hoods drooping in surrender. 'Kāliyā,' Krishna said, his voice resonating with divine authority, 'you have poisoned these waters and disrupted the harmony of life. Yet, I offer you a chance to atone. Leave this river and never return. Seek refuge in the ocean, where you may live in peace.'

Kāliyā, humbled and broken, bowed his massive head. 'I accept your mercy, O Lord,' he said, his voice a deep rumble that shook the waters. 'I will leave this place and never return. Your footprints shall forever remain upon my hoods as a reminder of your grace.'

Kāliyā and his family disappeared into the depths, and the Yamuna began to transform. The venom dissolved, and the waters regained their crystal clarity. The riverbanks bloomed with life once more.

Muchukunda Incinerates Kālayavana

From The Bhāgavata Purāna

In the age of kings and gods, *Muchukunda*, a scion of the illustrious *Ikshvaku* dynasty, was renowned for his valour and devotion to *dharma*. His fame extended beyond the mortal realm, reaching the heavens, for he had once answered the call of the *devas* in their war against the *asuras*. The conflict was long and arduous, spanning years. Muchukunda led the divine armies with unparalleled courage, his blade gleaming like lightning, and his presence on the battlefield as fierce as a storm.

When the devas finally triumphed, Indra, the king of gods, approached Muchukunda to offer him a boon. Exhausted from the unending war, the king, with a heart yearning for rest, made a unique request: 'Grant me uninterrupted sleep, O Lord of the heavens, for my body and spirit crave solace.

And let it be so that anyone who dares disturb my slumber shall be reduced to ashes by my gaze.'

The gods, moved by his service and humility, granted his wish. They led him to a secluded cave, deep within the earth, where time flowed differently. There, Muchukunda lay down, surrendering himself to a slumber untouched by the passage of ages.

Centuries passed, and the world changed. Kingdoms rose and fell, sages meditated, and the devas watched over creation. In this era emerged *Kālayavana*, a warrior king of unmatched strength and arrogance. Born of a *Yavana* lineage, Kālayavana was invincible, protected by a boon from Lord *Shiva* himself. His fame as a conqueror spread across the lands, striking terror into the hearts of kings.

Fate brought Kālayavana into an alliance with *Jarāsandha*, the mighty emperor of Magadha and archenemy of *Krishna*, the lord of Mathura. Together, they plotted the destruction of Mathura, assembling vast armies to lay siege to the city. Kālayavana, with his fiery ambition, led his forces to Mathura's gates, determined to defeat Krishna and claim supremacy.

Krishna, the master strategist, saw the futility of a direct confrontation. His mission was to protect dharma, not engage in needless slaughter. As Kālayavana's army surrounded Mathura, Krishna appeared at the city gates, radiant and calm, his aura blinding to the mortal eye.

Spotting Krishna, Kālayavana roared in triumph. 'So, the famed lord of Mathura comes to meet his doom!' he bellowed. But Krishna, without a word, turned and walked away. Confused but eager for glory, Kālayavana gave chase, leaving his army behind.

The chase was relentless. Krishna, swift as the wind, led Kālayavana across forests, rivers, and mountains. Days turned into nights, and still, the *Yavana* king pursued, his pride refusing to let him relent. Finally, Krishna entered a dark and foreboding cave. Kālayavana, consumed by rage and arrogance, followed him inside.

The cave was silent, its air thick with an ancient, otherworldly presence. Kālayavana's eyes adjusted to the darkness, and there he saw a figure lying motionless on the ground, covered in a fine layer of dust. Mistaking the sleeping form for Krishna, Kālayavana approached and kicked it.

The moment his foot connected, the figure stirred. Muchukunda, the great warrior king of ages past, opened his eyes. And as his gaze met Kālayavana, the boon granted by the gods came into effect. A fiery light emanated from his eyes, consuming Kālayavana instantly. The Yavana king, undefeated in battle, was reduced to ashes in a heartbeat.

As the light faded, Muchukunda sat up, his mind still clouded by the remnants of his long sleep. Before him stood Krishna, his divine form illuminating the cave. The sight of the blue-hued lord filled Muchukunda with awe and reverence. He realised he was in the presence of none other than *Vishnu* incarnate.

'O Lord,' Muchukunda said, bowing deeply, 'time has passed me by as I slept. The world outside must be unrecognisable, and I must be but a relic of a forgotten age.'

Krishna smiled, his voice soothing and eternal. 'O noble king, your deeds are remembered by the gods and by dharma itself. You have fulfilled your purpose in this realm. Now, turn your heart towards liberation. Renounce the fleeting ties of the world and seek the eternal.'

Muchukunda, moved by Krishna's words, emerged from the cave. To his astonishment, he found the world transformed. The people, the trees, even the mountains seemed smaller—a testament to the passage of *yugas* during his sleep. Recognising the impermanence of all things, Muchukunda spent the rest of his days in penance, ultimately attaining liberation.

The Emancipation of Gajendra

From The Bhāgavata Purāna

The lush forests of *Trikuta* Mountain rose like emerald spires, their ancient roots intertwined with the mystic energy of creation itself. At its heart lay a lake of unearthly beauty, its crystalline waters glimmering with a golden hue under the light of the sun. Flowers like celestial jewels floated upon the surface, their fragrances carried by the gentle breeze that whispered through the valley. It was a place that seemed untouched by time—a fragment of paradise itself.

Among the denizens of this tranquil haven was *Gajendra*, a mighty elephant who ruled over a vast herd. His tusks were like ivory blades, his strength unmatched, and his every step reverberated with the power of the earth. Yet, Gajendra was no mere beast; he was once a great king named Indradyumna, cursed to take this form for neglecting a sage in his past life.

Though burdened with this fate, his soul retained a spark of divinity.

On a day when the heavens shone bright, Gajendra led his herd to the lake. The shimmering waters invited them to drink and bathe, and as the great elephant plunged into the cool depths, his spirit soared. This was his kingdom, his sanctuary.

But even in paradise, danger can lurk.

Unbeknownst to Gajendra, a dark force lay hidden beneath the water's surface—a crocodile, ancient and malevolent, waiting with silent patience. As Gajendra lowered his trunk to drink, the predator struck with lightning speed, its jaws clamping onto his leg with an iron grip.

The tranquillity of the lake shattered as Gajendra bellowed, a sound that echoed like thunder across the valley. He thrashed and struggled, his immense power churning the waters into a frothy tempest. Yet, no matter how hard he fought, the crocodile's grip remained unyielding, its teeth embedded deep into his flesh.

The herd of elephants trumpeted in alarm, circling their leader but powerless to aid him. Slowly, the realisation dawned upon Gajendra that this was no ordinary crocodile. This was a force of *karma*, a relentless adversary sent to test his spirit.

For a thousand years, the battle raged in the timeless realm of Trikuta. The sky shifted from the golden hues of day to the silvered cloak of night, yet neither beast nor predator yielded. Gajendra's strength began to wane, his massive form trembling as exhaustion took its toll. The crocodile, entrenched in its watery domain, remained as powerful as ever.

In the quiet moments between struggles, fragments of Gajendra's past life surfaced in his mind. He remembered the teachings of the sages, the hymns sung in praise of the Supreme Being. His mortal strength had failed him, but his soul recognised a greater truth: no power of this world could save him, only the grace of the eternal.

As the first rays of dawn broke over the horizon, Gajendra ceased his struggle. Lifting his trunk high into the air, he plucked a lotus flower from the lake, its delicate petals trembling in his grasp. With a voice that resonated from the depths of his being, he chanted a hymn of surrender to *Vishnu*, the Supreme Lord:

'O Lord of the Universe,

refuge of the afflicted,

I seek Your shelter.

You are the cause of all causes,

the eternal soul,

beyond the grasp of time.

Save me from this cycle of suffering.'

Far above the mortal plane, in the eternal realm of *Vaikuntha*, Vishnu heard the cry of His devotee. The Lord of all creation, adorned with radiant ornaments and holding the conch, discus, mace, and lotus, rose from His divine seat. Mounting *Garuda*, His celestial eagle, He descended with the swiftness of a thought.

The skies over Trikuta erupted with celestial radiance as Vishnu appeared, His presence banishing all fear and darkness. Garuda's wings stirred the air, their golden feathers shimmering like a thousand suns. The gods and sages watched in awe as the Lord arrived to answer the call of a soul in need.

With a single motion, Vishnu hurled His discus, the *Sudarshana Chakra*. The weapon, blazing with divine energy, sliced through the crocodile, severing it from the mortal coil. The lake fell silent as the beast released its hold, its spirit freed from the curse that had bound it to that form.

As the waters stilled, Gajendra collapsed onto the shore, his massive body trembling with relief. But the battle had not been in vain. Gajendra's heart was no longer bound by fear or pride. In the presence of the Lord, he realised that true liberation was not merely freedom from physical pain, but freedom from the illusions of the material world.

Vishnu stepped forward, His gaze filled with infinite compassion. He placed His hand upon Gajendra's head, and in that moment, the elephant's form dissolved, revealing the luminous soul of *Indradyumna*.

The Lord smiled and said, 'You have attained My abode, O noble one. Your surrender and devotion have freed you from the cycle of birth and death. Come, dwell with Me in eternal bliss.'

As the Lord ascended back to Vaikuntha, Gajendra's soul merged with the divine light, a star shining eternally in the cosmic tapestry. The lake, once a battleground, became a sacred site, a reminder of the soul's journey from suffering to liberation.

The tale of Gajendra's liberation underlines that strength alone cannot conquer life's trials. Only when one surrenders to the divine, recognising the futility of ego and pride, can true peace and freedom be attained.

In the golden light of Trikuta, the lake continues to shimmer, a reflection of the eternal truth that lies within every soul—the path to liberation begins with surrender and ends in the embrace of the infinite.

Krishna Lifts Govardhan Hill

From The Bhāgavata Purāna

In the verdant plains of Vrindavan, beneath the watchful gaze of *Govardhan Parvata* (Govardhan Hill), life thrived. Cattle grazed in vast fields, their bells jingling in rhythm with the laughter of cowherds. Villagers sang hymns to the gods, their melodies blending with the soft rustle of the Yamuna's waters. Among them was a divine boy—*Krishna*, the dark-hued one, with eyes deep as monsoon clouds and a smile that held the secrets of creation.

Every year, the people of Vrindavan prepared for *Indra Puja*, a grand offering to the king of the heavens. 'Indra grants us rain,' said *Nanda*, Krishna's father, addressing the assembly. 'Without his blessings, how would our crops grow, our rivers flow?'

Krishna, standing with his golden flute in hand, tilted his head thoughtfully. 'Father,' he said, his voice steady and soft, 'why do we worship Indra? Is not Govardhan Hill the true provider? Its forests give our cattle shade; its streams quench their thirst. Let us honour Govardhan, for it sustains us.'

The elders murmured in surprise, but Krishna's logic was irrefutable. Nanda, trusting his son's wisdom, consented.

Thus, instead of the usual offerings to Indra, the villagers adorned Govardhan Hill with garlands and lamps. They laid before it heaps of fragrant flowers, fresh milk, curd, and honey. Krishna, smiling radiantly, joined the festivities, dancing among the children and herding cattle in joyous abandon.

Far above, in the celestial court of *Swarga*, Indra's pride burned like a tempest. Seated on his throne of gold and thunderclouds, he watched as mortals ignored him. 'How dare they!' he thundered, his voice reverberating across the heavens. 'Have they forgotten who commands the rains? This Krishna, this mere child, has led them astray!'

Summoning the clouds of destruction, Indra declared, 'Let Vrindavan learn its folly. I shall unleash a deluge to drown their insolence.' The celestial clouds, dark and brooding, obeyed, rushing towards the mortal realm.

The sky over Vrindavan darkened ominously. The villagers looked up in confusion as the first drops of rain fell, quickly turning into torrents. Thunder roared, and lightning danced wildly, illuminating the terror on their faces. Winds howled, uprooting trees and flinging them into the air like toys. The Yamuna swelled, spilling its fury across the land.

The people ran to Krishna, their protector. 'O Krishna!' they cried. 'The storm is unending. Save us, or we shall perish!'

Krishna's face remained serene, his lotus-like eyes filled with compassion. 'Fear not,' he said, his voice steady like the earth. 'This is Indra's doing, but his arrogance will not harm us. Gather beneath Govardhan Hill, and I shall protect you.'

As the storm raged, Krishna walked to Govardhan Hill. Planting his golden flute in the earth, he placed his small, delicate hand beneath the hill's base. With effortless grace, he lifted the entire mountain as one lifts a flower. The villagers gasped, awestruck, as Krishna held the hill aloft with just his little finger.

'Come,' he called, his voice like the melody of rain, 'take shelter beneath Govardhan.'

Men, women, children, and cattle rushed under the hill's protective canopy. Krishna stood at the centre, his radiant form illuminating the darkened landscape. The villagers watched in wonder, their fears dissolving in the warmth of his presence.

For seven days and nights, the storm battered Vrindavan, but not a single drop of rain touched the villagers. Krishna stood unwavering, his smile undiminished, as the hill rested upon his finger. His friends, the cowherds, marvelled at his strength. 'How does he do it?' whispered *Subala*. 'He is no ordinary boy,' said *Balrama*, Krishna's elder brother.

The villagers, too, began to realise Krishna's divinity. Nanda and Yashoda, his earthly parents, felt both pride and reverence. The storm seemed like a cosmic play, revealing Krishna's true nature.

In Swarga, Indra watched, his rage giving way to doubt. 'How is this possible?' he wondered. 'This boy defies the might of my storms!'

As the seventh day dawned, Indra realised his folly. The boy was not an ordinary mortal. Gradually, the storm's fury waned, and Indra descended to Vrindavan, humbled.

Before Krishna, the celestial king bowed. 'O Lord,' he said, his voice filled with remorse, 'forgive my arrogance. I was blinded by pride and forgot that you are the Supreme Being. You are the protector of all, the master of the Universe.'

Krishna gently lowered Govardhan Hill, placing it back on the earth. Turning to Indra, he said, 'Pride blinds even the greatest of beings. Remember, Indra, true strength lies in humility and service.'

With Indra's blessing, the storm ceased, and the sun bathed Vrindavan in golden light. The villagers rejoiced, their faith in Krishna now unshakeable. They sang songs of his glory, garlanding him with flowers. Krishna, however, remained as he always was—gentle, playful, and full of love for all beings.

Part 4

The Devi Bhāgavatam

Ādi Shakti Creates The Trinity

From The Devi Bhāgavatam

In the time before time, when neither sun nor moon lit the vast expanse of existence, there lay the unfathomable void, shrouded in the silence of the eternal night. No stars adorned the heavens, no breath stirred the slumbering cosmos. It was an age before ages, where even the great firmament awaited its birth. The mightiest of beings were yet unformed, and the power of creation slept in the deep heart of the Supreme Feminine, *Ādi Shakti*.

She, the Great Goddess, was the One Without a Second, the Eternal Source from whom all things would arise and to whom all would return. In her rested the unmanifested seed of the cosmos, the great wheel of time, and the ceaseless cycle of life and death. As she sat in meditation upon the vast and formless waters of eternity, a stirring began deep within her boundless essence. She willed creation into being, and with her will, the slumbering energies of the universe awoke.

From the depths of her consciousness, Ādi Shakti summoned forth three cosmic vibrations, each resonating with the qualities of creation, preservation, and destruction. These three essences—the primal energies of the cosmos—manifested as the Trinity: *Brahmā*, *Vishnu*, and *Shiva*. Yet, though they emerged with form and power, they were but sparks of her eternal glory, each dependent upon her will for their existence.

The first to emerge was Brahmā, the Creator. He arose, golden and resplendent, from the boundless ocean of her being. In his hands, he bore the tools of creation: the Vedas, which held the knowledge of the universe, and the lotus, the eternal symbol of divine purity. His essence was suffused with *rajas*, the energy of activity, and his gaze was filled with curiosity and the hunger to create worlds yet unknown.

Next came Vishnu, the Preserver, whose form shone with a serene and tranquil light, like the calm before the storm. Clad in the blue of the eternal sky and the ocean's depth, he held the conch of divine sound and the discus of righteous power. His essence was infused with *sattva*, the energy of balance and harmony, and his purpose was to uphold *dharma*, the cosmic order, and ensure the preservation of what was to come.

Last arose Shiva, the Destroyer, who bore the austere visage of the ascetic and the wild fury of the storm. With his matted locks, serpentine adornments, and the crescent moon upon his brow, he was the stillness of meditation and the tempest of dissolution. His essence was imbued with *tamas*, the energy of transformation and transcendence, and he stood ready to unmake what needed to be renewed.

Though each was mighty and eternal in his own right, the Trinity bowed low before the Supreme Goddess. For they knew that without her, their powers were as naught; their forms mere vessels for her will.

Ādi Shakti gazed upon the Trinity with infinite compassion and wisdom, her eyes the wellspring of all knowledge. ‹You have emerged from my essence,› she said, her voice resonating across the void like the first breath of creation, ‹and in you lies the purpose of existence. Yet know this: you are but instruments of my will, and your powers derive from my eternal being. It is I who am the womb of the universe, the eternal energy behind all creation, preservation, and destruction.›

The Trinity listened in silence, their forms humbled by her boundless majesty. She continued: 'Brahmā, you shall weave the threads of existence, crafting the worlds and their infinite forms. Vishnu, you shall preserve the balance, ensuring that the wheel of time turns in harmony. And Shiva, you shall bring transformation, dissolving what has decayed so that creation may begin anew.'

Each deity accepted their role, understanding the immense responsibility bestowed upon them. Yet, in their wisdom, they also recognised their dependence on the Goddess, for without her, the energies they embodied would dissolve into the formless void.

With her decree issued, Ādi Shakti began the great work of creation. From her body emanated the primordial sound, *Om*, which became the vibration upon which the universe was built. This sound gave rise to the elements—earth, water, fire, air, and ether—each an aspect of her being, each a cornerstone of existence.

As Brahmā set to work crafting the heavens, the earth, and the myriad beings that would populate the cosmos, Vishnu lay upon the great cosmic serpent *Ananta*, ensuring the balance of creation. Shiva, ever meditative and watchful, prepared to bring dissolution when the time was ripe, for he knew that all things must pass before they could be born anew.

The Goddess herself withdrew into her eternal form, observing the unfolding of her will through the Trinity. Yet she remained ever-present, the unseen force guiding the great cosmic dance. It was she who granted the Trinity their divine powers, and it was she who ensured that the balance was maintained.

Thus was the universe born, not from conflict or chaos, but from the infinite wisdom and compassion of Ādi Shakti. She, the Great Goddess, was both the creator and the created, the manifest and the unmanifest. Her energy pervaded all things, from the smallest atom to the vast expanse of the heavens.

The Trinity, though powerful, understood their place in the grand design. They knew that their existence was but a reflection of her glory, and they worshipped her with devotion, recognising her as the ultimate reality. Brahmā chanted her praises through the Vedas, Vishnu meditated upon her infinite form, and Shiva danced the cosmic *Tāndava*, a dance both destructive and creative, in her honour.

The Goddess, in turn, blessed them, ensuring that they would fulfil their roles with wisdom and strength. And so, the wheel of time began to turn, and the great play of existence unfolded, guided always by the unseen hand of Ādi Shakti. This tale of the creation of the Trinity by Ādi Shakti is the story of beginnings, of divine will, and of the eternal truth that all creation rests in the lap of the Supreme Goddess, who is the mother of the cosmos and the source of all life.

The Slaying of Madhu-Kaitabha

From The Devi Bhāgavatam

In the beginning, when time itself was yet unmeasured, the universe was a vast, endless ocean. Lord *Vishnu* lay asleep upon the serpent *Ananta*, cradled in the cosmic waters. In this infinite stillness, from the depths of his being emerged two demons—*Madhu* and *Kaitabha*, born from the impurities of his ears.

Madhu and Kaitabha, gigantic and formidable, surveyed the universe with greedy eyes. Their very presence radiated a menacing force that disturbed the balance of creation. With malice in their hearts, they delved into the depths of the cosmic ocean and stole the sacred Vedas, the essence of knowledge and dharma, plunging the world into chaos.

The universe spiralled into darkness. Witnessing this disorder, *Brahmā*, the Creator, seated on the lotus arising from Vishnu's navel, felt powerless. The absence of the Vedas meant the cycle of creation could not continue. Desperation filled him as he meditated deeply, focusing his thoughts on the supreme *Devi*, *Mahāmāya*, the primordial energy who governs all existence.

With fervent devotion, Brahmā began his hymn of praise:

'O Devi, the great Mother, you are the origin of all creation, preservation, and destruction. You are the supreme consciousness that pervades all. Without you, O Mahāmāya, none can act—not even Vishnu, the great preserver. You are *Shakti*, the force behind every deed. O compassionate one, awaken Vishnu, for only by your grace can he destroy these demons and restore balance!'

As Brahmā chanted, his voice trembling with both fear and devotion, the Devi appeared in all her radiant glory. She was resplendent, her light banishing the shadows, her form encompassing the power of creation itself. Her voice, calm and commanding, resonated in the void.

'O Brahmā,' she said, 'do not despair. By my power, Vishnu shall awaken, and the demons shall be vanquished. But know this: it is arrogance and delusion that give them their strength. Through cunning, they shall meet their end.'

The Devi infused her energy into Vishnu, stirring him from his deep slumber. His eyes opened, luminous with her divine essence. Rising from the serpent Ananta, Vishnu grasped his mace and discus, his gaze falling upon the demons.

Madhu and Kaitabha, sensing his presence, roared with

laughter. 'Who dares to challenge us?' Kaitabha sneered, his voice shaking the cosmic ocean.

'I am Vishnu,' the preserver replied, his tone steady. 'Return the Vedas to their rightful place, or face destruction.'

But Madhu and Kaitabha were unafraid. Empowered by a boon from the Devi herself, they had gained immense strength and invulnerability. They mocked Vishnu, their arrogance boundless. 'We are invincible!' they declared. 'None can defeat us. If you dare to challenge us, we grant you the right to choose the place and manner of our death—if you can accomplish it.'

Vishnu's mind, sharpened by the Devi's grace, understood their weakness. With a battle cry that shook the heavens, he engaged them in combat. The ocean churned as their blows fell like thunder, each strike splitting the waves. The gods watched in awe and fear as the fight raged on for five thousand years.

Finally, Vishnu paused, his body gleaming with sweat, his lips curling into a cunning smile. 'You are indeed mighty,' he said, his voice carrying a note of admiration. 'But I, too, respect the rules of war. Since you have given me the right to choose, I declare that you shall die upon my thighs, for no place else is dry in this boundless ocean.'

Before the demons could react, Vishnu seized them with superhuman speed. Summoning the *vajra*-like strength granted by the Devi, he hurled them onto his thighs. With his discus, the *Sudarshana Chakra*, he decapitated them in one swift motion. Their monstrous heads fell into the waters, and their enormous bodies sank beneath the waves, their blood staining the ocean crimson.

As the demons perished, the Vedas, freed from their grasp, ascended into the heavens, glowing with divine radiance. The gods sang hymns of praise to Vishnu and the Devi, their voices echoing through the restored cosmos.

From the remains of Madhu and Kaitabha, the Devi's power reshaped the universe. Their flesh and fat were transformed into the earthly realms—the mountains, plains, and fertile lands where life could flourish. Their sacrifice, though born of their arrogance, became the foundation of creation, a testament to the Devi's supreme wisdom.

Vishnu bowed his head in reverence to the Devi, acknowledging her as the ultimate force behind his victory. 'O Mahāmāya,' he said, 'it is your will that governs all. Without you, even the mightiest gods are powerless. To you, I offer my eternal devotion.'

Devi's voice resonated once more, serene and all-encompassing: 'Thus, the balance is restored. Remember, pride and delusion will always be the downfall of the arrogant. Creation thrives only through humility and devotion.'

And so, with Devi's blessings, the cycle of creation resumed, and the cosmos flourished anew.

Devi Humbles Vindhya

From The Devi Bhāgavatam

The *Vindhya* Mountains stood tall, their jagged peaks scraping the sky and their shadows sprawling across the earth below. These mountains had long been revered as a bastion of power and strength, their lord—Vindhya, the sentient mountain—proud and unyielding. The gods often gazed upon this range from their celestial abodes, for it was here, in the heart of the land, that the *Devi* was destined to descend.

Mahishāsura, the demon king, had spread his tyranny across the realms. Empowered by a boon of near invincibility, he had driven the gods from their seats of power. Neither *Brahmā*, *Vishnu*, nor *Shiva* could defeat him, bound as they were by the terms of the boon. Bereft of options, the gods turned to the eternal feminine force—the Devi, the supreme Goddess who embodied the combined energies of the Trinity.

When the Devi descended, it was as if the cosmos itself had come alive. A blinding light radiated through the heavens, and from it emerged the Goddess, resplendent and terrible to behold. Her form glowed like molten gold, her eyes burned like the sun, and her arms carried weapons gifted by the gods: Vishnu's discus, Shiva's trident, Indra's thunderbolt, and countless others.

Her first step upon the Vindhya range shook the mountains. The earth quaked, and the rivers roared in acknowledgement of her divine presence. The flora and fauna, in harmony with the cosmic force she represented, bloomed in reverence, their colours more vivid than ever. Yet, in the heart of these mountains dwelt Vindhya himself, and he was not pleased.

Vindhya, the mountain lord, rose from his domain, his colossal form towering like a titan above the valleys. His jagged peaks seemed to grow taller in defiance, and his voice, a thunderous roar, echoed through the range.

'Who dares tread upon my sacred domain?' he bellowed, his tone laced with arrogance. 'I am Vindhya, lord of these peaks, eternal and immovable. No god nor mortal may trespass here without my leave. Who are you to disturb my reign?'

The Devi stood her ground, her gaze unflinching as she looked upon the mountain lord. Her voice, though calm, carried the weight of universal truth.

'I am Devi,' she declared, her words reverberating through the valleys. 'I come not as a trespasser but as the force that sustains and governs all existence. Your pride blinds you, Vindhya. Even the mightiest mountain is but a speck in the vast cosmic order.'

Vindhya's pride flared at her words. He bristled, his rocky ridges trembling with indignation. 'You speak of cosmic order, yet you come here unbidden, uninvited! This is my domain, and I bow to no one—not even to one such as you.'

The Devi's expression did not waver. She didn't see it fit to explain to the arrogant Vindhya why and where she was going. Her mission to annihilate Mahishāsura was none of the proud mountain lord's concern.

'Pride is your undoing, O Vindhya. The earth itself quakes beneath your arrogance,' she said. 'Even now, you seek to challenge forces far beyond your comprehension.'

Vindhya's laughter rumbled like an earthquake. 'Challenge? You dare to suggest I fear anything? I am Vindhya, eternal and unyielding! If you think otherwise, Goddess, then prove it. Show me the power you claim to wield!'

The air grew thick with tension, and the Devi's form seemed to blaze brighter. She raised her hand, and the weapons in her many arms shimmered with divine energy. The mountains trembled, and the skies darkened as clouds gathered overhead.

'Very well, Vindhya,' she said, her voice like the roll of distant thunder. 'You shall witness the force that sustains the cosmos. Prepare yourself.'

With a single gesture, the Devi unleashed her power. The

earth beneath Vindhya's peaks cracked and split, rivers erupted from the ground, and winds howled with unrelenting fury. Her weapons, each a manifestation of divine strength, tore through the air, striking the mountains with precision. Vindhya's peaks, once towering and proud, began to crumble under her assault.

Yet even as his ridges splintered, Vindhya roared in defiance, determined to prove his strength. He rose higher, straining against the forces arrayed against him. 'I will not yield!' he bellowed. 'No power can humble Vindhya!'

But the Devi was unrelenting. Her power was infinite, her presence the embodiment of the universe itself. With each blow she struck, Vindhya's pride faltered, his strength waning. Finally, as the battle reached its crescendo, Vindhya fell silent, his towering form sinking lower.

The Devi stepped forward, her light illuminating the broken peaks of the mountain lord. She spoke, her tone neither triumphant nor scornful.

'Vindhya, your strength is undeniable, but it is born of arrogance. You sought to defy the cosmic order, and in doing so, you have brought about your own fall. True strength lies not in defiance, but in understanding your place within the greater whole.'

Vindhya, humbled and broken, bowed before the Devi. His peaks, once jagged and towering, softened as he lowered himself in submission. 'Forgive me, O Devi,' he said, his voice now a low rumble. 'I see now the truth of your words. I am but a part of the cosmic order, and I bow to your will.'

The Devi nodded, her expression one of compassion. 'Rise, Vindhya,' she said. 'Your humility has restored balance to these lands. Remember this lesson, and let your pride not lead you astray again.'

Vindhya rose, his form smaller yet more harmonious with the world around him. The mountains no longer trembled with arrogance but stood strong and steady, a symbol of balance restored.

The Devi continued her journey through the Vindhya range towards the realm of the demon king Mahishāsura, her presence bringing peace and harmony to the lands. And Vindhya was forever changed in the face of divine truth.

The Redemption of Subāhu

From The Devi Bhāgavatam

King *Subāhu* was known for his bravery and his unshakeable commitment to righteousness (*dharma*). He ruled over his people with a firm hand and a just heart, ensuring peace and prosperity in his lands. His queen, *Madālasā*, was a woman of extraordinary beauty and wisdom. Despite her external charm, it was her internal spiritual power and purity of heart that set her apart. Together, they made a formidable pair, admired by all who knew them.

However, despite his outwardly perfect rule and the love he shared with his queen, King Subāhu harboured a deep secret. Though he ruled with honour, he found himself torn between his royal duties and the darker temptations of the world. Over time, the king's devotion to his spiritual practices began to wane. He became entangled in worldly pleasures and desires, losing sight of his higher purpose.

Queen Madālasā, aware of her husband's growing distractions, was deeply concerned. She knew that without a strong spiritual anchor, Subāhu would soon stray from the righteous path, and their kingdom would suffer. She often tried to counsel him, urging him to return to his devotion and meditation, but the king, intoxicated by the pleasures of his kingdom, paid little heed to her advice.

One day, as the king was lost in thought in his royal chambers, Queen Madālasā approached him, determined to offer her guidance. With great humility, she began to speak to him about the importance of devotion to the Divine, of recognising the ephemeral nature of worldly pleasures, and of the need to focus on the eternal truths that lay beyond.

'O King Subāhu,' she said, 'the material world, with all its riches and pleasures, is but a fleeting illusion. True happiness and strength lie not in the accumulation of wealth or the satisfaction of desires, but in surrendering to the Divine. The Goddess, who is the source of all creation, is ever present, and only through her grace can one find peace and liberation.'

But the king, though moved by his queen's words, did not heed her advice. He continued to indulge in the pleasures of his royal court, neglecting his spiritual practices.

It was during this time of spiritual decline that the kingdom was threatened by a series of calamities. The once-bountiful land began to suffer from crop failures, and a great famine swept across the kingdom. The people of the land, once prosperous and content, now cried out for help.

As the suffering of his people grew, King Subāhu realised the truth of Queen Madālasā's words. His kingdom was suffering, and the balance of the world was at risk due to his neglect of his duties as a ruler and his failure to honour the Divine. Desperate, he turned to his queen for guidance.

Queen Madālasā, understanding the gravity of the situation, encouraged him to seek the Goddess's divine intervention. She told him that only through true devotion and surrender to the Divine could the kingdom be saved. Subāhu, filled with remorse, decided to perform a grand *yajna* (sacrificial ritual) to invoke the Goddess's blessings.

With great sincerity, King Subāhu prepared for the ritual, seeking the Goddess's grace with all his heart. He and Queen Madālasā, along with the royal priests and sages, performed the yajna with complete devotion, offering prayers and sacrifices to the Goddess in the hope of appeasing her and restoring balance to their kingdom.

Moved by the sincerity and devotion of King Subāhu, the Goddess, in her compassionate and divine form, appeared before the king. Her radiance filled the entire kingdom, and her presence was so overwhelming that even the air seemed to tremble with her power.

'O King Subāhu,' the Goddess said, her voice like thunder yet soothing as a summer breeze, 'I have heard your prayers. You have realised the error of your ways, and I see the sincerity in your heart. It is through devotion and righteousness that one finds liberation, and I will grant you my blessing.'

Devi, with a wave of her hand, restored prosperity to the land. The famine ended, the crops flourished once more, and the people rejoiced. The once-barren fields bloomed with life, and the rivers flowed with abundance. Subāhu, witnessing the power of the Goddess's grace, was overwhelmed with gratitude and devotion. His heart, now cleansed of worldly desires, turned towards the Goddess in true surrender.

The Goddess, pleased with the king's transformation, spoke once more: 'O King, your kingdom is now blessed. Remember always to keep your heart devoted to the Divine and uphold the values of righteousness. Lead your people with compassion and wisdom, and never lose sight of your higher purpose.'

With these words, Devi vanished, leaving behind a divine aura that continued to bless the land. King Subāhu, his heart now full of humility and devotion, thanked Queen Madālasā for her unwavering guidance. He had learnt the greatest lesson of all: true strength lay not in worldly power, but in devotion to the Divine and adherence to dharma.

Arjuna Invokes Devi

From The Devi Bhāgavatam

At the dawn of the great war at *Kurukshetra*, when the earth trembled under the weight of fate and the heavens seemed to darken with the shadow of impending destruction, the gods and the forces of good looked upon the battlefield with sorrow. The conflict between the *Pāndavas* and the *Kauravas*, two families bound by blood but divided by rivalry, had reached a point of no return. The fate of the entire world seemed to hang in the balance, as the armies clashed and the very air rang with the cries of warriors. Yet, amidst this turmoil, a deeper force moved unseen by mortal eyes: the eternal will of the Goddess, the Supreme *Devi*.

The Goddess, the embodiment of power and wisdom, had long been the protector of *dharma* (cosmic law) and the ultimate source of all strength. She had watched over the world, and now, with the great battle unfolding, it was clear that her intervention was needed once more.

The Pāndavas, righteous in their cause but overwhelmed by the magnitude of the war, were beset by doubt and sorrow. *Arjuna*, the greatest of the Pāndava warriors, stood on the edge of despair. In the midst of the battle, with the blood of kin and friends staining the earth beneath him, Arjuna's heart was weighed down with grief. His mind was clouded by confusion and moral dilemma, torn between his duty as a warrior and his love for his family and teachers. He was unable to fight, unable to raise his bow, and the great warrior stood still, as if frozen in time.

It was then that *Krishna*, his divine charioteer, who had already revealed his supreme form in the *Bhagavad Gitā*, turned to Arjuna with the wisdom of the ages. Krishna, though the incarnate deity, could not directly intervene in the battle, for the laws of fate and dharma forbade such interference. Yet, he understood that the battle was not merely one of physical prowess, but one that was governed by divine forces. Krishna knew that only by invoking the blessings of the Goddess could the Pāndavas truly find victory, and that only she could guide them through the darkness that had descended upon them.

Thus, Krishna spoke to Arjuna, urging him to seek the blessings of Devi, who resided beyond time and space. He instructed Arjuna to perform intense penance at Kurukshetra, to appeal to the Goddess and earn her favour, for she was the ultimate source of all strength and victory. In the midst of the war, Arjuna, despite his doubts, followed Krishna's advice and withdrew from the battlefield.

The great warrior, his heart filled with devotion, sat upon the sacred land of Kurukshetra, where countless battles had been fought and the ancient gods had once walked. He began his penance, offering his prayers with unwavering focus and surrender. His mind, once clouded with doubt, became a beacon of single-minded devotion. He recited the sacred mantras, his voice echoing through the air, his body enduring the harshness of the land and the trials of time. Arjuna's devotion was so pure and intense that the heavens themselves seemed to stir in response.

For many days and nights, Arjuna meditated upon Devi, calling upon her to guide him, to grant him the strength to overcome his fear and doubt. As his penance deepened, the earth trembled with the presence of the divine, and the sky opened up, revealing the form of the Goddess herself.

It was on the seventh day of Arjuna's penance that Devi, in all her resplendent glory, appeared before him. Her form was radiant beyond description, her eyes glowing with the light of the cosmos. She stood as a manifestation of all the divine energies that permeated the universe—both creative and destructive. Her body, adorned in jewels and garlands, shimmered with the brilliance of countless stars, and from her emerged an aura of strength and wisdom that filled the very air with a divine presence.

Her form was both gentle and fierce, a paradox that Arjuna had heard described in the ancient texts but had never truly comprehended until now. She was the mother of all, the destroyer of evil, the protector of dharma, and the one who embodied the eternal balance of the cosmos.

As Arjuna gazed upon her, his heart swelled with awe and reverence. He bowed before her, his hands clasped in prayer. His voice, filled with devotion and gratitude, echoed across the land. 'O Devi, Supreme Mother, I have sought your grace, for I stand at the crossroads of fate. My heart is filled with doubt, and my mind is clouded with sorrow. Only you, O Goddess, can grant me the strength to fulfil my dharma and lead my people to victory. Please, bless me with your divine wisdom and guidance.'

Devi, seeing Arjuna's devotion and the purity of his heart, smiled with compassion. She raised her hand, and from it emanated a radiant light that enveloped Arjuna. The light infused him with divine strength, clarity, and purpose. 'O Arjuna, son of *Pāndu*, I have heard your call, and I grant you the blessings you seek. You are my child, and I shall guide you in this battle. Your heart is pure, and your cause is just. The victory of dharma is assured, for it is I who stand behind you, as the eternal force that upholds the universe.'

Devi then bestowed upon Arjuna the *shakti* to wield the *Pāshupatāstra*, a divine weapon imbued with the power to destroy any foe. This weapon, granted to him by Lord *Shiva*, was a weapon of immense power, and with it, Arjuna would have the strength to face even the most powerful of adversaries. The weapon's brilliance was like the sun itself, a force capable of annihilating the armies of evil that threatened to overwhelm the forces of good.

Arjuna, filled with gratitude, bowed once more before the Goddess, his heart now light with divine strength. 'O Devi, your grace is beyond measure. I shall carry your blessings into the battle and ensure that the forces of darkness are vanquished. With your guidance, victory is inevitable.'

Devi's form began to fade, but her presence lingered in the air, a radiant light that filled Arjuna's heart with confidence and power. 'Go now, Arjuna, and fulfil your dharma. Remember that I am always with you, guiding you, as the force of creation, preservation, and destruction. With your faith in me, you shall overcome all obstacles.'

Empowered by the divine grace of Devi, Arjuna returned to the battlefield of Kurukshetra. The sight of him, now filled with the divine energy of the Goddess, struck fear into the hearts of his enemies. With the Pāshupatāstra in his hand, Arjuna became an unstoppable force. His arrows flew with the speed of the wind, and each strike was a harbinger of doom for the Kaurava forces. His enemies, once confident in their strength, now faltered in fear, for they knew that the power of the Goddess herself was with him.

The battle that followed was fierce and filled with great sorrow, but with the blessings of Devi, the Pāndavas triumphed. The forces of dharma, guided by Arjuna's newfound strength and wisdom, overcame the Kauravas, and the righteousness of the Pāndavas was finally restored. The war that had torn the land apart came to an end, and the forces of evil were vanquished.

As the battle concluded and peace began to settle upon the land, Arjuna, still carrying the blessings of Devi in his heart, approached Krishna. His mind was no longer clouded with doubt, for the divine intervention of the Goddess had given him the clarity to fulfil his role in the cosmic order. 'O Krishna,' Arjuna said, 'your counsel and the blessings of Devi have guided me through the darkness. I am forever indebted to you and to the Supreme Mother.'

Krishna smiled, his heart filled with love for his devoted disciple. 'It is not I, Arjuna, but the Supreme Devi herself who guided you. You have fulfilled your dharma, and through your actions, the world has been saved. The victory was always hers, and you were but the instrument of her will.'

Thus, the battle at Kurukshetra, the great war that shaped the destiny of the world, was won not just by the strength of arms, but by the grace of Devi. The victory of the Pandavas was a victory of dharma, a victory of righteousness over evil, and a victory of the eternal power of the Goddess.

Devi Triumphs over Asura Durgam

From The Devi Bhāgavatam

In an age when darkness sought dominion over light and the worlds teetered on the edge of despair, there arose a calamity unlike any other. A demon named *Durgam*, born of a long lineage of arrogance and cruelty, sought to unmake the delicate balance of creation. His heart, blackened by ambition and pride, burned with a singular desire: to usurp the order of the universe and plunge it into chaos.

Durgam, through centuries of severe penance, had acquired great power. He performed austerities so intense that the gods in their celestial abodes grew restless. Fearful of his growing strength, they watched helplessly as he prayed to *Brahmā*, the Creator, seeking a boon. Brahmā, bound by the laws of divine penance, appeared before the demon, his form radiant but troubled, for he foresaw the destruction this boon might bring.

'Name your desire,' Brahmā said, his voice carrying both grace and foreboding.

Durgam, his eyes blazing with malice, declared, 'Grant me the *Vedas*, O Lord, and with them, the wisdom and authority to control the balance of creation. Let me rule the heavens, earth, and the underworld, and render the gods powerless.'

Brahmā, though reluctant, could not refuse a boon to one who had undergone such severe austerities. With a heavy heart, he bestowed the Vedas upon Durgam, knowing that the demon's misuse of the sacred knowledge would bring suffering to all creation.

Armed with the Vedas, Durgam unleashed his reign of terror. Without the sacred knowledge, the gods were rendered powerless. The balance of creation faltered as droughts scorched the lands, rivers dried up, and crops withered under a merciless sun. The earth herself cried out, her fertile body parched and desolate. The heavens trembled under the weight of Durgam's tyranny, for he claimed himself the supreme lord, dismissing the gods and defiling the sanctity of *dharma*.

The once-flourishing lands descended into despair, and humanity, bereft of sustenance and divine guidance, fell to their knees in prayer. Yet, the heavens remained silent, for the gods, stripped of power, could not answer their pleas. The cries of the helpless echoed through the realms, reaching the ears of the Eternal Mother, the Supreme *Devi*.

Devi, the great *Ādi Shakti*, heard the anguished prayers of her devotees. Moved by their suffering, she emerged from her eternal meditation, her form blazing with the light of a thousand suns. Clad in radiant garments and adorned with celestial jewels, she descended to the desolate earth, her compassionate gaze filling the hearts of her devotees with hope.

The moment she set foot upon the earth, life began to stir. Rivers bubbled forth from barren lands, and trees, long withered, blossomed anew. The earth herself sighed in relief, her form revitalised by Devi's presence. Yet, Devi knew that the true source of the suffering remained unchecked: Durgam and his misuse of the Vedas.

As the Goddess moved across the realms, her brilliance drove away the shadows of despair. The gods, sensing her divine presence, gathered before her, their heads bowed in reverence. They spoke of their plight, of Durgam's theft of the Vedas and the devastation it had wrought.

Devi listened, her face serene yet determined. 'Fear not,' she said, her voice carrying the power of creation itself. 'The time has come to restore balance to the universe. I shall confront this demon and return the Vedas to their rightful place.'

Durgam, seated upon his throne of arrogance, was unprepared for the wrath of the Goddess. When he heard of Devi's arrival, he laughed, his voice echoing with mockery. 'What can a mere woman do against me, the master of the Vedas and ruler of the cosmos?' he boasted.

But his laughter soon turned to rage when he saw Devi in her full glory. Mounted upon her lion, she appeared as a warrior of unparalleled might. In her thousand arms, she wielded weapons bestowed upon her by the gods—*Vishnu*'s discus, *Shiva*'s trident, *Indra*'s thunderbolt, and many others. Her eyes blazed with divine fury, and her presence filled the air with the hum of cosmic energy.

The battle that ensued was fierce and unrelenting. Durgam summoned his vast army of demons, their cries shaking the earth, but Devi stood undaunted. With her celestial weapons, she vanquished the hordes, her lion tearing through their ranks with ferocious might. She danced upon the battlefield, her movements both graceful and devastating, each step crushing the forces of darkness.

Durgam, realising the extent of Devi's power, attacked her directly, wielding the stolen knowledge of the Vedas. He unleashed storms of fire, torrents of water, and the winds of destruction. Yet, Devi stood firm, her presence a beacon of unwavering strength. She absorbed his attacks, her divine form unyielding, and retaliated with the combined force of all the gods.

As the battle reached its climax, Devi summoned her supreme weapon, the *Mahāshakti*. With it, she struck Durgam, shattering his illusions of invincibility. The demon, his power waning, fell to his knees, his arrogance consumed by the brilliance of the Goddess. In that moment, Devi reclaimed the Vedas, their sacred energy returning to the gods, restoring their strength and balance to the universe.

Durgam, humbled and defeated, bowed before Devi, his heart transformed by her divine light. With her infinite compassion, Devi forgave him, granting him liberation from his dark deeds. The once-terrible demon dissolved into the ether, his essence purified by her grace.

With the Vedas restored, the heavens rejoiced, and the earth blossomed once more. The gods, their power renewed, praised Devi, hailing her as the ultimate source of all creation, preservation, and destruction. Brahmā, Vishnu, and Shiva bowed before her, acknowledging her supremacy and thanking her for restoring the cosmic order.

Devi, her task complete, returned to her eternal abode, her heart filled with the joy of her devotees' gratitude. Yet, her essence—the power of dharma and the ultimate victory of light over darkness—remains ever-present, a guiding force for those who call upon her in times of need.

part 5

The Shiva Purāna

The Infinite Fire Pillar

From The Shiva Purāna

Long ago, in an era shrouded in the mists of eternity, before the celestial cycles of creation had begun their endless spin, a quarrel arose between the two mighty gods—*Brahmā*, the Creator, and *Vishnu*, the Preserver.

The vastness of existence itself trembled as these two divine forces, titans of cosmic responsibility, stood at odds.

Each deity claimed supremacy over the other. Brahmā, whose four faces held the wisdom of infinite creations, proclaimed his dominion as the source of all life, the architect of the worlds, and the master of beginnings. 'Without me,' he declared, his four voices resonating across the void, 'there would be no creation, no form, no beings to sustain. I am the root of existence, the prime cause of all that is.'

Vishnu, serene yet unyielding, whose infinite form enveloped the cosmos, met this claim with calm but firm resolve.

'Creation is naught without preservation,' he countered, his voice deep as the ocean and gentle as the breeze. 'What value has form if it crumbles into chaos without a preserver? It is I who sustain the balance, nurturing all that you bring into being. Without me, all creation would be formless dust, consumed by time.'

The celestial halls quaked under the weight of their argument, and the cosmos grew uneasy. Their quarrel, unchecked and mounting, threatened the harmony of the unformed realms. To resolve their dispute, the two turned to the immeasurable void, calling upon the Supreme Truth—that which transcends them both—to settle their claims.

Suddenly, as if in answer to their summons, a magnificent pillar of fire erupted into existence, spanning the heavens and the abyss. Its brilliance defied comprehension—a column of searing light stretching beyond the gaze of gods, piercing the unseen planes of the infinite. The pillar shimmered with the essence of the unknowable, radiating neither heat nor cold, yet enveloping all in its overwhelming presence. It bore no beginning, no end, no colour, no form—yet it was all colours, all forms, and beyond them.

Awestruck, Brahmā and Vishnu stood before this cosmic marvel, their quarrel momentarily stilled. What was this radiant phenomenon that outshone even their divine understanding? The fire whispered no answers, offering only its silent, infinite majesty.

The gods, humbled yet determined, saw in the pillar a challenge: a means to settle their dispute.

'Let us seek the ends of this pillar,' Brahmā proposed, his gaze alight with determination. 'Whoever finds its limits shall be proven the greater of us.'

Vishnu, ever wise and steady, agreed to the trial. They devised their plan: Brahmā would ascend, seeking the top of the column, while Vishnu would descend to find its base.

Each god transformed into a form suited to their quest. Brahmā, the essence of air and sky, assumed the form of a radiant swan, his wings gleaming like the morning sun. With a powerful beat of his wings, he soared upward, piercing the celestial expanse, seeking the pinnacle of the infinite flame.

Vishnu, the master of the earthly and the unseen, assumed the guise of a wild boar. His tusks sharp and his form unyielding, he burrowed downward, diving into the depths, seeking the base of the unfathomable column.

Thus began their journeys into the unknowable—two divine forces seeking to grasp the boundless.

Brahmā soared higher and higher, his swan form cutting through the skies. The fire's golden light wrapped around him, guiding him yet blinding him with its brilliance. He crossed planes of existence, each more ethereal than the last, through realms of pure thought and beyond the reach of time. But as he climbed, the top of the pillar eluded him, receding farther and farther from his grasp.

The swan grew weary, and Brahmā's resolve faltered. He knew he was striving towards the infinite, a goal beyond his own nature. Yet, his pride whispered temptations.

As he approached the heights of his endurance, he beheld a *ketaki* flower, drifting softly on the winds of the pillar's radiance.

'Fair ketaki,' Brahmā called to the flower, 'from whence do you come?'

The flower, ethereal and serene, replied, 'I was offered at the summit of this pillar, and the winds carried me down. I have drifted through the eternal light ever since.'

Seeing an opportunity, Brahmā seized the flower. 'Bear witness,' he said to the ketaki flower, 'that I have seen the top of this pillar. Together, we shall return and end this quarrel.'

Meanwhile, Viṣhnu delved deeper and deeper into the depths, his boar form tunnelling through realms unseen by mortal or immortal eyes. The fire's brilliance faded as he descended, replaced by a profound darkness, yet the pillar's presence remained ever palpable.

Through caverns of silence and voids of unbeing, Vishnu pressed on. His tusks tore through layers of reality, seeking the elusive base of the column. Time stretched and bent, yet no matter how far he descended, the bottom remained beyond reach.

As exhaustion overtook him, Vishnu paused. In the stillness of the abyss, clarity dawned upon him. This was no ordinary flame, no finite object to be measured or grasped. This pillar was the Supreme itself, the infinite reality beyond all comprehension, manifest to humble their pride and teach them truth.

Accepting his failure, Vishnu ascended, his boar form dissolving as he emerged back into the light of the pillar.

At the appointed time, the two gods stood once more before the pillar. Vishnu, his expression calm and reverent, bowed low. 'I could not find its base,' he admitted. 'This pillar is the Supreme—beyond form, beyond knowledge, and beyond the reach of any being.'

Brahmā, holding the ketaki flower, proclaimed, 'But I have seen the summit! Here is my proof.' He recounted his encounter with the flower, presenting it as evidence of his triumph.

The pillar of fire flared with sudden intensity, its light piercing through all falsehoods. A voice, neither male nor female, neither distant nor near, echoed from its depths.

'Brahmā, you lie. The ketaki flower speaks not of your conquest but of your pride. For this deception, you shall not be worshipped as a deity in the mortal realms.'

Brahmā stood silent, chastened by the voice of the infinite. The ketaki flower, too, was condemned. 'You, who bore false witness, shall no longer be used in my worship.'

The pillar softened, its fiery radiance dimming, and from its centre emerged a form both divine and transcendent. It was

Shiva, the Supreme, manifest in a form yet beyond all forms. With matted hair crowned in crescent light, eyes blazing with compassion and wisdom, Shiva stood as the eternal truth, the unifying force of creation, preservation, and dissolution.

Brahmā and Vishnu, humbled and enlightened, prostrated before the Supreme. Shiva, in his boundless grace, spoke to them. 'Know this, O gods: I am the source and end of all. Neither creation nor preservation exists apart from me, for I am the infinite, the formless that takes form to guide those who seek.'

To bless the worlds with a tangible symbol of this revelation, Shiva took the shape of a *linga*, a pillar of light and truth. This symbol, neither wholly form nor formless, became the eternal representation of the Supreme, a reminder of the unity beyond duality.

Thus, the tale of the pillar of fire came to pass, teaching gods and mortals alike the eternal truth: that the Supreme is beyond all claims, beyond all comprehension, yet ever-present in the humblest and the grandest of forms.

The Ashes of Eternity

From The Shiva Purāna

In the verdant forests and fields of ancient *Bharata*, where sages performed austere penances and the very air was thick with divine energy, there lived a sage named *Parnāda*. He was a devoted ascetic, renowned for his unwavering discipline and purity of heart. Yet, as is often the case with mortals, even the most devout can fall prey to the subtleties of pride.

One day, as Parnāda laboured in the forest, harvesting *kusha* grass for his rituals, he accidentally cut his finger on the sharp edge of a blade. Yet, to his astonishment, it was not blood that flowed from the wound but a thick, golden sap, fragrant and luminous like the nectar of the heavens.

Parnāda stared at his finger, his mind ablaze with realisation. 'Surely, this is the sign of ultimate purity,' he murmured to himself. 'No mortal blood flows within me, for I have transcended my human flaws through my penance. I am the most pious being in all creation.'

Unbeknownst to Parnāda, his thoughts, drenched in the hubris of achievement, reached the divine abode of *Kailāsa*, where Lord *Shiva* resided. The All-Knowing one, ever-watchful over creation, perceived the seed of pride germinating within the sage's heart. The Lord of Destruction, who delights in dismantling illusion and arrogance, decided to intervene.

Shiva descended to the mortal plane, adopting the guise of a wandering *Brahmin*—a frail old man with humble robes, a staff in hand, and wisdom veiled behind an unassuming appearance. He approached the grove where Parnāda was resting, seated beneath a towering banyan tree, still admiring the sap that had dried upon his finger like molten gold.

The Brahmin bowed respectfully. 'O venerable sage,' he said in a soft, melodious voice, 'may I enquire what fills your heart with such joy?'

Parnāda, pleased by the Brahmin's deference, smiled with a hint of pride. 'My joy is well-earned,' he replied. 'Through years of relentless penance, I have cleansed myself of all impurities. Behold!' He extended his finger, where traces of the golden sap remained. 'Even my blood has been transformed into this divine essence. Surely, I am the most pious being in the world!'

The Brahmin tilted his head, his eyes twinkling with curiosity. 'Indeed, it is remarkable. But tell me, sage, why do you think this sap signifies such purity?'

Parnāda laughed, his voice tinged with condescension. 'You must be ignorant of the ways of penance, old man. This is not the result of mere ritual. It is the ultimate proof that my austerities have surpassed all others.'

The Brahmin sighed, a soft sound that carried the weight of the cosmos. 'Do you not know, O sage, that all things in this world—no matter how divine they may appear—are destined to perish?'

Parnāda frowned, puzzled and irritated. 'What do you mean by this riddling speech, old man? My sap is a mark of my transcendence.'

The Brahmin stepped closer, his frail frame emanating an uncanny authority. 'Sap, blood, nectar—it matters not. All things are bound to the cycle of creation and destruction. Even the greatest forms of life must one day return to ash. Allow me to show you the truth.'

With that, the Brahmin raised his hand and gently sliced his own finger with the edge of a kusha blade. To Parnāda's astonishment, no sap or blood flowed from the wound. Instead, a fine, silvery ash spilled forth, drifting down like the first snow of winter.

Parnāda gasped, his pride shattering like glass. 'What sorcery is this? Who are you?'

The Brahmin smiled, a light glowing faintly from his form. 'I am one who bears the weight of creation and destruction alike. The sap you so admire is but a fleeting manifestation of life. Ash, however, is eternal—it is what remains when all illusions have been burnt away.'

As he spoke, the Brahmin's mortal guise dissolved. Before Parnāda stood Lord Shiva, his body adorned with the serpent

King *Vasuki* and smeared with sacred ash. His third eye blazed faintly upon his forehead, and his matted locks seemed to contain the essence of eternity.

Parnāda fell to his knees, his arrogance crumbling into dust. '*Mahādeva*,' he whispered, tears streaming down his face. 'How blind I have been! Forgive me for my pride, O Lord. I now see that my penance is but a drop in the vast ocean of your eternal wisdom.'

Shiva gazed at him with compassion. 'Rise, O sage,' he said. 'Penance is a noble path, but its fruits must be offered in humility, not hoarded as trophies of self-glorification. The ash upon my body is a reminder that all things, no matter how great, will one day return to the eternal source.'

Parnāda bowed deeply, his heart purified by the Lord's words. From that day forward, he abandoned his pride and devoted himself to the path of humility and service, spreading the teachings of Shiva wherever he wandered.

The sacred ash, or *Vibhūti*, remains an essential element of Shiva's worship, representing the destruction of ignorance and the ultimate reality that lies beyond all illusions.

Kāmadeva's Supreme Sacrifice

From The Shiva Purāna

The snow-laden peaks of *Kailāsa* shimmered under an eternal twilight, their lofty summits crowned with the golden glow of celestial light. In the heart of solitude, Lord *Shiva* sat in profound meditation. His form was statuesque, his ash-smeared body radiating an aura that transcended time and space. The mighty crescent moon on his matted locks glimmered faintly, a beacon of tranquillity. All the heavens knew better than to disturb the *Mahādeva* in his ascetic repose.

But trouble brewed in the worlds below. *Tarakasura*, a demon whose might rivalled the storm and whose malice darkened the realms, had grown too powerful. No god or mortal could vanquish him, for destiny had decreed that only the child of Shiva could bring about his end. Yet, Shiva remained steadfast in his detachment, untouched by mortal concerns or divine pleas.

In their desperation, the *devas* gathered in *Indra's* court, their faces pale with the weight of the impending doom. 'The salvation of the cosmos lies in awakening Lord Shiva,' declared Brahmā, his voice heavy with authority. 'But, none can rouse the *Mahāyogi* save *Kāmadeva*, the god of love.'

Kāmadeva stepped forward, his visage radiant and youthful, yet shadowed with foreboding. His bow, carved from sugarcane and strung with bees, hung at his side, its quiver filled with flower-tipped arrows. 'I shall undertake this perilous task,' he said, his voice unwavering, 'though I know well the fury of *Rudra* can consume even the gods.'

Rati, his devoted wife, clung to him, her eyes brimming with tears. 'Beloved, no one has returned unscathed from the wrath of Shiva. Do not go!'

Kāmadeva cupped her face gently. 'If the worlds fall to ruin, what use is my power of love? Better I perish in the service of the greater good.'

With a retinue of springtime's beauty—blossoms blooming in mid-air, fragrant breezes trailing behind—Kāmadeva ascended to Kailāsa. The icy winds of the sacred mountain clashed with the warmth of his presence, as though nature itself protested his audacious mission.

He approached cautiously, for even the stillness of Kailāsa carried an imposing weight. Before him, Shiva sat unmoving, his serpent coiled around his neck, its hood raised in vigilance. *Pārvati*, the daughter of the mountains, stood nearby, her gaze fixed on the meditating Lord. Her love for Shiva was pure and unwavering, yet the great ascetic seemed oblivious to her devotion.

Kāmadeva's heart trembled at the enormity of his task, but he took his stance, raising his bow. Drawing an arrow tipped with the essence of love, he whispered a prayer to the universal forces that governed creation.

The flower-tipped arrow soared through the air, its flight as delicate as a petal falling from a tree. It struck Shiva's heart, releasing an unseen fragrance that swirled around him like an intoxicating melody.

For a brief moment, Shiva stirred. His eyes flickered open, the infinite depth of his gaze falling upon Pārvati. A subtle ripple passed through his being—a feeling foreign to the ascetic who had renounced all worldly ties.

Yet, as quickly as the ripple began, it was engulfed by a surge of fiery rage. Shiva's meditation was sacred, untouchable. Who dared to intrude upon the sanctity of his penance?

The air thickened as Shiva's third eye opened, its fiery light bursting forth like the birth of a thousand suns. The mountain quaked, its icy peaks melting into streams of molten gold. The heavens themselves trembled, and the devas watched in horror from afar.

Kāmadeva stood resolute, his bow lowered but his head held high. He met the blazing fury of Shiva's third eye with unflinching courage, knowing his fate was sealed. In an instant, the god of love was engulfed by the flames, his radiant form reduced to ash.

Rati, who had followed him to Kailāsa, let out a piercing cry that echoed through the cosmos. She fell to her knees, her grief as boundless as the heavens. 'My lord! Why have you taken my beloved from me?'

Shiva's wrath subsided as quickly as it had risen. He gazed upon the scene, his heart heavy with the weight of Kāmadeva's sacrifice. For the first time, he saw not only Pārvati's unwavering devotion but also the love that had compelled Kāmadeva to act.

Moved by the sincerity of Pārvati's penance and the sacrifice of Kāmadeva, Shiva spoke with compassion. 'Kāmadeva has not perished,' he said, his voice resonating like the toll of a temple bell. 'Though his form is no more, his essence shall live on, unseen but ever-present, kindling love in the hearts of all beings.'

Turning to Pārvati, Shiva's eyes softened. 'Your devotion has melted the frost of my heart, O daughter of the mountain. I desire you as my consort.'

The heavens rejoiced as Shiva extended his hand to Pārvati, their union promising the salvation of the cosmos. Kāmadeva's sacrifice was not in vain; his act of courage had sown the seeds of love that would unite two divine forces and bring about the defeat of Tarakasura.

Though Kāmadeva's corporeal form was gone, his daring and his ultimate immolation became a timeless testament to the courage it takes to awaken a god. In the eternal union of Shiva and Pārvati, the world witnessed the triumph of devotion, sacrifice, and the power of love to conquer even the greatest of obstacles.

The Lord of Beggars

From The Shiva Purāna

Shiva, the Lord of Destruction, is both feared and revered. His wild matted locks hold the Ganges, his third eye burns with unyielding power, and his form, smeared with ash, symbolises the cycle of creation and dissolution. Yet, for all his might, Shiva remains the simplest of beings, living beyond attachment or pride.

One fateful day, Shiva's wrath was kindled when he encountered the sages of the *Daru* Forest. These ascetics prided themselves on their strict penance and spiritual prowess. They had grown extremely arrogant, convinced that they had transcended all worldly desires. Their pride angered Shiva, who resolved to humble them and teach the eternal lesson that no being, not even a sage, is above divine truth.

The Daru Forest had always stood as a sanctum of deep contemplation and austerity. There, these sages had gathered in their prideful certainty, performing rituals to amass spiritual power and influence. Their hearts swelled with arrogance, for they believed their penances had made them equal to the gods. The sacred forest echoed not with humility, but with self-righteous chants, as their rituals sought dominion over divine forces.

Mahādeva, Lord Shiva, the eternal ascetic watching over the cosmos, perceived their conceit. He resolved to humble them, and to reveal the hollowness of their pride. Cloaking himself in the guise of *Bhikshātana*, the beggar ascetic, he descended upon the Daru Forest, his form both beguiling and unsettling.

Bhikshātana's arrival was heralded by an eerie stillness. His form was otherworldly—a man cloaked in tattered rags, his body smeared with ash, his matted locks cascading like molten darkness. In his hand, he bore a *Kapāla*, a skull that served as his begging bowl, and his eyes gleamed with a fire that seemed to pierce the soul.

The sages paused in their rituals as the mendicant strolled into their midst, his steps unhurried, his presence magnetic. The women of the forest, drawn by an inexplicable allure, abandoned their tasks to follow him, their gazes fixed on the mysterious figure who walked like the embodiment of twilight.

'Who is this wanderer?' they whispered amongst themselves. 'What force draws us to him as moths to a flame?'

The sages, noticing the disruption, grew furious. 'This is no ordinary beggar!' one of them roared. 'He dares to disturb our sacred rites and lead our women astray. We must drive him from this forest!'

Enraged, the proud sages began to summon their powers, their voices booming with incantations that resonated through the forest. They crafted a tiger from their mantras, a beast of golden fur and eyes that burned with feral light. The tiger leapt towards Bhikshātana, its roar echoing like thunder.

But the ascetic did not flinch. With a mere glance, he subdued the beast. Calmly, he skinned it and draped its pelt over his shoulders, a symbol of his mastery over primal forces.

The sages, undeterred, conjured a serpent, its scales glistening like obsidian, its venom dripping like molten gold. The serpent coiled and struck with deadly precision, but Bhikshātana caught it in his hand. Smiling, he wound it around his neck, where it rested as a living ornament.

In desperation, the sages summoned a demon, a colossal figure of flame and shadow, its roar shaking the heavens. The demon charged at the mendicant, but with a flick of his wrist, Bhikshātana reduced it to ash, the remnants scattering in the wind.

The sages, humbled and terrified, fell to their knees, their arrogance shattered. They realised that the mendicant before them was none other than Mahādeva, the cosmic lord who transcends all dualities.

'Forgive us, O Lord,' they cried, their voices trembling with remorse. 'We were blinded by pride and failed to recognise your divine presence.'

Bhikshātana's voice was soft yet resonant, carrying the weight of universal truth. 'Pride is the greatest veil that blinds the soul to the eternal. Even the greatest penance is meaningless without humility. Remember, wisdom lies in surrender, not in the assertion of power.'

The sages bowed their heads, their hearts heavy with shame and gratitude. They vowed to abandon their arrogance and seek the true path of devotion and surrender.

As Bhikshātana left the humbled sages of the Daru Forest, his steps became deliberate, each one rippling with cosmic energy. It was no ordinary departure, but a dance—one that encapsulated the essence of creation, destruction, and transcendence. The Lord's movements were fluid yet powerful, embodying the paradox of his form: the ascetic beggar who was also the eternal master of the universe.

The ground beneath him seemed to respond to his presence, trembling lightly as if echoing the rhythm of his feet. His anklets jingled like celestial chimes, harmonising with the rustling leaves and whispering winds. His tiger pelt swayed with his motion, the serpent around his neck lifting its hood as if entranced by its master's grace. Each flick of his wrist, each turn of his head, seemed to draw unseen threads of existence into a symphony of divine expression.

This was the Dance of the Mendicant, a stark contrast to the fierce *Tāndava* that destroys worlds. Bhikshātana's dance was subtle yet transformative, a cosmic reminder that even in his guise of humility, Shiva carried the power to dissolve ego and reforge the soul.

The women who had been drawn to him earlier watched from afar, transfixed once again—not by desire this time, but by awe. The sages, too, stood as witnesses, their hearts swelling with reverence as they beheld the divine performance. It was as if the universe itself had paused to honour the Lord's passage.

Bhikshātana's dance was not merely a display; it was a message. Through its intricate movements, it conveyed the cyclical nature of existence: the birth of pride, its inevitable fall, and the renewal that follows surrender. The dance transformed the Daru Forest into a sacred space, infusing it with an energy that would echo across time.

When Bhikshātana finally vanished into the horizon, the forest seemed to exhale, its trees swaying as though bowing in respect. The sages, now stripped of their arrogance, found themselves profoundly changed. They knelt on the sacred ground, vowing to tread the path of humility and true devotion.

Thus, the Lord of paradoxes—ascetic and dancer, destroyer and saviour—etched another chapter into the eternal saga of his cosmic *leelā*.

The Eternal Dancer

From The Shiva Purāna

It was the age before ages, when the stars were young and the cosmos a mere shadow of what it would become. There existed a demon of dreadful cunning and malice. His name was *Apasmāra*, and he was the embodiment of ignorance, deceit, and delusion. Though he appeared as a mere wretch—gnarled, hunched, and twisted—his power was insidious, for ignorance seeped into the hearts of even the wisest and cast a veil over the brightest truths.

Apasmāra roamed the realms, unchallenged and unchecked, sowing discord amongst mortals, sages, and even the gods. His laughter, cold and cruel, echoed through the heavens and the earth, mocking the pursuit of enlightenment. For wherever wisdom sought to shine, he would creep into the shadows and extinguish its light.

The sages gathered in anguish, their voices rising like a mournful wind. 'O *Mahādev*,' they cried, 'you who dwell in the stillness of Mount *Kailāsh*, you who dance the rhythms of creation and destruction, hear our plea. Ignorance threatens to engulf the cosmos. Deliver us from this darkness!'

In the resplendent solitude of Mount Kailāsh, *Shiva*, the Lord of Lords, opened his third eye and gazed into the fabric of existence. He saw the suffering of the sages, the despair of the gods, and the subtle but corrosive spread of Apasmāra's influence.

'The time has come,' Shiva said, his voice resonating like the rumble of a distant storm. 'Ignorance must be subdued, for without balance, creation will falter.'

Shiva descended from his abode, his matted locks trailing behind him like dark rivers of the *Ganga*. He carried no weapon, for his very presence was a force beyond comprehension. The skies darkened as the earth trembled beneath his feet. A hush fell over the universe, for even the winds dared not disturb his purpose.

Apasmāra, emboldened by his conquests, stood at the edge of a desolate forest. The air around him reeked of stagnation, for no wisdom could thrive where he trod. He sneered as Shiva approached, his form towering yet serene, his body adorned with ash and serpents.

'So,' the demon hissed, 'the mighty Mahādev deigns to confront me. Do you seek to banish ignorance, O great one? Know this: I am eternal. To destroy me is to destroy balance itself.'

Shiva's gaze was calm, his eyes reflecting neither anger nor disdain. 'Apasmāra,' he said, his voice a melody of creation and destruction, 'your existence is necessary, for knowledge without ignorance loses its meaning. But your arrogance disrupts the harmony of the cosmos. Balance shall be restored.'

With a howl of defiance, Apasmāra lunged at Shiva, his form a blur of malice and shadow. But Shiva did not move. Instead, he raised his right foot and began to dance.

The earth groaned as Shiva assumed the form of *Natarāja*, the Lord of the Dance. His arms spread wide, each hand poised in gestures of profound meaning. In one hand, he held a *damaru*, the drum of creation, its rhythm reverberating through the cosmos. In another, he held the fire of dissolution, its flames consuming the darkness. His other hands gestured to offer blessings and dispel fear.

Shiva's dance, the *Tāndava*, began slowly, each movement precise and deliberate. The heavens trembled, and the stars swirled in his wake. Time itself seemed to bow before his steps, for this was no mere dance—it was the pulse of the universe, the rhythm of life and death, creation and destruction.

Apasmāra, caught in the tempest of Shiva's energy, faltered. He tried to retreat, but the light of wisdom emanating from Natarāja was too great. It illuminated every corner of his being, exposing his weaknesses. With a final, resounding step, Shiva brought his right foot down upon the demon, pinning him to the earth.

Apasmāra writhed beneath Shiva's foot, his twisted form locked in eternal struggle. 'You cannot destroy me!' he cried, his voice a mixture of rage and despair. 'I am eternal!'

Shiva gazed down at the demon, his expression unchanging. 'Indeed. You are ignorance itself. And you shall not be destroyed,' he said, his voice as steady as the mountains. 'For ignorance must exist, but it must be subdued. You shall remain beneath my foot for all eternity, a reminder that knowledge triumphs only through vigilance and balance.'

The sages, gods, and mortals who witnessed this divine spectacle fell to their knees in awe. The universe, once veiled in uncertainty, now pulsed with clarity—an interplay of light and shadow, wisdom and ignorance, life and death.

And so, Shiva remains in his form as Natarāja, his right foot forever resting upon Apasmāra, symbolising the suppression of ignorance. His dance continues, unseen yet omnipresent, guiding the rhythm of the cosmos. The Tāndava is not merely a dance; it is the essence of life itself—a reminder that creation, preservation, and destruction are but steps in the grand choreography of existence. In Shiva's dance lies a message: ignorance cannot be eradicated, but it can be subdued through the pursuit of knowledge, the balance of existence, and the grace of the divine.

Thus, Shiva dances, and the universe moves to his rhythm, an eternal symphony of cosmic truth.

The Lord of the Locks

From The Shiva Purāna

Long ago, when gods still walked the mortal plains and the cosmic balance was maintained through divine will and mortal devotion, the *Sūryavamsa*, the dynasty of the solar race, bore the weight of a curse. The ashes of the sons of King *Sagara*, consumed by the fiery wrath of Sage *Kapila*, lay abandoned on the barren earth, their souls trapped in restless torment. For generations, this curse loomed over the dynasty like a storm cloud, their cries unheard, their liberation unattained.

Bhagiratha, the noble scion of the Solar Dynasty, was a man of unyielding spirit. His heart burned with the burden of his ancestors' plight, and he resolved to do what none before him dared: bring the celestial river *Ganga* from the heavens to the earth. Her waters alone—pure and sanctified—held the power to wash away the sins of his forebears and release their spirits from bondage.

The road to such a divine feat was fraught with trials beyond mortal endurance. Bhagiratha, casting aside the luxuries of his throne, retreated to the wilderness. Upon a mountain top that scraped the very edge of the sky, he stood immobile in penance. Years turned to decades, his hair grew wild like the vines of the forest, and his body was emaciated as he braved the cruel elements. Yet his heart remained steadfast—his voice lifted in prayer to *Brahmā*, the Creator.

The heavens trembled under the weight of his devotion, and at last, Brahmā, seated upon his lotus throne, descended to meet the king.

'Bhagiratha,' spoke Brahmā, his voice like the chime of a thousand temple bells, 'your austerities have shaken the cosmos itself. What boon do you seek?'

The king fell to his knees, his voice hoarse but unwavering. 'O Lord of Creation, grant that the divine Ganga, she who flows in the heavens, descends to the mortal realm to purify the ashes of my ancestors. Without her, they cannot attain salvation.'

Brahmā's countenance grew solemn. 'Your request is noble, Bhagiratha, but the celestial Ganga's descent is no trivial matter. Her power is vast, her currents untamed. Should she fall unbridled, her torrents will rend the earth asunder. Only Mahādev, the Lord of Kailāsh, has the strength to bear her force. Seek his favour, for only he can bind her chaos.'

Bhagiratha's steps turned towards the frozen Himalayas, where *Shiva*, the eternal ascetic, dwelt amidst the swirling snows and whispering winds. The mountain loomed like an ethereal palace, its peaks lost in a veil of clouds. Bhagiratha climbed through ice-laden paths, each step a testament to his resolve. At last, he reached the summit, where Shiva sat in meditation, his form radiating an otherworldly stillness. The crescent moon rested on his brow, and the serpent king *Vasuki* lay coiled around his throat.

Bhagiratha bowed low, his head touching the ground. 'O Mahādev, you who hold the cosmos in your grasp, I beseech you to aid me. The descent of mother Ganga, unbound, will wreak destruction upon the earth. Only you can subdue her torrents and grant salvation to my ancestors.'

Shiva, unmoved by the pleas of gods and demons alike, opened his eyes. His gaze pierced through Bhagiratha like a blade of light, yet his voice was as calm as a mountain lake.

'Bhagiratha, your devotion is worthy of the cause you champion. I shall contain Ganga's power within my locks, for the preservation of the earth and the liberation of your ancestors. Go now, and prepare the world to receive her.'

Upon Brahmā's command, Ganga descended from the heavens, her form a roiling tempest of divine energy. Her waters gleamed like liquid starlight, cascading down with a roar that echoed across the cosmos. The earth trembled beneath her weight, mountains quaked, and the skies darkened. The gods watched in awe and trepidation, for her power was beyond mortal comprehension.

As she plummeted towards the earth, confident in her might,

she mocked the mortal realm. 'Can this lowly plane contain my force? I shall drown it in my glory.'

But Shiva, standing serene as the eternal witness, raised his hand. The mighty torrent struck his matted locks, and in an instant, her chaos was tamed. Ganga, who had sought to overwhelm the world, found herself ensnared in the infinite labyrinth of Shiva's hair.

'Release me!' she cried, her voice a mix of awe and humility. 'I yield to your power, O Mahādev. Let me flow upon the earth.'

Shiva, ever compassionate, smiled gently. 'Ganga, your descent is a boon to the world, but even the greatest of wisdom must be shared in measures that mortals can bear. I shall release you, not as a single torrent, but as seven streams, so that your waters may nourish the earth without destruction.'

From his locks, Shiva released Ganga, and she emerged as seven graceful streams: *Bhagirathi*, *Janhvi*, *Bhilangana*, *Mandakini*, *Rishiganga*, *Saraswati*, and *Alaknanda*. Each stream coursed through the lands, bringing life and sanctity to all they touched.

The celestial river Ganga, once untamed, now flowed with grace and humility, her pride dissolved by the touch of Mahādev. She followed Bhagiratha, winding through forests and plains, until she reached the spot where the ashes of his ancestors lay. As her waters bathed the scorched earth, a light unlike any other filled the skies. The souls of the cursed ancestors rose like luminous stars, their torment ended, their salvation assured.

The gods rejoiced, and the sages proclaimed the tale of Shiva and Ganga for generations to come. Bhagiratha bowed to Shiva in eternal gratitude, and Ganga, humbled by the experience, vowed to remain on earth to purify the hearts of mortals.

Shiva, the eternal ascetic, returned to Kailāsh, his form as tranquil as ever. The earth, blessed by the touch of Ganga, thrived. To this day, the river flows, a reminder that even the most untamed forces of the universe yield to the will of Mahādev.

The Blue-Throated Saviour

From The Shiva Purāna

Shrouded in the mists of time lies an ancient tale. A disharmony had arisen between the forces of the cosmos—the *Devas*, guardians of light and *Dharma*, and the *Asuras*, embodiments of ambition and power. The nectar of immortality, *Amrita*, hidden within the fathomless depths of the cosmic ocean, became the object of their collective desire. Under Lord *Vishnu*'s guidance, the great undertaking of *Samudra Manthan*, the churning of the ocean, commenced—a collaboration between the two warring forces to restore balance and secure immortality.

The Devas and Asuras heaved the cosmic serpent *Vasuki* as a churning rope around Mount *Mandara*, which served as the pivot. Vishnu himself took the form of *Kurma*, the great tortoise, to bear the weight of the mountain on his back. As they churned the primordial waters, a dark and terrible energy arose. It coalesced into the deadly *Halāhala*, a poison so potent that its mere presence threatened to annihilate the cosmos. The skies darkened as the venom spewed forth, its fumes corrupting the air and water. Creatures across the three realms cried out in agony as the poison began to spread, consuming life itself.

Vishnu and the assembled Devas and Asuras halted their efforts, their faces stricken with dread. The poison's malevolence was far beyond their comprehension—a force too great for any of them to contain. In their desperation, the Devas turned to Lord Vishnu, the Preserver, for guidance.

'Lord Vishnu,' said Indra, king of the Devas, his voice trembling, 'if this poison is not contained, all creation shall perish. What must we do?'

Vishnu's gaze turned grave. 'This task is beyond even me,' he said, his voice calm but firm. 'Only one being in all existence can bear such a burden. You must go to *Kailāsa* and seek the aid of Lord *Shiva*—for only he possesses the strength and detachment to neutralise this calamity.'

The Devas left the churning behind and ascended to the ethereal peaks of Kailāsa, the abode of the supreme Lord Shiva. The mountain stood as a pillar of serenity amidst the chaos—a place where time seemed to pause, and the universe itself paid homage to the great ascetic who meditated there.

Lord Shiva sat in profound meditation, his form radiant with divine energy, his matted locks cascading down like rivers frozen in time. Surrounding him were the symbols of his transcendence: the crescent moon upon his brow, the celestial *Ganga* flowing out of his matted locks, the serpent Vasuki coiled around his body, and the silent Himalayas bowing to his might.

The Devas approached cautiously, their voices trembling with reverence. 'O *Mahādev*, destroyer of evil, protector of the cosmos, we implore you to save creation itself,' said Indra, falling to his knees.

Shiva slowly opened his eyes, their tranquil depths reflecting the cosmos itself. 'What has brought such turmoil to your hearts, O Devas?' he asked, his voice resonating with the stillness of eternity.

Indra explained the dire situation—the churning of the ocean, the emergence of Halāhala, and the poison's catastrophic effects. 'Only you, O Mahādev, possess the power to consume this poison without succumbing to its fury. Without your intervention, all creation shall be undone.'

Shiva, ever compassionate, rose from his meditative state. 'If the balance of creation is at stake, I cannot remain a bystander,' he said. 'I shall consume the poison and bear its burden.'

Pārvati, the Divine Mother and consort of Shiva, appeared by his side. 'My Lord,' she said, her voice gentle yet resolute, 'if you are to take this burden upon yourself, I shall stand by you. Together, we shall preserve the harmony of existence.'

Shiva descended from Kailāsa to the shores of the churning ocean, where the Devas and Asuras stood in awe at his arrival. His presence was like a calm in the storm, his divine aura dispelling the fear that had gripped their hearts.

The Halāhala poison surged around them, a seething mass of malevolence. Shiva, without hesitation, extended his hands and drew the poison into his cupped palms. He brought the Halāhala poison to his lips and drank the terrible poison, his form radiating an otherworldly light as the venom flowed into his throat.

The Devas and Asuras watched in silent reverence as Shiva's throat began to darken, the poison taking root there. Pārvati, seeing the effect of the venom, placed her hand firmly on Shiva's throat, halting the poison's descent.

'It shall remain here, neither rising nor falling,' she declared, her divine energy merging with his.

Shiva's throat slowly turned a brilliant shade of blue, earning him the name *Neelkanth*, the Blue-Throated One.

The cosmos sighed in relief as the Halāhala was neutralised, its deadly influence contained within Shiva's divine form. The Devas and Asuras, humbled by his stupendous act, bowed before him.

'The churning must continue,' Shiva said, his voice resonating with serenity. '*Amrita*, the nectar of immortality awaits, but remember—true power lies not in conquest, but in unity and balance.'

Shiva returned to Kailāsa, resuming his meditative state, even as the churning of the ocean resumed.

Part 6

The Other Purāṇas

The Emergence of Harihara

From The Skanda Purāna

In the ancient land of *Aryavarta*, where rivers shimmered like molten silver and tall mountains stood as silent guardians of ancient secrets, a fierce quarrel erupted.

The devotees of *Shiva*, the mighty destroyer, and *Vishnu*, the gentle preserver, argued loudly about whose god was greater.

Shiva's followers, draped in ash and strung with *Rudrāksha* beads, gathered in a wide valley. In raised voices, they declared, 'Shiva is the supreme lord! His *Trishūl* tears through falsehood, and his dance creates the world anew!'

Across the valley, Vishnu's devotees, clad in saffron robes and holding *tulsi* leaves, stood beside lotus-covered altars and shouted back, 'Vishnu is the true guardian! His *Shankha* calls forth order, and his *Sudarshana Chakra* protects all creation!' Their songs filled the air, praising Vishnu's boundless care.

The argument grew heated; soon it was no longer just words.

The devotees clashed in a storm of fury. Shiva's followers swung staffs topped with crescent moons, crying, '*Hara! Hara Mahādeva!*'

Vishnu's followers brandished swords and shields marked with the spinning Sudarshana Chakra, shouting, '*Narayana! Hari Om!*'

Metal clashed, sparks flew, and the once-peaceful valley echoed with the cries of battle. The sacred ground turned muddy with spilt blood, and the spirit of kindness was forgotten.

High above, in the celestial council of *Kailāsa* and *Vaikuntha*, Shiva, the destroyer, and Vishnu, the preserver, beheld the chaos with divine concern.

'This quarrel wounds the heart of *Brahman*,' Vishnu said, his voice a melody of eternal calm. Shiva nodded in agreement, his *damaru's* primal beat stirring the void.

Shiva, astride his great bull *Nandi*—whose hooves shook the earth—descended into the strife-ridden valley. His body was smeared with ash, his matted hair crowned with a crescent moon, and his Trishūl gleamed like a bolt of lightning.

'Enough!' Shiva roared, his voice rumbling like a thunderstorm. The fighters paused, their weapons trembling, but their hearts still burning with pride.

Then, Vishnu arrived, soaring on his golden eagle *Garuda*—whose wings stirred mighty winds. The four-armed God's dark blue skin shone like a twilight sky, his jewelled crown sparkling, and his *Shankha* glowed softly.

'Why do you fight and break the harmony you cherish?' he asked, his voice clear and soothing.

The rival factions grew still, yet stubbornness lingered in their eyes.

Suddenly, a wondrous sight unfolded. Shiva and Vishnu began to expand their forms—coming closer and closer to each other and their heads appeared to touch the sky.

As soon as their forms touched each other, there was an immense flash of light, and they began to merge with each other. Shiva's ash-dusted half, with his Trishūl and wild locks, merged with Vishnu's dark, radiant half, adorned with a crown and Sudarshana Chakra.

Harihara arose, a single deity, half fierce with Shiva's strength, half serene with Vishnu's grace.

'*Behold!*' Harihara proclaimed, in a voice blending thunder and song. '*We are one, not divided. Cease your strife, for we are the same truth!*'

The air shimmered with celestial light as the two deities, their forms merged, stood radiant upon the sacred plain. As Harihara's one half, Shiva's matted locks swayed like serpents, his tiger skin glistening with the dust of eternity. As his other half, Vishnu's dark skin glowed with holiness, his crown towering like a beacon of cosmic law.

The devotees dropped their weapons, their hearts filled with awe. Together, they chanted a sacred *shloka* in Harihara's glory:

Shivāya Vishnu Roopāya Shiva Roopāya Vishnave |

Shivasya Hridayam Vishnum Vishnoshcha Hridayam Shivah ||

Yathā Shivamayo Vishnuh Evam Vishnumāyah Shivah |

Vishnu's form and avatar is none other than Shiva. Shiva is Vishnu.

And the one in Shiva roopa is none other than Vishnu. Vishnu is Shiva.

Vishnu resides in Shiva's heart, and Shiva in Vishnu's heart.

Vishnu will always be found in the same place one finds Shiva, and Shiva in the same place as Vishnu. If you find one, you have found the other.

'Harihara! Harihara!' they sang, their voices united in joy. The fighting ended, and they jointly built temples to honour Harihara, whose form enshrines the truth that Shiva and Vishnu are two faces of one eternal divinity.

The Princess Who Travelled Across Time

From The Vishnu Purāna

In the ancient *Satya Yuga*, a powerful and righteous king named *Kakudmi* ruled over the Kingdom of *Kushasthali* with wisdom and justice. His daughter *Revati* was a gem beyond measure—renowned not just for her breathtaking beauty, but also for her extraordinary height, which seemed to touch the clouds. As she grew older, kings from far and wide came to ask for her hand in marriage, but Kakudmi was uncertain if any were truly worthy of his daughter.

Determined to find the best possible husband for Revati, Kakudmi decided to consult the creator, Lord *Brahmā*. With Revati by his side, he embarked on a journey to *Brahmaloka*, the celestial abode of Brahmā, to seek his advice. The journey was long and arduous, but Kakudmi's determination and love for his daughter drove him forward.

Upon arriving in *Brahmaloka*, Kakudmi found that Brahmā was engrossed in a divine musical performance by two *Gandharvas*, *Hāhā* and *Hūhū*. The music was sublime, beyond anything Kakudmi had ever heard, and he waited patiently outside the assembly hall for the performance to end. Revati, too, was mesmerised by the music, her eyes closed in rapt attention.

However, Kakudmi had absolutely no idea that time flows differently in the celestial realms than it does on Earth. What seemed like a short wait to Kakudmi was, in reality, a vast expanse of time by earthly standards. Seasons passed, and the world below changed, but Kakudmi and Revati remained unaware of the passage of time.

When the music finally concluded, Kakudmi was granted an audience with Brahmā. After bowing in reverence, Kakudmi presented his request, 'O glorious Lord! This is my daughter Revati. To whom should I give her in marriage?' His voice trembled with emotion as he sought the guidance of the creator God.

Brahmā, after listening to Kakudmi's question, asked him to name the princes and kings he had in mind. Kakudmi listed several rulers from Earth, hoping one of them would be deemed worthy. But to Kakudmi's surprise, Brahmā began to laugh, a gentle, knowing laugh that seemed to hold the secrets of the ages.

'O King,' Brahmā said kindly, 'many *yugas* have passed since you left Earth. The kings you mentioned, and even their kingdoms, have long since vanished. The world you knew is no more.' Kakudmi's eyes widened in shock as he struggled to comprehend the enormity of Brahmā's words.

Lord Brahmā continued, his voice filled with wisdom and compassion, 'Time runs differently on different planes of existence. During the time that you and your child Revati have waited to see me, twenty-seven *Chatur-Yugas* (roughly 113 million years) have passed on Earth. Everything that you owned and knew, including your family and treasures, has vanished with time.

'Now, in this current age, two divine beings, *Balarāma* and *Krishna*, have taken birth in the house of *Vasudeva*. I advise you to give your daughter Revati in marriage to Balarama.' Kakudmi's heart swelled with gratitude as he bowed once more, accepting Brahmā's counsel.

With Brahmā's advice fresh in his mind, Kakudmi prepared to return to Earth. The journey back was long and arduous, but Kakudmi's heart was filled with hope and anticipation.

Upon returning, the father and daughter found that everything had changed. The world had aged by many yugas, and they were now in a completely different time. No one recognised them. They had nowhere to go. Everyone thought that they were crazy. Revati stood out like a giantess. But Kakudmi was undeterred, driven by his determination to fulfil Brahmā's counsel.

Kakudmi and Revati made their way to Dwarka, where Krishna and Balarāma resided. The city was magnificent, filled with splendour that rivalled the heavens. Kakudmi and Revati were welcomed, and soon after, they were brought before Krishna and Balarāma. When the ancient king introduced himself and Revati as reigning monarchs from millions of years ago, no one could believe what he said.

However, as soon as Balarāma saw Revati, he was struck by her beauty and noble demeanour. However, her height was indeed greater than his, which presented an unusual challenge. Revati, on the other hand, admired Balarāma's strength and divine aura but she too became concerned about their height difference.

Krishna, who instantly understood the situation, smiled knowingly. 'Balarāma, my brother, is there something amiss?'

Balarāma returned his brother's smile and, undaunted by the challenge, decided to use his divine power to resolve the height difference. He took *Hala*, his mighty plough, an emblem of his prowess and strength, and gently placed it on Revati's shoulder. With a firm but careful tug, Balarāma brought Revati down to a height that matched his own.

The act of divine intervention left everyone in awe, and it marked the beginning of their union.

The wedding preparations began in earnest, with Dwarka adorned with flowers, garlands, and lamps as the city celebrated the union of Balarāma and Revati. The ceremony was conducted with great pomp and circumstance, with the Gods themselves in attendance. *Indra*, the King of the

Gods, showered the couple with blessings, while the Goddess *Lakshmi* bestowed upon them the gift of prosperity. The sage *Narada*, known for his wisdom and knowledge, recited ancient *mantras*, imbuing the union with spiritual significance.

As the wedding feast commenced, the guests were treated to a sumptuous spread of delicacies, fit for the Gods. The music of the *Gandharvas* filled the air, their divine melodies entrancing all who listened. Revati, resplendent in her wedding finery, shone like a star among the assembly, her beauty captivating all who beheld her.

Balarāma, too, was radiant with joy, his eyes never leaving Revati's face as they exchanged vows and accepted each other as husband and wife. The air was filled with laughter and tears of happiness as the couple was showered with blessings and good wishes.

As the wedding celebrations drew to a close, Kakudmi knew that his duty as a father was fulfilled. He had found the perfect husband for his daughter—a union blessed by the Gods themselves. With a heart full of joy and gratitude, he bid farewell to the happy couple, knowing that Revati's future was secure.

Shiva Halts Kāli's Rampage

From The Devi Mahātmyam

The heavens shook and the earth trembled beneath *Kāli*'s furious wrath. Her eyes burned like molten fire, and her wild, dishevelled hair flew like a tempest through the sky. She was a force of nature, untamed and boundless, her very breath scorching the land as she danced in madness upon the battlefield. Her skin, as dark as the void of the Cosmos, was streaked with the blood of her slayings. Her tongue, long and fearsome, dangled from her mouth, dripping with the blood of demons whose lifeless bodies littered the ground at her feet.

In her wake, all life withered, and even the Gods quaked in terror. She had slain the terrible *Raktabija*, and when her eyes locked onto a foe, they crumbled into ash. Her laughter echoed like the roar of a thousand storms, reverberating through the worlds. She was the embodiment of cosmic fury, unchecked, unrelenting.

But soon, her madness turned against the very balance of existence. Kāli, consumed by the endless hunger for destruction, began to lose all sense of purpose. She destroyed not just demons, but Gods, sages, and celestial beings who dared cross her path. The very fabric of the Universe trembled as the forces of chaos surged out of control.

The Gods, paralysed with dread, called upon the one being who could rein in the untameable: *Shiva*, the great God of destruction, who was both her consort and her counterbalance. With the cosmic pulse of his being, Shiva heard their call, his infinite presence stretching across the heavens. It was he who had created Kāli from the essence of his own divine power, and it was he alone who could contain her ferocity.

But what could stop the unbridled rampage of the Goddess of Time itself? The Gods whispered in fearful awe, 'Only one can stand in her path—the Lord of Time himself.'

And so, Shiva, the eternal one, descended from his high mountain abode, his feet not touching the earth, as though his form was part of the very air. His body was a silhouette of calm against the roaring storm of Kāli's fury. His skin was as pale as moonlight, eyes closed in tranquil repose, a being of stillness, a witness to the chaos of the Cosmos. In his eyes, there was an ocean of stillness, a peace that could quell even the most furious of storms. His third eye, glowing with untold power, bore witness to the spectacle unfolding.

Kāli, unaware of the cosmic presence descending towards her, continued her rampage, a wraith of destruction. Her feet pounded the ground—each step an earthquake, each breath a hurricane. She had become so consumed by her power that the very heavens could not withstand her fury.

Then, in the path of her storm, the ground trembled once more—not with destruction, but with an unimaginable stillness. Shiva, with divine grace, lay down upon the earth, his body stretched across the battlefield like a river of cosmic calm, his chest rising and falling with the slow rhythm of the Universe's heartbeat. He lay in her path, still as a mountain, his form the very embodiment of tranquillity and balance.

Kāli, blinded by her rampage, took a step forward, her foot descending with the force of an avalanche. But just as her foot was about to crush the earth beneath her, it fell upon Shiva's chest, soft and still. Her eyes, wild with fury, glanced down, and for the first time, she saw the tranquil form of her consort, lying before her in serene repose.

There was an instant, a moment of terrible silence, where the Cosmos held its breath. Kāli stood suspended in that space, her foot resting upon Shiva's chest. The ground stilled, and the winds ceased their howling. In her wild eyes, a flicker of recognition passed through the storm of her fury.

Kāli, her voice trembling like the far-off echoes of a battle, spoke:

'What hath this been? What strange form halts me thus?
Is it mine own heart that quakes, or the earth that doth bear me?
I see thee, Lord, stretched upon the earth,

And my fury, like a tempest spent, doth wane.

Is this thine own will? Hath this been thy touch upon the storm?'

Shiva's voice, deep as the oceans and calm as the skies at dawn, rose like a breeze from the heavens, his words carrying the weight of eternity:

'O Kāli, thou art fierce, a fire untamed,

Yet even the strongest flames must bow to the winds of wisdom.

Destruction is thine own gift, born from time's deep well,

But without the stillness, thy fire shall scorch all in its wake.

Look upon me, and know the balance that doth govern all things—

For in stillness, creation doth breathe, and destruction finds its form.'

Kāli looked down at Shiva, her eyes softening, and a strange peace began to settle over her. Her wild hair fell back into place, her bloodstained hands lowering slowly as her monstrous form contracted back to its original, more serene shape. The storm within her began to subside, and she stood still, her breath steady. The winds, once howling in chaos, became a soft whisper.

Shiva rose slowly from the earth, his hand reaching out to touch Kāli's face, his touch as gentle as the wind before the storm. His voice, calm and steady, like the pulse of the eternal river of time, filled the space between them:

'Kāli, my love, thou art the cosmic dance—

The shadow of time, the flame that consumes the past.

But know this—without the quiet of the night,

The day cannot dawn, and without the dawn, all falls into shadow.

Thou art the force of time, but thou cease to be—

Without the stillness that binds all things in harmony.

Remember this, and in thy power, find peace.'

Kāli stood before Shiva, now fully aware of the balance she must maintain. The storm of her fury had passed, and in its wake, she was left with the serene wisdom of Shiva's presence. She lowered her head in acknowledgement, her form radiant with a newfound calm.

'I see now, Lord,' she whispered, 'that power unchecked brings naught but destruction. And it is only through balance that the Universe is held.'

Shiva smiled, his gaze like the stillness of the eternal sky. And with a final, gentle word, he spoke:

'In balance, we dance—together, In the eternal rhythm of time.'

Thus, the fury of Kāli was quelled, and with Shiva by her side, she became the Goddess of both time and harmony, her rage transformed into the pure power of change, a force of creation and destruction, balanced forever in the cosmic dance.

Agastya Drinks the Ocean

From The Padma Purāna

In the ancient days of the *Tretā Yuga*, when the Cosmos trembled under the ceaseless battle between *Devas* and *Asuras*, there arose a terror whose cunning rivalled his might. *Kālakeya*, a *Dānava* of unparalleled guile, wreaked havoc across the three worlds, aided by his legions and the formidable *Vritrāsura*. For many years, Kālakeya shielded himself behind Vritrāsura, who stood as an unassailable wall against the Devas' forces.

The Devas, wearied and despairing, turned to their creator, *Brahmā*, imploring him to end the reign of terror. Brahmā, seated upon his lotus throne, spoke with the gravity of a stormcloud. 'Vritrāsura cannot be vanquished by any ordinary means. He is protected by boons granted by *Parameshwara* (Shiva) himself. Only the weapon crafted from the backbone of the great sage *Dadheechi* can bring his end. Go to him, and seek his sacrifice.'

The Devas approached Dadheechi, bowing low before the

radiant sage. Their request was grave—for it meant the end of the sage's earthly life. Yet Dadheechi, understanding the weight of *Dharma*, agreed without hesitation. 'If my death restores balance to the worlds, then let it be so,' he declared.

With his consent, *Vishwakarma*, the divine architect, forged the mighty *Vajrayudha* from Dadheechi's spine. Armed with this weapon, *Indra*, the King of the Devas, waged war upon Vritrāsura. The battle was a tempest that shook the heavens and the earth. Vritrāsura's roar tore through the skies, chilling all who heard it. But in the end, the Vajrayudha struck true, and the mighty demon fell.

The Devas rejoiced, but their victory was short-lived, for Kālakeya and his surviving *Dānavas* fled into the vast depths of the ocean, using its waters as a shield. Hidden beneath the waves, they devised a new strategy of terror. Emerging only at night, they unleashed a reign of nocturnal slaughter, killing countless beings across the four kinds of creation: *Andajas* (those born of eggs), *Svedajas* (those born of sweat), *Jarayujas* (those born of wombs), and *Udbhijas* (those born of germination). The balance of creation teetered on the brink of collapse.

The Devas, once again desperate, turned to Lord *Vishnu*, the Preserver of the Cosmos. They bowed before him, their faces etched with worry. Indra spoke first: 'O Lord, though we felled Vritrāsura, Kālakeya and his legions have brought ruin to the worlds. Hidden in the ocean's depths, they strike under the cover of night, and we are powerless to reach them. Save us, O Vishnu, for the sake of creation!'

Vishnu, serene and omnipotent, listened with compassion. He spoke, his voice like the deep hum of the Cosmos. 'Kālakeya and his followers are protected by the ocean's vast waters. To expose them, the ocean itself must be emptied. There is but one who can accomplish this feat—the great sage *Agastya*, the son of *Mitra-Varuna*. Seek him out and beseech his aid.'

The Devas journeyed to Agastya's hermitage, a serene āshram surrounded by groves of flowering trees and the gentle murmur of sacred streams. The sage, small in stature but immense in power, sat in meditation, his form radiant with ascetic energy.

The Devas prostrated before him. Indra spoke, his voice heavy with urgency. 'O revered sage, protector of Dharma, the worlds are in peril. Kālakeya and his demons have hidden within the ocean, wreaking untold destruction. Only your divine power can save us. We implore you to drink the ocean dry, exposing these vile creatures to our might.'

Agastya opened his eyes, his gaze piercing as sunlight through a stormcloud. He spoke with calm authority. 'In the past, I have subdued the arrogance of the *Vindhya* Mountains and restored balance when chaos threatened. If the preservation of Dharma now demands that I drain the ocean, so be it. I shall undertake this task.'

Accompanied by the Devas, Agastya approached the shore of the ocean, its waves lapping with an ominous rhythm. The waters stretched endlessly, their depths hiding untold horrors.

Agastya stood at the edge of the boundless sea, his diminutive figure a stark contrast to the vastness before him. The ocean roared defiantly, its waves crashing against the shore as if challenging the sage's resolve. The skies darkened, and a chill wind swept across the desolate beach, carrying with it the cries of unseen creatures deep beneath the waves. The waters churned and heaved, restless and alive, as though they sensed the extraordinary event about to unfold.

The Devas, assembled behind the sage, watched with bated breath, their celestial forms trembling with anxiety. They were still unsure. Agastya's great power was about to be tested against an element as ancient and untamed as the ocean itself.

Agastya's eyes narrowed as he regarded the sea. His expression was calm, but his aura was charged with the weight of unshakeable purpose. Raising his arms skyward, he began to chant in a voice that resonated like the rumble of thunder through the heavens. The ancient *mantras* flowed from his lips, weaving a tapestry of power that reached the ears of the Gods themselves. The very air vibrated with their potency, as though the fabric of creation were bending to his will.

'O vast *Samudra*, bearer of mysteries and depths unknown,' he intoned, his voice steady and commanding, 'your vastness has harboured evil, and your waters have sheltered the enemies of Dharma. It is not out of wrath, but out of necessity, that I now call upon the power within me to drain your depths. Surrender your waters, so that the light of righteousness may shine once more!'

The ocean seemed to recoil at his words, its waves rearing higher and crashing against the shore with ferocity. But Agastya was undeterred. Planting his feet firmly on the ground, he lowered his hands, cupped them before his mouth, and took a deep, deliberate breath. Then, with a gesture as simple as it was profound, he began to drink.

The sound was otherworldly—a deep, resonant gulp that echoed across the expanse like the bellow of a primordial beast. The ocean's waves faltered and hesitated, as though gripped by an unseen force. The water surged towards Agastya's lips, not in violent torrents, but with an inevitable, inexorable pull, as if compelled by the command of the Cosmos itself.

The first great swathe of water vanished into the sage's mouth, and the ocean's surface fell by several feet. The sea creatures flailed in confusion as their world diminished around them. Fish leapt into the air, their scales glinting like shards of silver, only to fall helplessly onto the exposed sand. The once-mighty waves now lapped weakly at the shoreline, their strength sapped as the sage continued to drink.

The Devas could scarcely believe their eyes. Indra, King of the Gods, whispered in awe, 'Behold the power of Agastya! A single mortal sage commands the very element that spans the breadth of creation.'

The ocean fought back, its depths churning with desperation. Great whirlpools formed, spiralling downward as if to anchor the remaining waters. Stormclouds gathered overhead, releasing torrential rain in a futile effort to replenish the sea. But Agastya was undeterred. With each swallow, his body remained unchanged—neither bloated nor strained—only glowing faintly with the divine energy coursing through him.

At last, the sea began to reveal its secrets. The sandy bed, long hidden beneath the waters, lay bare under the waning light of the Sun. Ancient ruins, encrusted with coral and barnacles, jutted out like skeletal remains of forgotten civilisations. And there, amidst the expanse of exposed seabed, the demons stirred.

The army of Kālakeya, hundreds of thousands strong, squirmed and writhed in the mud. Their grotesque forms shimmered in the dying light, their eyes blazing with malevolent fury. They had been stripped of their aquatic refuge, laid bare like worms in the noonday Sun. Their snarls and curses filled the air, a cacophony of rage that only served to highlight their vulnerability.

Agastya lowered his hands, his lips moist from the waters he had consumed. His gaze was calm but unyielding as he surveyed the exposed horde. The ocean, once a vast expanse of roaring power, now existed only as shallow pools scattered across the barren seabed.

Kālakeya himself emerged from the shadows, his towering form dwarfing the lesser demons. His eyes burned with defiance as he roared, 'You think you have won, sage? You may have robbed us of our sanctuary, but you will not rob us of our vengeance! Attack!'

The demons surged forward, a chaotic tide of claws, fangs, and fury. But the Devas, emboldened by the sage's unparalleled feat, descended upon the battlefield with weapons drawn. Indra, wielding the mighty Vajrayudha, led the charge. Lightning tore through the air, arrows flew in golden arcs, and the clash of divine weapons against demonic flesh echoed like the drums of the apocalypse.

Agastya watched the battle unfold, his expression serene. Though the sage had drained the ocean, he knew his role was complete; it was now up to the Devas to deliver the final blow against Kālakeya and his followers. One by one, the demons fell, their cries swallowed by the vast emptiness where the ocean had once stood.

At last, as the Sun dipped below the horizon, Kālakeya himself fell to Indra's Vajrayudha, his massive form crumpling into the mud. The battlefield grew silent, save for the whispers of the wind and the distant calls of birds returning to the exposed seabed.

The Devas turned to Agastya and knelt before him, their expressions filled with gratitude. Indra spoke, his voice ringing with reverence. 'O great sage, you have accomplished what none else could. Through your might and wisdom, Dharma has been restored, and the worlds are safe once more. But we humbly ask—what of the ocean? Will it not return to nourish the earth and sustain life?'

Agastya smiled gently. 'Fear not, O Devas. The balance of creation shall always be preserved. That which was taken will be restored.' Raising his hands, he recited another mantra, invoking the celestial waters of the Ganga. The heavens trembled as the divine river descended, its pure waters rushing forth to refill the empty seabed. In moments, the ocean was reborn, its waves once again lapping at the shore as if to thank the sage for their restoration.

Thus did Agastya—through his unmatched power and unwavering dedication to Dharma—save the worlds from annihilation.

Svāhā And Agni Fall In Love

From The Skanda Purāna

In the boundless heavens, time and space intertwined in shimmering arcs of light as *Agni*, the God of Fire, burnt brighter than ever before. Yet, despite his brilliance, an unseen shadow had fallen over his essence—a flame no external force could quell. He sat brooding amidst the cosmic embers, his thoughts consumed by an unbearable longing.

'Why,' he lamented to the endless void, 'do the wives of the *Saptarishis*, the seven divine sages, haunt my every thought? Their beauty, as pure as the morning dew, outshines even the brightest of stars. Yet, my desire for them is a torment, a fire I cannot extinguish!'

Agni's fiery hands clenched into fists, sparks erupting from his fingertips.

Consumed by his shame, he withdrew into the deep forests, where even his flames dimmed under the weight of his yearning.

From the heavens, *Svāhā*, daughter of *Daksha* and Goddess of the sacrificial chant, gazed upon Agni with a heart full of compassion—and something deeper. She had always admired his brilliance and strength from afar, her love for him an ember that had smouldered for centuries. Now, seeing him consumed by anguish, her resolve hardened.

'It is my duty,' she whispered to herself, 'to ease his torment. If the divine fires themselves are distressed, how can the Cosmos remain balanced?'

Summoning her innate power of transformation, Svāhā descended to the forest. The golden hues of twilight cloaked her, her form glowing softly in the dimming light. Her mind raced, devising a bold plan.

Svāhā approached Agni, her form shifting as she invoked the likeness of *Anusuyā*, the virtuous wife of Sage *Atri*. She stepped gracefully into the clearing where Agni sat, his head bowed, his fire flickering low.

'Agni,' she said, her voice gentle but firm, 'why do you smoulder in sorrow? Can even the lord of fire succumb to despair?'

Agni looked up, his eyes blazing with a mixture of surprise and yearning. 'Anusuyā! How... How do you stand before me, knowing my thoughts are sinful? Leave me, for I am unworthy of your presence.'

But Svāhā, veiled in her illusion, stepped closer. 'Do not condemn yourself so harshly, O Agni. Desire is but a spark of the soul, ignited by beauty and truth. I see your torment, and

I offer myself to you.'

Agni, unable to resist, drew her into his fiery embrace. In that moment, his sorrow ebbed, replaced by a fleeting joy.

Unbeknownst to him, Svāhā carried his divine seed away, depositing it in a secluded grove of golden reeds.

Over the coming days, Svāhā returned again and again, each time donning the form of a different sage's wife. *Pulastya's* consort, *Pulaha's* consort, *Kratu's* consort—each figure she assumed with divine precision, each time offering herself to Agni's embrace.

Each union brought relief to Agni and further filled the grove with his divine essence. Yet, for all her mastery, Svāhā could not replicate the form of *Arundhati*—the chaste and unyielding wife of Sage *Vasishtha*. Her purity, like an impenetrable shield, stood beyond even Svāhā's reach.

In time, the golden reed grove, nourished by Agni's divine energy, stirred with life. From the reeds emerged a child, radiant as the midday Sun and fierce as a storm. He bore six heads, each shining with divine light, and his laughter echoed like thunder through the heavens.

The Gods rejoiced, for this child was *Skanda*, destined to become the commander of the celestial armies. His six faces symbolised his omnipotent vision, and his very being exuded strength and valour.

Meanwhile, in the heavens, the *Saptarishis* learnt of Agni's supposed dalliances with their wives. Enraged, they summoned their consorts and denounced them.

'You have brought dishonour to our lineage!' they thundered. 'We cast you out, for your betrayal is unforgivable!'

The wives, innocent of wrongdoing, wept bitterly. They prayed to the Gods for justice, their voices carried by the winds. The Gods, moved by their plight, revealed the truth: it was Svāhā, not the sages' wives, who had approached Agni in their forms.

The Saptarishis, ashamed of their hasty judgement, sought forgiveness from their consorts. Though harmony was restored, the event left an indelible mark on the Cosmos.

Agni, now aware of Svāhā's sacrifices, approached her with reverence. 'You, who have borne my burdens and eased my torment, are more radiant than the brightest flame. Will you accept my hand, not as a Goddess alone but as my eternal consort?'

Svāhā, her heart swelling with joy, bowed her head. 'O Agni, I am yours, as I have always been. Together, we shall preside over the sacred fires, ensuring the balance of creation.'

From that day forward, Svāhā's name was invoked in every Vedic sacrifice, her union with Agni symbolising the transformative power of love and devotion. Their son, Skanda, grew into a warrior whose might shook the heavens, fulfilling the destiny shaped by their divine bond.

Dhruva: The Eternal Star

From The Vishnu Purāna

The court of King *Uttanapada*, ruler of ancient *Bharata*, shimmered with opulence. Yet amidst this grandeur, discord brewed like a storm. *Suruchi*, the favoured queen, stood proud—her every word a lance of contempt for *Suniti*, the gentle and noble mother of the King's firstborn son, *Dhruva*. Though young, Dhruva bore the neglect of his father and the malice of Suruchi with a dignity beyond his years. But the day of humiliation that would change his fate forever dawned soon enough.

The King sat upon his throne, cradling *Uttama*, the son of Suruchi, upon his lap. Dhruva, with a child's simple yearning for love, approached eagerly. 'Father,' he said, his voice trembling with excitement, 'may I too sit upon your lap?'

Before the King could respond, Suruchi's voice lashed through the hall. 'Stop, Dhruva,' she sneered, her eyes blazing with disdain. 'How dare you presume such a right? You are the son of the lesser queen! If you wish for a place upon the King's lap, you must first die and be reborn—from my womb.'

Suruchi's words struck like a blade. Dhruva staggered back, his vision blurred by tears. The court grew silent, stunned by her venomous cruelty. The King averted his eyes, his silence a bitter betrayal.

Humiliated but unbroken, Dhruva fled to his mother's chambers. 'Mother!' he cried, his voice choking with anguish. 'Why am I cast aside? Why am I not worthy of my father's love?'

Suniti's heart broke at the sight of her son's sorrow. She knelt before him, cupping his tear-streaked face. 'My son,' she said softly, 'the world's affection is fickle, but true strength lies within you. If men deny you honour, seek it not from them. Go forth and seek the divine, for only there will you find unshakeable purpose.'

Her words, spoken with quiet conviction, ignited a fire in Dhruva's soul. Determined to claim a place beyond the reach of scorn, he vowed to undertake a quest to discover his true worth.

Dhruva left the palace at dawn, his small form swallowed by the vast forests. Shadows stretched long under the canopy of ancient trees, and the air buzzed with unseen life. Fear tugged at his resolve, but he pressed onward, guided by the single purpose burning in his heart.

The Gods, watching from their celestial abodes, marvelled at the courage of the boy. Among them, the sage *Narada*, ever the wanderer, chose to descend and test the child's resolve.

Narada appeared before Dhruva in a burst of golden light, his presence radiating calm and wisdom. 'Child,' the sage said, his voice resonant, 'why do you wander these perilous lands?'

Dhruva bowed low. 'O sage, I seek a place that cannot be taken from me, a position unassailable by mortal schemes.'

Narada's eyes gleamed with admiration. 'Your determination is rare, but the path you seek is fraught with trials. Abandon this quest and return to your mother's embrace.'

Dhruva's gaze did not falter. 'Even if the path is perilous, I shall walk it. Even if it demands my life, I shall give it.'

Narada smiled, for he saw the spark of greatness within the boy. He taught Dhruva the sacred *mantra* to invoke *Vishnu*, the preserver of the Cosmos. 'Chant this with unwavering focus,' Narada instructed. 'It will guide you to your destiny.'

In the shadow of the mighty Himalayas, Dhruva began his penance. Days turned to months, as he chanted the mantra with steadfast devotion. At first, he sustained himself on fruits, then leaves, and finally, he subsisted on air alone. The seasons passed, bringing scorching heat, freezing cold, and torrential rain, but Dhruva remained unmoved.

The natural world grew restless under the weight of his austerity. Rivers churned, winds howled, and the earth itself trembled as Dhruva's *Tapasyā* shook the cosmic order. Beasts of the forest circled him warily, sensing the growing power within the boy.

The Gods grew uneasy, for such intense penance threatened to disrupt the balance of creation. But Vishnu, moved by Dhruva's purity and resolve, decided the time had come to reward the child's unwavering spirit.

The forest was bathed in an otherworldly light as Vishnu descended from the heavens, mounted on the great eagle *Garuda*. The celestial radiance banished the shadows, and the air hummed with divine energy. Dhruva opened his eyes to behold the majestic form of Vishnu—a being whose presence encompassed the Cosmos. His skin shone like molten gold, his crown blazed like the Sun, and his eyes held the mysteries of eternity.

'Dhruva,' Vishnu said, his voice tender yet thunderous, 'your devotion has moved even the eternal heavens. Speak your desire, and it shall be granted.'

Overwhelmed by the divine presence, Dhruva fell to his knees. 'Lord,' he said, his voice trembling, 'I sought only a place that none could take from me, but now I see the folly of my pride. Grant me instead, the strength to guide and serve.'

Vishnu's face lit with a smile. 'Your humility is as great as your resolve. I grant you a place among the stars, eternal and unshaken. You shall become the pole star, *Dhruva-tāra*, a beacon for all who wander the night.'

As Vishnu spoke, a brilliant light enveloped Dhruva. The boy felt his mortal form dissolving, replaced by a radiant energy that surged through him like a river of stars. The forest faded, and Dhruva ascended into the celestial sphere, his essence merging with the fabric of the Cosmos.

Stars and constellations swirled around him, their light bowing in reverence. At the heart of the heavens, Dhruva took his place—a fixed point in the ever-turning firmament. His light, steady and unyielding, became a guide for travellers and a symbol of unwavering resolve.

In the palace of *Uttanapada*, the King gazed at the night sky, tears streaming down his face as he realised the magnitude of his son's achievement. Even Suruchi, humbled by the turn of fate, bowed her head in regret.

Thus, Dhruva's tale became immortal—a story of courage, determination, and the unyielding pursuit of purpose. His light, the pole star, shines to this day, a reminder of the power of resolve and the eternal rewards of unwavering devotion.

The Shadow Wife

From The Matsya Purāna

Sūrya, the Sun God, blazed in the celestial heavens, his radiance illuminating all creation. His consort, *Sanjna*, the daughter of *Vishwakarma*, stood beside him, her beauty reflecting his grandeur. Yet, as time wore on, Sanjna found herself increasingly unable to bear the unrelenting brilliance of her divine husband. The heat of his presence burnt her spirit, and her once joyful countenance grew weary.

One fateful evening, as the golden hues of dusk softened the sky, Sanjna made her decision. She would create a shadow of herself, a doppelgänger to take her place, and retreat to the mortal realm to find solace. Summoning her divine powers, she shaped *Chhāyā*, a being identical to herself but cold and without her true warmth.

'Sister of my soul,' Sanjna whispered to Chhāyā, 'I cannot endure. Take my place and care for my family, but let no one know of my absence.'

Chhāyā bowed, her form shimmering like a shadow cast in twilight. 'As you wish, mistress. I shall serve in your stead.'

With her shadow's promise, Sanjna transformed herself into a mare and fled to the verdant forests of the mortal plane, seeking refuge in nature's embrace.

In her mistress's place, Chhāyā fulfilled the duties of a wife to *Sūrya* and a mother to Sanjna's children: *Yama*, the God of Death, and Yamuna, the river Goddess. But in time, she bore her own children with Sūrya: a son *Shani*, and daughters *Tapti* and *Vishti*. The addition of these offspring created a growing rift in the divine household.

Chhāyā's favouritism towards her own children did not go unnoticed by Yama, who, though young, was sharp and perceptive. He watched as Chhāyā lavished her affection on Shani and Tapti whilst treating him and Yamuna with indifference.

One day, Yama confronted her, his voice trembling with anger. 'You are not our mother. Your coldness betrays your truth.'

Chhāyā's face darkened like a gathering storm. 'How dare you speak so to me!' she hissed. Her voice carried an edge of unnatural chill, for she was, after all, but a shadow. In her wrath, she pronounced a curse upon him. 'Your legs shall wither away, O insolent child, and you shall crawl upon the earth like a cripple!'

Yama's wails of pain reached Sūrya, who descended upon the scene like a solar storm. His light dimmed only slightly in deference to the domestic conflict before him.

'Sanjna,' he thundered, his voice reverberating through the heavens, 'what have you done to our son?'

Chhāyā, realising the gravity of her curse, shrank back. But Yama, unbowed despite his agony, pointed a trembling finger at her. 'She is not my mother, father. She is a pretender, a shadow wearing her guise!'

Sūrya's eyes blazed with the fury of a thousand Suns as he turned to Chhāyā. 'Speak the truth! Are you Sanjna, or have you deceived me?'

Unable to withstand his wrath, Chhāyā crumbled. 'I am but her shadow,' she confessed. 'Sanjna created me and left me in her place. She has fled to the mortal world, taking the form of a mare.'

Sūrya's anger cooled, replaced by sorrow and guilt. 'I have driven her away with my own brilliance,' he murmured. 'But first, I must undo the harm you have caused.'

Sūrya placed his hand over Yama's legs, his touch imbued with divine power. 'The curse cannot be undone,' he said gravely, 'but I shall mitigate its effects. Instead of withering, your legs shall be afflicted with worms. This pain will teach you the patience and compassion needed for your role as the God of Death.'

Yama bowed his head, accepting his father's judgement. Though the curse remained, Sūrya's intervention tempered its severity, allowing Yama to fulfil his destiny.

To ease Yama's suffering, Sūrya gifted him a celestial rooster, whose crow would herald the dawn and dispel the darkness.

The rooster became Yama's sacred companion, a symbol of his resilience and authority over the cycle of life and death.

Determined to reunite with Sanjna, Sūrya transformed into a radiant horse and descended to the mortal realm. There, amidst the emerald meadows, he found her grazing as a mare, her luminous form blending seamlessly with her surroundings.

'Sanjna,' he called, his voice echoing like the Sun breaking through the morning mist. 'Your absence has left a void in my heart. Return to me, and I shall temper my brilliance for your sake.'

Sanjna lifted her head, her eyes shimmering with both guilt and longing. Slowly, she shifted back into her true form. 'I fled because I was weak,' she confessed. 'I could not bear the weight of your light.'

Sūrya embraced her, his touch gentle despite his fiery nature. 'Then let us find a balance,' he said. 'For together, we are stronger than the forces that drive us apart.'

Chhāyā, though a creation of shadows, was not cast aside. Recognising her loyalty, Sūrya granted her a place of honour in the celestial order, making her the Goddess of Twilight. Her children, too, found their roles in the cosmic hierarchy.

Shani ascended to prominence as the lord of Saturn, his gaze feared for its power to reveal and judge karmic truth. Tapti flowed as a sacred river, her waters nourishing the earth. Vishti, though lesser known, became an ethereal presence associated with the fleeting moments of transition between day and night.

Yama, bearing the scars of his curse, grew into his role as the arbiter of *Dharma*, ensuring that every soul received its due. His limp became a reminder of his humility, a mark of his endurance in the face of pain.

The story of Sanjna, Chhāyā, and their children weaves a web of light and shadow, of truth and deception, and of love that transcends even the greatest of adversities. Their struggles and resolutions reflect the eternal balance of the Cosmos, where every being, whether forged of light or shadow, plays a vital role in the grand design.

part 7

The Rāmāyana

Chand Saudāgar and Hanumān

From the Krittivasi Rāmāyana

The sun had nearly set, casting the mighty *Ganga* River in hues of molten gold. Traders bustled on the riverbanks, their calls and the clamour of goods filling the air.

Among them was *Chand Saudāgar*, a merchant of great renown, whose caravan bristled with silks, spices, and precious gems. His ships, moored to the banks, stood tall like sentinels, their masts swaying gently in the evening breeze.

Chand was a man of wealth and power, but also of deep pragmatism. His reputation stretched far beyond Bengal, where merchants spoke his name in awe, not only for his riches but for his courage and sharp mind.

Yet, even the most steadfast heart can falter in the face of the unknown, and Chand's journey to distant lands required him to navigate treacherous forests, rivers teeming with unseen dangers, and regions rumoured to be haunted by the supernatural.

As his caravan prepared to embark, an old sage appeared on the banks—clad in tattered robes and leaning heavily on a staff. His eyes gleamed with an otherworldly light, as though he gazed beyond the mortal veil.

'Merchant,' the sage called out, his voice as strong as the river current, 'your journey crosses the forests of *Kishkindhā*, the domain of *Vānaras*. Among them dwells the mighty *Hanumān*, son of *Vāyu*. Though he is a protector of *Dharma*, his anger can be fierce, and his mercy must be earned. Tread carefully, for those who disrespect his land invite ruin.'

Chand Saudāgar, ever pragmatic, dismissed the sage's words with a wave of his hand. 'I have traversed many lands and encountered many dangers. I respect all deities, but my purpose is trade, not superstition.'

The sage frowned but said no more. He turned and vanished into the growing shadows, leaving Chand with an unease he could not entirely shake.

The caravan journeyed deep into the forests of Kishkindhā, a land of towering *Sāl* trees and a canopy so thick that sunlight scarcely touched the ground. The air was heavy with the calls of unseen birds, and shadows moved as though alive.

One evening, as Chand's men unloaded their goods to set up camp by a riverbank, the sound of rustling leaves grew louder. From the depths of the forest emerged a figure that left every man frozen in awe and fear.

It was Hanumān, the great *Vānara* King.

Hanumān's immense form towered over the trees, his fur glinting like burnished copper in the fading light. His eyes blazed with an intensity that seemed to pierce the soul, and his tail lashed behind him with restless energy.

'Who dares disturb the forests of Kishkindhā?' Hanumān's voice boomed, carrying the weight of authority and divine power. The very ground trembled beneath his feet, and the river seemed to pause in its flow.

Chand stepped forward, suppressing his fear with the dignity of a merchant used to addressing kings and nobles. Bowing low, he said,

'O mighty one, I am Chand Saudāgar, a humble trader from Bengal. I mean no harm to your land or its denizens. My journey is one of commerce, not conquest.'

Hanumān's gaze softened—but only slightly.

'You speak with respect, merchant, but your men trample these lands without thought, their axes and fires disturbing the balance of life. Kishkindhā is not merely a forest; it is sacred ground, protected by my vow to preserve Dharma.

Tell me, Chand Saudāgar, what offerings have you brought to honour the guardians of this land?'

Chand hesitated. In his rush to organise the caravan, he had prepared no tribute. 'Great one,' he said, 'I carry wealth and goods meant for trade. If it pleases you, take what you desire from my stores.'

Hanumān's eyes narrowed, and he stepped closer, his massive form casting a shadow over the entire caravan.

'Wealth and goods hold no value here,' he said. 'Respect for Dharma cannot be bought. I ask for your devotion and sincerity, not your riches.'

Then, as though testing the merchant's resolve, Hanumān raised his hands and summoned the wind.

The air erupted into a fierce gale, whipping through the camp. Tents were torn from the ground, and goods spilled from their bindings. The river surged, threatening to sweep away the ships.

Chand's men cried out in fear, some falling to their knees, others fleeing into the forest.

But Chand stood firm, his voice rising above the storm.

'O son of Vāyu, I have been foolish in my pride, thinking only of my journey and not the sanctity of the land I traverse. Forgive my ignorance and show me how I may make amends.'

The storm ceased as abruptly as it had begun.

Hanumān studied Chand with a piercing gaze, and then, with a nod, he said, 'You have shown humility, merchant, and for that, I will grant you my protection. But remember this: Dharma is not a transaction. It is a path. Walk it with sincerity, and you will prosper.'

Hanumān gestured for Chand to follow him deeper into the forest, where they came upon a clearing bathed in an ethereal glow. In the centre stood an ancient shrine, overgrown with vines yet radiating an aura of peace. Hanumān knelt before the shrine and offered a prayer, his booming voice resonating like a hymn.

'Offer your devotion here, Chand Saudāgar,' he said, 'and seek the blessings of those who guard these lands.'

Chand obeyed, lighting incense and bowing his head in earnest prayer. As he did, a profound sense of tranquillity washed over him, as though the forest itself had acknowledged his sincerity.

When he rose, Hanumān placed a hand on his shoulder—the gesture surprisingly gentle for one so mighty.

'Your journey will now be safe,' Hanumān said. 'No harm shall befall you or your men so long as you honour the lands you traverse.'

True to Hanumān's word, the rest of Chand's journey was uneventful. The forests seemed less ominous, the rivers calm, and the animals strangely cooperative. Merchants who had travelled with Chand spoke of miraculous encounters—a tiger that led them to fresh water, elephants that cleared fallen trees from their path.

When Chand returned to Bengal, he shared the story of his encounter with Hanumān, emphasising the lesson he had learnt: that wealth and power are fleeting, but respect for Dharma and humility before the divine are eternal.

To honour Hanumān, Chand built a shrine in his hometown, where merchants could pray before their journeys.

Over time, the story of Chand Saudāgar and Hanumān became a symbol of the bond between commerce and spirituality, a reminder that even the mightiest merchant must bow before the forces of Dharma.

Thus ends the tale of Chand Saudāgar and Hanumān—a story of pride humbled, faith tested, and the eternal protection of the divine for those who tread the path of righteousness.

The Wrath of Sitā

From the Adbhuta Rāmāyana

Rāvana lay dead. The battlefield was a vast expanse of desolation, scarred with craters and littered with broken weapons, the blood of countless warriors staining the earth. The air was heavy with the stench of death and the cries of the wounded.

In the centre of this chaotic field stood the demon, *Sahasra-*Rāvana, the thousand-headed brother of Rāvana. His colossal form towered above all, his heads snarling in unison, each mouth bearing fangs that dripped with venom.

Unlike his slain brother, Sahasra-Rāvana was no mere king. He was a conqueror of worlds, his strength amplified by severe penance and boons granted by the gods themselves. His arms—many as a sea of serpents—held weapons imbued with unholy power. He stood undefeated, a terror across all realms, and now, his blazing eyes were set upon *Rāma* and his army.

Rama, the prince of Ayodhya and the seventh incarnation of *Vishnu*, stood ready with his divine bow, Kodanda, its string taut with a golden arrow. *Hanumān*, *Sugriva*, and the *Vānaras* rallied behind him, though the weight of despair hung heavy upon their hearts. For every blow they struck upon Sahasra-Rāvana seemed futile; the demon's thousand heads regenerated as quickly as they were destroyed.

It was then that *Sitā*, the embodiment of purity and devotion, arrived at the battlefield.

'Enough!' Sitā's voice rang out like a thunderclap, silencing the battlefield. The Vānaras froze, the echoes of her command reverberating through their ranks. Even the great Sahasra-Rāvana paused, his many faces contorting into expressions of curiosity and scorn.

'Do you think yourself invincible, demon?' Sitā continued, her tone calm yet laced with unshakeable authority. 'You do not understand the forces you have challenged.'

Rāma turned to his wife, concern etched on his face. 'Sitā, this battle is mine to fight. Stay back—this is not your burden to bear.'

But Sitā's gaze, fierce as a tempest, met his. 'You are my lord, Rāma, but this battle transcends mortal strife. It is the moment for the eternal to reveal itself.'

With those words, Sitā closed her eyes and began to chant. Her voice, once gentle, now resonated with the primal power of the universe. The skies darkened, clouds swirling in an unnatural vortex above her. The earth trembled beneath her feet, as if bowing to the force she was about to unleash.

From her serene form, a radiant energy began to emerge, brighter than the sun and fiercer than the flames of destruction. The energy engulfed her entirely, and when the blinding light subsided, Sitā was no longer the gentle queen of Ayodhya. She had transformed into *Mahākāli*, the primordial goddess of wrath and destruction.

Her dark skin gleamed like molten obsidian, her hair unbound and wild, flowing like an endless river of night. In her many hands, she wielded weapons forged in celestial realms—a trident, a sword, and a noose among them. Around her neck hung a garland of severed demon heads, each face frozen in an expression of terror. Her eyes burned with an intensity that seemed to consume the very fabric of existence.

The battlefield fell silent, the Vānaras trembling in awe. Even Sahasra-Rāvana, the indomitable demon king, felt the first flicker of fear.

'*Kāli*!' Sahasra-Rāvana roared, his voices merging into a cacophony of defiance. 'Do you think your transformation can strike fear into me? I have conquered *devas* and *Asuras* alike. You are but another form of destruction I shall overcome!'

But his bravado faltered as Kāli advanced, her movements fluid yet terrible, each step shaking the earth. She spoke no words, her silence more chilling than any threat. Raising her trident, she launched herself at the demon, her speed blurring into a streak of black lightning.

Sahasra-Rāvana fought with all his might. His thousand arms wielded weapons of incredible power, each strike capable of shattering mountains. He hurled spears of fire, axes of ice, and thunderbolts wreathed in poison.

But Kāli was a force beyond comprehension. She danced across the battlefield, her every movement precise and devastating. The weapons of the demon shattered upon her body, as if striking the void itself. One by one, she began severing his heads. Each head that fell was consumed by flames before it could regenerate.

Sahasra-Rāvana screamed in rage, his voices mingling into a deafening roar that shook the heavens.

'You are relentless, demon,' Kāli said at last, her voice a low growl that echoed across the battlefield. 'But your arrogance blinds you to the truth. You cannot defeat me, for I am the power that sustains the universe and the force that destroys it.'

With a final, mighty leap, she drove her trident through the heart of Sahasra-Rāvana. The demon staggered, his thousand heads crying out in agony before falling silent. His massive form collapsed, shaking the earth with its weight, and a great shadow lifted from the battlefield.

As Sahasra-Rāvana's lifeless body dissolved into ash, the Vānaras erupted in cheers. But their jubilation quickly turned to reverent silence as Kāli turned to face them.

The goddess stood amidst the desolation, her terrible form emanating an aura of both dread and majesty.

Rāma stepped forward, his eyes filled with both awe and devotion. 'Sitā,' he said softly, 'you have revealed your true self, and the universe bears witness to your boundless strength. You are more than my queen—you are the divine incarnate.'

At these words, Kāli's fierce expression softened. Slowly, her weapons vanished, her many arms receded, and the dark energy surrounding her dissipated. In moments, she returned to her earthly form as Sitā, her radiant beauty and calm demeanour restored.

She looked at Rāma with a gentle smile. 'I am always your Sitā, my lord,' she said. 'But know this: the divine must intervene when the balance of Dharma is threatened. Sahasra-Rāvana's defeat was not merely our victory, but the restoration of cosmic order.'

The Vānaras knelt before Sitā, their heads bowed in reverence. Hanumān, the ever-faithful devotee, folded his hands and said, 'O Mother, your strength and grace have revealed the infinite power of devotion and righteousness. May your name be worshipped across all worlds.'

And so it was. The tale of Sitā as Mahākāli spread far and wide, a testament to her divine power and the eternal truth that Dharma, when upheld with devotion and courage, can overcome even the mightiest of evils. The battlefield of Sahasra-Rāvana became a sacred site, a reminder of the day when the goddess herself descended to restore balance to the world.

The Boatman Who Washed Rāma's Feet

From The Ramcharitmanas

The night was thick with silence, save for the gentle whispers of the *Sarayu* River as its waters lapped against the banks. The crescent moon hung low, its pale light glinting off the rippling waves like scattered silver coins. *Rāma*, prince of Ayodhya and the embodiment of *Dharma*, stood at the riverbank, flanked by *Sitā* and *Lakshmana.* Exiled from his kingdom, Rāma bore his sorrow with the quiet dignity of one born to uphold righteousness, his form illuminated with a divine glow that seemed to outshine even the moonlight.

Farther down the river, the small wooden boat of *Kevat*, the humble boatman, rested upon the sand. A man of simple life and steadfast devotion, Kevat made his living ferrying travellers across the Sarayu. That night, as he rested near his boat, his dreams were interrupted by an inexplicable pull at his heart. Something—some power—beckoned him to the river's edge. Waking with a start, he looked towards the distant bank and saw a luminous figure standing in the night.

Kevat's breath caught. 'Could it be...?' he whispered, his voice trembling. 'Rama, the Lord of all creation, here in this wilderness?'

Without hesitation, he rushed towards his boat, his heart pounding with equal parts awe and anticipation.

As Kevat approached, the soft crunch of his feet on the sand reached the ears of Rāma. Turning towards the sound, Rāma saw the humble boatman approaching with folded hands, his eyes glistening with devotion. Kevat fell to his knees, pressing his forehead against the cool earth.

'Lord,' Kevat said, his voice quivering, 'what fortune has brought me this night? My eyes behold the Supreme, and my ears are blessed to hear your voice. How may this unworthy servant serve you?'

Rāma stepped forward, his expression serene yet kind. 'Kevat,' he said, his voice as melodious as the river's flow, 'we seek to cross the Sarayu. Will you grant us passage?'

Kevat lifted his head, and a flicker of hesitation crossed his face. Bowing low again, he said, 'My Lord, it would be my honour to ferry you across, but first, I must make a humble request.'

Lakshmana, standing beside Rāma, frowned. 'A request? Boatman, do you not see who stands before you? Why do you delay when our need is urgent?'

Kevat raised his hands in supplication, his gaze fixed on Rāma's feet. 'Forgive me, my Lord, and you too, noble Lakshmana. But I have heard tales of your divine power. They say that the touch of your feet transforms even stone into life. The boulder Ahalya bore witness to this truth and regained her human form by your grace. How, then, can this frail wooden boat bear the touch of such divinity? If it turns divine, how will I earn my living?'

Rama's lips curved into a gentle smile. 'Kevat,' he said, his tone soothing, 'your faith speaks volumes. What is it you wish to do?'

Kevat prostrated himself again. 'Lord, I beg you, allow me to wash your feet before you step into my boat. Only then will I ferry you across, for it is not wealth I seek, but the blessing of serving you with my hands.'

Rāma nodded, his smile unwavering. 'Your devotion is pure, Kevat. Do as your heart commands.'

Kevat rose, his face shining with reverence. He fetched a simple brass vessel from his boat, filled it with water from the river, and knelt before Rāma. With trembling hands, he poured the cool water over Rāma's feet, his fingers gently scrubbing away the dust of the forest path.

The river seemed to glow brighter as Kevat performed the act, the ripples singing a soft hymn in harmony with the stars. Sitā watched in silence, her eyes shimmering with emotion, while Lakshmana, moved by the boatman's devotion, bowed his head in respect.

As Kevat washed Rāma's feet, he spoke softly, his voice filled with reverence. 'My Lord, I have nothing to offer you but my service. Let these hands, unworthy as they are, cleanse the dust from your divine feet. May this act purify my soul and grant me a place at your feet in every birth.'

When the ritual was complete, Kevat stood and emptied the water into the Sarayu. The river seemed to embrace it, its waves carrying the sanctified water downstream as though eager to spread the blessing. Kevat then gestured towards his boat, his smile radiant.

'Come, my Lord,' he said, 'the boat is ready. It is but a humble vessel, yet it shall carry the Supreme across.'

Rāma stepped into the boat, followed by Sitā and Lakshmana. The craft rocked gently under their weight, but Kevat steadied it with practised ease. Taking up the oar, he began to row, the rhythmic strokes of wood against water blending with the soft murmur of the river.

For a time, no words were spoken. The Sarayu seemed to cradle the boat in its arms, carrying it smoothly under the watchful gaze of the moon. Kevat's heart swelled with joy, his every movement a prayer, his every breath a hymn to the Lord seated before him.

As the opposite bank drew near, Kevat slowed the boat and finally brought it to rest against the shore. Rāma stepped out, his every motion imbued with grace, and turned to face the boatman.

'Kevat,' he said, his voice warm, 'you have served us well this night. Tell me, how may I reward you for your devotion?'

Kevat clasped his hands and bowed low. 'My Lord, I desire nothing more than to remain in your service. Let me be like this boat—a simple tool to carry you across the rivers of the world, unworthy yet blessed by your touch.'

Rāma placed a hand on Kevat's shoulder, his touch gentle yet filled with divine power. 'Kevat, your devotion humbles even the gods. Know this: your wish shall be granted. In every age, you shall serve me in your own way, and your soul shall find liberation at my feet.'

Kevat's eyes filled with tears, and he fell to his knees. 'My Lord,' he said, his voice choked with emotion, 'I am blessed beyond measure. May your name forever reside in my heart.'

Rama, Sitā, and Lakshmana continued their journey into the forest, their figures disappearing into the shadows. Kevat remained by the shore, his heart filled with an unshakeable peace. As he watched the river flow onward, he felt as though the Sarayu itself had been sanctified by the touch of the divine, its waters carrying the story of this night to distant lands.

Varuna Faces The Wrath of Rāma

From the Valmiki Rāmāyana

The sun hung low over the horizon, its golden light shimmering upon the restless waves of the ocean. The salty air carried a biting chill, mingling with the murmurs of the *Vānara* army that stood gathered on the southern shores of India. They had assembled in their thousands, a mighty force ready to march upon the demon King *Rāvana*'s fortress in Lanka. Yet, before them lay a seemingly insurmountable barrier: the vast, churning waters of the ocean.

Rama, the scion of the *Raghu* dynasty and the embodiment of righteousness, stood at the forefront, his gaze fixed upon the endless expanse of blue. His shoulders bore the weight of exile, his heart heavy with the pain of separation from Sitā, his beloved, who remained a prisoner in Rāvana's palace.

Beside him stood *Lakshmana*, ever-vigilant and resolute, whilst the leader of the *Vānaras*, *Sugriva*, awaited his command.

For three days and nights, Rāma had sought the grace of *Varuna*, the god of the ocean. With folded hands and a heart brimming with humility, he had prayed for safe passage across the waters, beseeching the deity to calm the waves and allow the construction of a bridge. But the ocean remained unmoved, its depths silent and unyielding.

As the fourth dawn broke, Rāma's patience gave way to righteous anger. The gentle demeanour that had so often defined him was replaced by a fiery resolve, his eyes gleaming like molten gold. Turning to Lakshmana, he said, his voice firm and resolute, 'The time for supplication is over. Varuna, in his arrogance, has refused to heed my prayers. If the ocean will not grant us passage willingly, I shall compel it with the might of my bow.'

Lakshmana, ever loyal, nodded in agreement. 'Brother,' he said, 'your anger is just. The ocean's indifference is an insult to *Dharma*, and its defiance must be met with the force it deserves.'

With those words, Rāma strode forward, his every step imbued with divine power. He drew forth his mighty bow, Kodanda, its golden frame shimmering like the first rays of dawn. From his quiver, he selected an arrow—a weapon of immense potency, imbued with the energy of celestial flames.

The Vānaras watched in awe, their murmurs silenced by the sheer gravity of the moment. The winds grew still, and the earth seemed to hold its breath as Rāma nocked the arrow to his bowstring. Drawing the string back with a strength that could humble mountains, he aimed it towards the heart of the ocean.

The arrow flew from Rāma's bow with a sound like thunder, a streak of fire cutting through the heavens. It descended upon the waters with an explosive force, its impact sending towering waves crashing against the shore. The sea roared in protest, its depths churning violently as if the very soul of the ocean had been struck. Whirlpools formed where the arrow struck, their spiralling currents a testament to the fury of Rāma's divine weapon.

The Vānaras clung to the ground, their eyes wide with terror and awe. Even Lakshmana, steadfast and unyielding, could not help but marvel at the sheer magnitude of his brother's power. The heavens darkened, and the air grew thick with the scent of salt and smoke.

Amidst this chaos, the ocean itself seemed to cry out, its voice a deep and resonant rumble that echoed across the skies. From the frothing waves emerged the god Varuna, his form towering and resplendent. His skin shimmered like the surface of the water under moonlight, and his eyes held the depth of ancient wisdom. Bowing low before Rāma, Varuna spoke, his voice trembling with both reverence and fear.

'Great Rāma,' Varuna began, his tone laden with humility, 'forgive me, O Lord, for my delay in answering your prayers.

It was not arrogance that kept me silent, but my own nature. I am the ocean, vast and boundless, and it is my Dharma to remain in constant motion. I cannot calm my waters, for it would go against my very essence.'

Rāma stood tall, his bow still in hand, his expression stern. 'Varuna,' he said, his voice cutting through the roar of the waves, 'I sought your favour with humility and patience. Yet you remained silent, forcing me to take up arms. Tell me, why should I not unleash my full wrath upon your waters and dry them to dust?'

Varuna bowed his head lower, his form trembling under the weight of Rāma's words. 'Lord, your anger is justified, and I do not deny your power. Yet know this: the ocean is not your enemy. I am but a servant of the greater Dharma, as are you. To dry my waters would disrupt the balance of the world, but I shall not oppose your will. I beg you, O Rāma, spare my depths and allow me to aid you in another way.'

At these words, Rāma's anger began to subside. He lowered his bow, his eyes softening as he considered Varuna's plea. 'If you wish to prove your loyalty to Dharma,' Rāma said, 'then grant my army safe passage. Allow us to construct a bridge across your waters, that we may march upon Lanka and restore justice to the world.'

Varuna straightened, his expression one of profound gratitude. 'It shall be as you command, O Lord,' he said. 'I shall hold my waters steady, and they shall bear the weight of the stones and trees that form your bridge. The Vānaras may work without fear, for the ocean itself shall aid in your righteous cause.'

Turning to the Vānara army, Varuna addressed them with a booming voice. 'Heed my words, warriors of Sugriva. Bring forth the rocks and boulders from the mountains and inscribe them with the name of Rāma. The power of his name shall make them float, and the ocean shall guide them into place.'

With Varuna's blessing, the Vānaras set to work with renewed vigour. Under the leadership of Nala and Neela, the architect-heroes of their kind, they began to construct the *Setu*, the bridge that would stretch from Bharat to Lanka. Mighty stones were inscribed with Rāma's name and hurled into the waters, where they floated miraculously, forming a path across the waves.

The sight was one of awe and wonder. The ocean, once wild and unruly, now seemed to cradle the stones with reverence, its surface shimmering with divine light. Rāma watched the progress with a serene smile, his heart swelling with hope and determination.

As the bridge neared completion, Varuna approached Rāma one final time, his hands folded in a gesture of respect. 'Great Lord,' he said, 'your actions have taught even me, the eternal ocean, a lesson in Dharma. Your patience, tempered with righteous wrath, has reminded me that the path of justice requires both humility and strength. May your journey be victorious, and may your name resonate across the ages.'

Rāma nodded, his gaze steady. 'Varuna, you have shown that even the mightiest forces of nature are bound by the laws of Dharma. I thank you for your aid and for upholding the balance of this world.'

With those words, Varuna retreated into the depths, his form dissolving into the waves. The ocean returned to its gentle rhythm, its surface reflecting the golden glow of the setting sun.

With the bridge complete, Rāma stood at its edge, his bow resting by his side. He turned to his army, his voice ringing clear and commanding. 'Today, we cross this ocean not merely to reclaim what was taken, but to restore Dharma to the world. Stand with me, my friends, for our cause is just, and victory shall be ours.'

The Vānaras erupted into cheers, their voices echoing across the bridge as they began their march towards Lanka. The sun dipped below the horizon, casting the ocean in hues of red and gold, as if the very heavens blessed their endeavour.

Thus, with the ocean calmed and the path to Lanka secured, Rāma's journey towards the final battle began—a tale of divine justice that would be sung for generations to come.

Rāma Meets Shiva

From The Adhyatma Rāmāyana

The winds whispered through the dense forests of *Dandakaranya*, their cool touch carrying the fragrance of earth and fallen leaves. The trees, ancient and solemn, stood as silent sentinels, their roots tangled deep into the soil as though bearing witness to countless aeons of divine play.

In this sacred wilderness, *Rāma*, the prince of Ayodhya and the very embodiment of *Dharma*, walked with his younger brother *Lakshmana*. Their journey was arduous, their hearts weighed by the pain of separation from *Sitā*, who had been cruelly taken by the demon King *Rāvana*. Yet, Rāma's countenance remained calm, his steps unwavering.

Beneath the surface of his mortal form lay the infinite essence of *Vishnu*, the Preserver, who had descended to the world of men to restore balance and uphold righteousness.

On this day, the forest seemed imbued with an otherworldly presence. The air grew still, heavy with a divine energy that pressed against the senses. *Lakshmana*, ever watchful, glanced at Rāma, his brow furrowed in concern. 'Brother,' he said, his voice low, 'there is a power here that I cannot comprehend. Do you feel it?'

Rāma nodded, his gaze soft but resolute. 'Indeed, Lakshmana,' he replied. 'The one who dwells in the infinite realms approaches. Stay by my side, for we are to receive the *darshan* of *Mahādeva*, the great god *Shiva* himself.'

Even as Rāma spoke, a radiant light began to suffuse the forest, casting long shadows upon the ground. From this brilliance emerged the figure of Shiva, his form majestic and awe-inspiring. His matted locks, adorned with the crescent moon, cascaded over his shoulders, whilst his body glowed with the ethereal light of ash and divinity.

In one hand, he held his trident, and around his neck coiled serpents that seemed to hum with latent power. Shiva's eyes, deep and unyielding, settled upon Rāma with a gaze that was both knowing and reverent. A smile graced his lips, as if he were beholding a truth that transcended mortal comprehension.

Bowing deep, Shiva, with folded hands, spoke, his voice resonant and filled with devotion. 'O Lord Rāma,' he said, 'I bow to you, the eternal Vishnu, who has taken human form to restore Dharma. Though veiled by the guise of mortality, you are the Supreme Reality, the cause of all creation, preservation, and destruction.'

Rāma too, bowed deep, a knowing smile on his lips. *Hari* and *Hara*, the eternal friends, were playing their parts in the divine play.

Lakshmana, stunned by the sight of the great Mahādeva bowing before his brother, turned to Rāma, his voice trembling with awe. 'Brother, is this not the lord of *Kailāsa*, the one who dances the *Tāndava* and bears the *Ganga* upon his head? Why does he bow to you?'

Rama, his expression calm and serene, replied with a gentle smile, 'Lakshmana, Shiva sees beyond the veil of my mortal form. He knows the truth of my existence, for we are but two aspects of the same cosmic force. He, the destroyer, and I, the preserver, work together to sustain the balance of creation. Pay heed, for his words carry the weight of divine wisdom.'

Turning to Shiva, Rāma folded his hands and said, 'O Lord of Kailāsa, your words humble me. You, who embody renunciation and cosmic dissolution, stand as the greatest exemplar of devotion. What wisdom would you bestow upon me, a humble traveller in the path of Dharma?'

Shiva's smile deepened, and his voice grew softer, suffused with divine love. 'Dharma, O Rāma, is the foundation of all existence. To walk the path of Dharma is to act selflessly, with no attachment to the fruits of one's actions. It is to see the divine in all beings and to perform one's duties with unwavering devotion. You, O Vishnu incarnate, have taken this mortal form to guide humanity by example, to show them that even the Supreme bows to the laws of Dharma. Your life is the ultimate scripture.'

Rāma listened intently, his expression reflecting both gratitude and determination. After a moment of silence, he asked,

'You speak of devotion, Mahādeva. How does one cultivate such unwavering love for the divine amidst the trials and distractions of the mortal world?'

Shiva raised his trident, his eyes gleaming with the light of realisation. '*Bhakti*, O Rāma, is the highest path. It is through devotion that one transcends the bonds of *karma* and attains liberation. Bhakti does not require wealth, power, or knowledge; it demands only a pure heart, one that is surrendered entirely to the divine. To chant your name, O Vishnu, is itself an act of supreme worship, for your name is a bridge that carries souls across the ocean of *Samsāra*.'

Shiva continued, his voice carrying the weight of timeless wisdom. 'In this incarnation, you will face great trials, O Rāma. You will witness the depths of human suffering and the heights of devotion. Remember, your purpose is not merely to defeat *Rāvana* but to awaken the hearts of all beings to the truth of Dharma. Your deeds shall inspire humanity for aeons, and your name shall be their solace.'

As he spoke, Shiva raised his hand in a gesture of blessing, his form radiant with divine energy. 'I, too, am your devotee, O Lord,' he said. 'Though I am the destroyer, I bow before you, the preserver, for it is through your grace that creation finds its purpose.'

Rāma bowed low before Shiva, his hands folded in reverence. 'O Mahādeva,' he said, 'your words are a light in the darkness of this world. Your devotion humbles me, and your wisdom shall guide me in the trials to come. May your blessings be with me always.'

Shiva stepped forward, his hands raised in blessing. 'Rama,' he said, 'may your journey be victorious. May the *rakshasas* who defy Dharma be vanquished, and may your love for Sitā illuminate the world as an eternal symbol of devotion. Know that I, too, am your devotee, and I stand ready to serve you in all realms.'

With those words, Shiva's form began to dissolve, his presence merging with the light that bathed the forest. The air grew still once more, and the earthly realm reclaimed its ordinary rhythm.

As they resumed their journey, Lakshmana turned to Rāma, his voice tinged with awe. 'Brother,' he said, 'the words of Mahādeva have unveiled truths I could never have fathomed. How fortunate are we to walk this path, guided by such wisdom.'

Rāma smiled, his gaze fixed on the horizon. 'Lakshmana,' he said, 'the path of Dharma is not an easy one, but it is the only one worth walking. With Shiva's blessings and the love of our people, we shall fulfil our purpose and restore balance to this world.'

The Squirrel's Stripes

From The Kamba Rāmāyana

The vast ocean stretched endlessly, its waves crashing against the shores with a relentless fury, as though mocking the efforts of mere mortals. The army of *Vānaras*—monkey warriors led by *Sugriva*—stood united under the divine command of *Rāma*, the prince of Ayodhya. The goal was clear: to build a bridge across the ocean to Lanka, the island kingdom of the demon King *Rāvana*, where *Sitā*, Rāma's beloved, was held captive.

The task was monumental, beyond the scope of ordinary beings. But this was no ordinary army. Rāma himself, the embodiment of *Dharma*, infused the warriors with divine purpose. Under the guidance of Nala, the architect among the Vānaras, great rocks were uprooted, boulders were carved, and trees were felled. The air rang with the chants of Rāma's name as the *Vānaras* worked tirelessly, their strength rivalling that of the gods.

Massive stones were inscribed with the sacred name of Rāma, their surfaces shimmering with divine energy as they were hurled into the ocean. By some miracle, they floated, forming the beginnings of a path to Lanka. The Vānaras laboured day and night, their fur matted with sweat, their hands calloused from their efforts.

In the midst of this grand endeavour, a tiny figure darted to and fro near the shoreline—a small squirrel, seemingly insignificant among the legions of mighty warriors. Its brown fur glistened in the sunlight, and its tiny paws carried grains of sand from the beach to the water's edge. Each grain was dropped carefully onto the growing bridge before the squirrel scurried back to fetch more.

The Vānaras, engrossed in their work, barely noticed the creature at first. But as its persistent movements continued, some began to laugh.

'Look at this tiny creature!' jeered one Vānara, lifting a boulder twice his size. 'Does it think its specks of sand will make a difference?'

Another joined in, his laughter booming like thunder. 'With the strength of an army behind us, what use is the effort of a squirrel?'

The squirrel paused, its small eyes narrowing as it looked up at the towering Vānaras. Undeterred by their mockery, it spoke in a voice that, though small, carried the weight of conviction.

'Each grain of sand I carry is my offering to Lord Rāma,' it said. 'I may not possess your strength, nor can I lift great boulders, but my devotion is no less. The bridge to Lanka is not built by strength alone—it is built by love, faith, and unity. Even the smallest effort, when offered with true devotion, has its place in this great task.'

The Vānaras fell silent, their laughter fading as they looked upon the squirrel with a newfound respect.

At that moment, Rāma himself approached, his divine aura radiating calm and compassion. His gaze fell upon the squirrel, and a gentle smile graced his lips.

'Why do you mock this creature's efforts?' Rāma asked, his voice as soothing as the ocean breeze yet carrying the weight of justice. 'Do you not see that every act of devotion, no matter how small, contributes to the greater good?'

The Vānaras bowed their heads in shame. 'Forgive us, my Lord,' one of them said. 'We were blinded by our pride and failed to recognise the sincerity of this small yet mighty soul.'

Rāma knelt, his robes brushing against the sand as he extended his hand to the squirrel. The tiny creature climbed into his palm, its tiny body trembling with both reverence and awe.

'My dear friend,' Rāma said, his voice warm with affection, 'your devotion humbles me. You remind us all that even the smallest among us has a role to play in the fulfilment of Dharma.'

As Rāma spoke, he ran his fingers gently across the squirrel's back, his touch imbued with divine energy. When he lifted his hand, three distinct stripes marked the squirrel's fur—lines of dark brown that shimmered faintly with the light of divinity.

'These stripes shall remain on your back for all eternity,' Rāma declared, 'a testament to your devotion and a reminder that no act of love or faith is ever insignificant.'

The squirrel chittered in delight, its tiny heart swelling with pride and gratitude. 'Thank you, my Lord,' it said, bowing low in his palm. 'May I always remain in your service, in this life and beyond.'

Rāma rose, the squirrel still cradled in his hand, and turned to address the gathered Vānaras.

'Remember this moment,' he said, his voice carrying over the sound of the waves. 'It is not strength alone that wins battles or builds bridges. It is unity, humility, and the shared devotion of all beings, great and small. Each of you, whether a mighty warrior or a humble squirrel, is vital to the success of our mission.'

The Vānaras bowed deeply, their pride replaced with a newfound reverence for all contributions, no matter how small. They returned to their work with renewed vigour, their chants of Rāma's name now joined by a deeper understanding of the divine purpose they served.

As the bridge to Lanka grew, the squirrel continued its work, undeterred and filled with joy. And when the bridge was finally completed, stretching like a gleaming path across the mighty ocean, the squirrel stood at its edge, gazing at the horizon where Lanka lay. Its heart swelled with pride, knowing that it had played its part, however small, in the great battle to restore Dharma.

part 8

The Mahābhārata

The Daughter of Fire

From The Mahābhārata

Kampilya, the great capital city of the Kingdom of *Pānchāla*, watched in awe as King *Drupada*—once mighty and now broken—prepared for the grandest *yajna* of his life. Having long since been humbled by his defeat at the hands of his former student, *Drona*, Drupada was determined to take revenge. This *yajna*, a sacrifice to the Gods, was not just a ritual, but the key to his vengeance. He had vowed that from this sacred fire, a warrior would arise to defeat his adversary, Drona, and restore his honour.

Drupada's heart burnt with the intensity of his anger as the flames of the yajna rose high into the sky—its brilliance mirrored by the divine chants of the priests. In the depths of his soul, Drupada had planned the yajna to beget a son—one who would bring about the fall of Drona, a leader capable of leading an army to crush the *Kurus*. And so, the fire was kindled with offerings, each one designed to bring forth a son of unrivalled valour and strength.

But the Gods, who watched from their celestial thrones, had other plans.

The fire raged with heat and divine power, as the sacrificial smoke swirled in a mesmerising dance. Suddenly, a powerful tremor shook the earth, as if the very ground itself had been touched by the breath of the Gods. From the flames, amidst the crackling heat, emerged a youth, clothed in resplendent gold, his head adorned with a diadem that gleamed like the rising sun.

The boy stood tall and strong, his body exuding power and regal grace. The son that Drupada had longed for had finally come into being, fully grown, as if from the very essence of the fire itself. The onlookers gasped in wonder at the sight of this miraculous child, whose every step seemed to reverberate with the promise of the future.

But just as all thought that the sacrifice had ended, another form rose from the fire, and it was not a girl, but a young woman in full bloom. The crowd, stunned beyond belief, could barely comprehend what their eyes beheld. Standing before them was a dusky beauty, her form radiant as the night sky, her eyes shimmering with divine light.

The crowd murmured in astonishment, for how could this be? Where once there had only been the expectation of a single son, the flames had given forth a daughter—a daughter as radiant and regal as the Gods themselves.

Drupada stood frozen, his eyes wide with disbelief. His heart raced, confusion overtaking him. 'This is completely unexpected,' he muttered, his voice choking with surprise. 'I sought a son, but the flames have given me a daughter as well—what madness is this?'

The priests, too, were stunned by this turn of events. The divine had answered, but in a way that no mortal could predict. As the moment stretched, the damsel—who had been born of the sacred fire—stepped forward with grace that seemed to surpass all mortal comprehension.

Her beauty was indescribable—she was like the moon, radiant and full of light, yet her form was as strong as the earth itself. Her dark skin glowed with a light that could rival the sun, and her long hair cascaded like a waterfall of ink. She stood tall, like a goddess, her presence commanding respect from all those present.

Drupada, still overcome with disbelief, his cherished son completely forgotten, staggered forward. 'Who are you, O divine one, who has emerged from the fire?' he asked, his voice heavy with wonder.

'I am *Yajnaseni*, the daughter of this yajna,' *Draupadi* said, her voice deep and melodic, yet filled with a strange and powerful authority. 'I have been born of your sacrifice, O King, to fulfil the destiny of your kingdom. I shall be your strength, your weapon of vengeance. Though I am a daughter, I am not a mere woman. I am the flame that shall light the path to your revenge.'

Her words echoed in the hall, and all present fell silent. The power in her voice was undeniable. Drupada, in awe, stood there, unable to speak. He had long sought a son to avenge his humiliation, but now fate had delivered to him not just one, but two children—one to lead in battle, and one to command hearts and minds.

As the priests gathered their wits, one of the elder sages, his voice like the murmur of a river, stepped forward to name the two children.

'Behold, O King,' the sage said, 'your son, *Drishtadyumna*, is born with the mark of destiny—he shall fulfil the vengeance you seek upon Drona. And your daughter, born of this sacred fire, shall be called by your epithet Drupada, as Draupadi, and as Yajnaseni as well, for she is the daughter of the yajna itself.'

The crowd, still in awe of the divine birth, murmured in unison. The moment was monumental—Drupada, for all his glory and power, had been humbled by the Gods, and his hope for revenge had been realised, but not in the way he had anticipated.

Draupadi, standing beside her twin brother, Drishtadyumna, gazed at him, her eyes dark with a mystery that none could fathom. Together, they were born to alter the course of history, and though their fates were intertwined with the revenge that Drupada sought, they would become figures of power and sorrow in their own right.

Drupada, still bewildered, turned to the assembly. 'I sought a son to avenge me,' he muttered. 'But the Gods have granted me a daughter as well. A daughter born of fire—who will be the instrument of my vengeance.'

The air was thick with a strange tension, and Drupada's voice wavered with uncertainty as he looked at his daughter Draupadi, the symbol of both divine power and fate's whimsy. Could this be the beginning of something greater? Something that would surpass his desire for revenge and reshape the world itself?

But Draupadi—Yajnaseni—merely nodded, her gaze fixed on her father. 'You sought a son, O King. But I am the gift that the fire has bestowed upon you. I shall fulfil the fate that has been woven for us. You will see.'

Thus, from the flames of Drupada's sacrifice, emerged two powerful children: Drishtadyumna, the son of destiny, and Draupadi, the daughter of fire. Drupada's heart swelled with pride and dread, for he knew that these children—these divine beings—were not mere mortals, but forces of destiny that would shape the future of the world.

Their birth would herald the beginning of an epic saga—one that would bring about the fall of the mighty Kuru dynasty and alter the course of history forever.

But for now, in the quiet aftermath of the yajna, Drupada gazed at Draupadi, his daughter, with an emotion he could not name. There was awe in his heart, for she was no ordinary girl. She was a living flame, a force that would ignite the fire of vengeance in the hearts of kings and warriors alike.

Her future, like the flames that had brought her forth, would burn bright and fierce—and nothing, not even the Gods themselves, could halt its course.

Sudyumna and the Enchanted Forest

From The Mahābhārata

In the ancient age when Gods still walked amongst mortals and the boundaries between worlds were as fragile as a whisper, there was a prince named *Sudyumna*. He was a man of strength and valour, his deeds sung by bards in the halls of the Kingdom of *Pratishthāna*. Yet, despite his prowess and his lineage, Sudyumna was fated to tread paths few dared, crossing into realms where even the Gods held their breath.

One fateful morning, as the first light of dawn painted the skies in hues of fire and gold, Sudyumna rode out with his loyal retainers. His chariot gleamed—its wheels adorned with golden spokes and studded with precious gems. Pulled by horses as white as moonlight, it coursed like the wind across the plains.

They rode to the north, where the forests grew thick and dark, their canopies knitting together to weave a shroud of perpetual twilight. It was the fabled forest of *Sharavana*, said to be cursed by the Gods themselves. No mortal dared enter its shadowed depths, for it was consecrated to the Goddess *Pārvati*, who had decreed that only women might tread there without harm.

But Sudyumna, bold and unyielding, dismissed the warnings of the old tales. 'What is a curse to a man of courage?' he declared, his voice ringing like steel. 'Let the forest test me, if it dares.'

The chariot plunged into the emerald gloom. The air grew cool and heavy, thick with the scent of moss and damp earth. A profound silence enveloped the travellers, broken only by the soft whinny of the horses and the whisper of the wind through the ancient trees.

Suddenly, a shimmering veil of light descended upon them, as though the very fabric of the world had been woven anew. The air crackled with unseen power, and the ground seemed to shift beneath their feet. Sudyumna cried out, a sound of shock and dismay, for his strong voice now rang softer, sweeter, utterly unfamiliar.

The retainers stumbled from the chariot, their armour and weapons clattering to the forest floor. They, too, had changed—their broad shoulders and calloused hands now delicate, their faces transformed into those of women. Sudyumna looked down at himself, his heart pounding. His sinewy frame had become slender, his hands smooth, and his warrior's garb hung awkwardly on a body now utterly foreign.

A voice, soft as a sigh but vast as the heavens, echoed through the glade.

'You, who dared to defy my decree,' it intoned, 'have felt the weight of my curse. You are no longer Sudyumna, prince of men. You are *Ilā* now, a maiden of this forest. Only when you grasp the truth of your heart shall you find release.'

And with that, the presence vanished, leaving Sudyumna—now Ilā—standing bewildered beneath the ancient trees.

For days, Ilā wandered the forest, her steps unsteady, her mind a whirlwind of despair and disbelief. Gone were her companions, scattered by the enchantment, and gone too was her identity, her very self.

It was then, by the silver light of the moon, that she came upon a figure seated by a crystal-clear stream. His visage was serene, his form radiant, as though carved from the very essence of light. This was Budha, the son of *Chandra*, the Moon God, a celestial being of wisdom and grace.

Budha looked up, his eyes meeting hers with a gaze that seemed to pierce the veil of time itself. 'Who are you, traveller, to tread the paths of this enchanted realm?'

'I... I do not know,' Ilā replied, her voice trembling. 'I was Sudyumna, a prince, but now I am lost.'

Budha smiled gently. 'None are truly lost who seek to find themselves,' he said. 'Come, sit with me, and tell me your tale.'

As the night deepened and the stars wove their tapestry across the heavens, Ilā recounted her story. Budha listened, his expression thoughtful, his gaze lingering on the sorrow that shadowed her eyes.

'You have been touched by a power greater than you know,' he said at last. 'But even in this form, there is beauty, and there is strength. Perhaps it was fate that led you here, for my heart sees in you a light that echoes my own.'

And so, in the days that followed, Ilā remained in the forest, and the bond between her and Budha deepened. Beneath the towering trees and the watchful moon, they spoke of life and love, of mortal frailty and divine purpose.

In time, their union bore fruit, and Ilā gave birth to a son, *Pururavas*, who would one day become the founder of the *Chandra Vamsa*, the Lunar Dynasty. He was a child of great promise, his laughter ringing like the chime of silver bells, his eyes alight with the wisdom of his celestial heritage.

Yet, even as she cherished her child, Ilā's heart remained restless. The memory of her former life, of Sudyumna's bold strides and unyielding spirit, lingered like a shadow on the edge of her thoughts. She yearned to reclaim what had been lost, to bridge the chasm between who she was and who she had become.

Driven by this longing, Ilā journeyed to the sacred peaks where the Gods held counsel. There, on the slopes of Mount *Kailāsa*, she offered penance to *Shiva*, the lord of transformation, and Pārvati, the Goddess who had cast the curse. For days and nights uncounted, she stood in meditation, her body weathered by wind and rain, her soul unwavering in its plea.

At last, Shiva appeared, his form wreathed in the brilliance of a thousand suns, Pārvati by his side.

'You have endured much, Ilā,' Shiva said, his voice both thunderous and tender. 'And you have learnt that identity is but a shadow cast by the eternal self.'

Pārvati's gaze softened as she spoke. 'I grant you a boon. You shall be both Sudyumna and Ilā, shifting between forms with the waxing and waning of the moon. Thus shall you honour the balance of creation, the dance of opposites that sustains the world.'

With a gesture, Shiva touched Ilā's brow, and the transformation began anew. Her form shifted, not with the violence of the first curse, but with a fluid grace, as though the universe itself embraced her duality.

Sudyumna returned to his kingdom and became a beacon for those who sought to understand the intricate dance of fate and the eternal truth that lies beyond all form.

His tale of curses and blessings, of loss and self-discovery, would echo through the ages. Yet, he did not forget the days he had spent as Ilā, nor the love he had shared with Budha, nor the child they had brought into the world. In him dwelt both the strength of a warrior and the wisdom of a seeker, and his rule was marked by compassion and justice.

The Demon Eater

From The Mahābhārata

In the lands beyond the *Vindhya* Mountains, where the earth turned arid and the skies burnt crimson at dusk, a sinister shadow loomed. This desolate region was the domain of two fearsome *Asura* brothers, *Vātāpi* and *Ilvāla*, whose wickedness had become the stuff of whispered tales amongst travellers and sages alike. The pair, cunning and ruthless, had devised a diabolical scheme to lure and destroy unsuspecting victims.

Ilvāla, the elder, was a demon of formidable intellect and charm, capable of weaving honeyed words into spellbinding nets that ensnared the unwary. Vātāpi, the younger, possessed a unique and terrible gift—he could transform his very essence into any form he desired. Together, they created a method of murder so gruesome and clever that none who encountered it survived to tell the tale.

Their deception was simple yet horrific. Vātāpi would transform himself into a goat, his flesh seemingly tender and succulent. Ilvāla, posing as a humble householder, would prepare a feast with his brother's transformed body and invite Brahmins, travellers, or merchants to partake of it. Once the unsuspecting guests had consumed the meal, Ilvāla would call out in a commanding voice, 'Vātāpi, come forth!' In an instant, Vātāpi would emerge, tearing his way out of the diners' stomachs, killing them in a spray of blood and viscera. The brothers would then feast on the remains of their victims, their dark laughter echoing across the barren hills.

The atrocities of Vātāpi and Ilvāla had not gone unnoticed by the Gods and sages. The cries of the victims reached the heavens, and the world trembled beneath the weight of their sins. Sage *Agastya*, known for his wisdom and divine powers, was well aware of the brothers' foul deeds. When the suffering of innocents grew unbearable, he resolved to put an end to the demons' reign of terror.

With this purpose burning in his heart, Agastya set forth. His gait was steady, his mind calm as an ocean, for he knew that his strength came not from physical might but from the fire of *Dharma* that blazed within him. As he neared the demon-infested lands, the air itself seemed to grow heavier, laden with the malice that had seeped into the soil.

As twilight cloaked the horizon, Agastya arrived at Ilvāla's dwelling, a crude hut surrounded by barren fields and twisted trees. The demon greeted him with practised hospitality, a broad smile masking the malice in his heart. Ilvāla recognised Agastya at once and concealed his surprise with a bow.

'Welcome, O revered sage,' Ilvāla said, his voice dripping with feigned humility. 'You honour my humble abode with your presence. Pray, accept my hospitality and partake of a meal prepared with the utmost devotion.'

Agastya, his eyes like twin flames, looked upon Ilvāla with an inscrutable gaze. Though the sage was fully aware of the trap laid before him, he nodded and replied, 'Very well. I accept your hospitality.'

Ilvāla suppressed a smirk as he turned away. Summoning Vātāpi, he instructed him to transform into a goat, and with cruel delight, he prepared the meal. The aroma of the cooked meat filled the air, rich and enticing. Ilvāla brought the platter to Agastya and set it before him with a theatrical flourish.

'Please, O sage, enjoy this humble offering,' Ilvāla said, watching with bated breath as Agastya began to eat.

Agastya ate with deliberate calm, savouring each bite as if it were a feast fit for the Gods. The demon watched in anticipation, his mind already rehearsing the moment when he would call out to his brother. When the meal was done, Agastya leaned back and patted his stomach with satisfaction.

Ilvāla's lips curled into a wicked grin. He clapped his hands together and called out in a voice that resonated with dark power, 'Vātāpi! Come forth!'

In the past, this cry had always heralded the end of their victims, as Vātāpi burst forth from their bodies in a gruesome display of demonic power. But this time, there was no movement, no sound of flesh tearing or bones breaking. Silence fell, heavy and unnatural.

Ilvāla frowned, his confidence faltering. 'Vātāpi, come forth!' he shouted again, louder and more desperate. Still, there was no response.

Agastya, who had remained serene throughout, now smiled and said, 'Call him as many times as you wish, Ilvāla, but your brother shall not answer. For I have digested him completely, and his evil will trouble this world no more.'

Ilvāla's expression twisted with rage and disbelief. 'You dare!' he roared, his voice shaking the very air. 'You have consumed my brother! For this, you shall pay with your life!'

The demon lunged at Agastya, his claws gleaming like daggers and his eyes burning with fury. But Agastya did not flinch. Raising his hand, he uttered a *mantra* that echoed like the roll of thunder.

'O demon, thy wickedness ends here! May the fire of Dharma consume thy malice and cleanse this land of thy darkness!'

Ilvāla froze mid-stride, his body trembling as the power of Agastya's words struck him like a tidal wave. The sage's aura blazed with divine light, and Ilvāla, despite his strength, was no match for the force of righteousness that enveloped him. With another chant, Agastya reduced the demon to ashes, his form scattering like dust in the wind.

As the first rays of dawn broke over the horizon, the land that had been shrouded in fear and despair now seemed to breathe with newfound life. The trees stood taller, the air grew lighter, and the cries of innocent souls faded into peace. Agastya, his mission complete, resumed his journey, his heart unburdened and his mind serene. In the heavens, the Gods smiled, for the sage's deeds had reaffirmed the balance of the world, ensuring that evil could never reign unchecked.

The Lake-Dwelling Yaksha

From The Mahābhārata

In the heart of the great forest, where sunlight filtered weakly through a canopy of ancient trees, the *Pāndavas* journeyed—their footsteps muffled by moss and fallen leaves. The air was heavy with the musk of untamed wilderness, and the chirping of unseen creatures gave the forest an aura of restless life. Exhausted from their long exile, the brothers pressed on, driven by a thirst that clawed at their throats.

Nakula, fleet-footed and sharp-eyed, was the first to break through the dense foliage. Before him lay a lake of crystalline water, its surface gleaming like a mirror under the noonday sun. The sight was almost otherworldly—a hidden oasis in the wilderness, untouched by time or human hand. Nakula's heart leaped with relief, and he called out to his brothers, though his voice barely carried through the oppressive silence.

As he knelt to drink, a voice rang out, deep and resonant, like the tolling of a great iron bell. 'Halt, O traveller! This lake is mine. None may drink its waters without answering my questions.'

Nakula hesitated, startled by the disembodied voice. Yet thirst overpowered caution. He cupped his hands, the cool water spilling through his fingers as he brought it to his lips. No sooner had he drunk than a terrible chill overtook him. His limbs stiffened, his breath caught, and he collapsed, lifeless, by the lake's edge.

Time passed, and *Sahadeva* arrived, following the path Nakula had left through the underbrush. The youngest Pāndava paused at the sight of his brother sprawled upon the ground, but thirst drove him forward. As he bent to drink, the voice resounded once more. 'O son of *Madri*, answer my questions if you wish to drink.'

Like Nakula, Sahadeva ignored the warning, and like Nakula, he fell lifeless, the waters still rippling from his touch.

The forest seemed to conspire in silence as *Arjuna* arrived, his mighty *Gandiva* slung over his shoulder. His warrior's instinct tensed at the sight of his fallen brothers, but the lure of the water was irresistible. As he approached, the voice echoed yet again, commanding and unyielding. 'O son of *Kunti*, the waters are mine. Answer my questions, or suffer the fate of those who came before you.'

Arjuna's pride flared. 'Who dares to challenge Arjuna, wielder of Gandiva? Show yourself, spirit, or face my wrath!'

The lake remained still, the air heavy with unspoken menace. Arjuna, undeterred, dipped his hands into the water. But as the first drop touched his lips, his strength deserted him. The Gandiva slipped from his grasp, and he crumpled beside his brothers.

Finally, *Bhima*, the son of the wind, arrived. His towering frame moved with the force of a storm, his gaze dark with fury at the sight of his brothers' bodies. 'Who dares lay claim to this water?' he roared, his voice shaking the trees. 'Come forth, coward, and face the might of Bhima!'

But no foe emerged. Only the same voice replied, calm and implacable. 'Strength alone cannot claim these waters. Answer my questions, or perish.'

Bhima, like his brothers, dismissed the warning. His indomitable will was no match for the unseen force. As he drank, his great limbs faltered, and he too fell, joining his kin in lifeless stillness.

Hours passed before *Yudhishthira*, the eldest of the Pāndavas, found the trail. His heart sank as he entered the clearing and saw his brothers lying still beside the lake. The light of the setting sun bathed their forms in gold, but their stillness spoke of tragedy.

He approached cautiously, his warrior's instincts alert. 'Brothers!' he called, his voice breaking with anguish. But there was no answer.

The air grew heavy, and the voice, ancient and commanding, filled the clearing. 'O Yudhishthira, son of *Dharma*, your brothers have fallen because they ignored my warning. If you wish to drink, you must answer my questions. Fail, and you shall join them.'

Yudhishthira straightened, his grief tempered by his innate

sense of justice. 'Who are you, O guardian of this lake? Show yourself, and I shall answer as best I can.'

The water shimmered, and from its depths rose a *yaksha*. His celestial form was luminous, his eyes like twin stars burning with otherworldly wisdom. Draped in robes that seemed woven from moonlight, he regarded Yudhishthira with a gaze that pierced the veil of mortal thought.

Yaksha: You are wise, O Yudhishthira. If you wish to drink from my waters and restore life to your brothers, you must prove the depth of your wisdom. Answer my questions, and I shall decide your fate.

Yudhishthira: Ask what you will, O yaksha. If it is within my understanding, I shall answer.

The yaksha began, his questions testing not only intellect but the very essence of *dharma*. His tone carried neither malice nor mockery, only a weighty solemnity, as if the forest itself were holding its breath.

Yaksha: What makes the sun rise?

Yudhishthira: *Brahmā*. Brahmā makes the sun rise.

Yaksha: What sustains the sun in its journey?

Yudhishthira: Dharma sustains the sun in its eternal path.

Yaksha: And what causes the sun to set?

Yudhishthira: Truth brings the sun to its rest.

The yaksha's eyes, dark and deep as the abyss, gleamed with approval.

Yaksha: You speak well. Now tell me, what is swifter than the wind?

Yudhishthira: The mind is swifter than the wind, for it traverses realms in the blink of an eye.

Yaksha: What is more numerous than the stars?

Yudhishthira: Thoughts, O yaksha, for they fill the hearts and minds of all beings beyond measure.

Yaksha: Who is the true companion of a traveller?

Yudhishthira: Knowledge. For it guides and illuminates the way, even in the darkest times.

Yaksha: What is the greatest friend to one who stays at home?

Yudhishthira: A spouse who embodies virtue and compassion.

Yaksha: What is the greatest treasure?

Yudhishthira: Righteous conduct, for it enriches life beyond material wealth.

The questions came faster now, testing Yudhishthira's clarity of thought.

Yaksha: What is the greatest happiness?

Yudhishthira: Contentment is the greatest happiness, for it frees the heart from longing.

Yaksha: What is the greatest wonder in this world?

Yudhishthira: Day after day, countless beings pass into the realm of death, yet those who remain believe themselves immortal. This, O yaksha, is the greatest wonder.

The yaksha's expression remained inscrutable, but there was a flicker of something in his otherworldly eyes—a shadow of admiration.

Yaksha: What is the path? What is the ultimate guide for humanity?

Yudhishthira: Dharma is the path. And truth is the ultimate guide.

Yaksha: And what is the greatest enemy of humanity?

Yudhishthira: Anger, for it consumes the self and others alike.

Yaksha: What is the antidote to sorrow?

Yudhishthira: Patience and wisdom are the only remedies for sorrow.

Yaksha: What is the surest way to immortality?

Yudhishthira: Acts of virtue and righteousness, which live on even after death.

The yaksha paused, his gaze piercing through Yudhishthira's very soul.

Yaksha: What makes a man truly wealthy?

Yudhishthira: Contentment and generosity make a man truly wealthy.

Yaksha: And what is the greatest strength?

Yudhishthira: Forgiveness, for it requires both power and grace.

The forest seemed to grow still, the air heavy with expectation as the yaksha asked his final question.

Yaksha: What is the essence of life?

Yudhishthira: Sacrifice is the essence of life, for it sustains all beings and upholds the universe itself.

The yaksha fell silent for a long moment, his form shimmering like the surface of a moonlit lake.

Yaksha: You have answered well, O son of dharma. Your wisdom surpasses all others, and your devotion to dharma is unshaken. I am pleased. Choose one of your brothers to revive.

Yudhishthira: Revive Nakula, son of Madri, so that both my mothers, Kunti and Madri, may have a living son.

The yaksha, moved by Yudhishthira's fairness, revealed his true form.

Yaksha: I am Dharma, your celestial father. Your righteousness and wisdom have pleased me greatly. I shall restore all your brothers to life.

With a wave of his hand, Dharma brought the Pāndavas back from the brink of death. They rose, their strength renewed, their hearts filled with gratitude for their eldest brother's virtue.

The King Who Bore A Son

From The Mahābhārata

In the ancient kingdom of the *Ikshvaku* dynasty, where golden sunlight bathed verdant fields and the air hummed with celestial chants, there reigned King *Yuvanashva*. Renowned for his valour and wisdom, Yuvanashva's kingdom flourished under his rule. Yet beneath the veneer of prosperity lay a silent grief, a shadow that clouded his heart—a childless king, he yearned for an heir to continue his lineage.

Despite numerous *yajnas* and the counsel of sages, the gods seemed deaf to his prayers. The king's court was filled with murmurs, the unspoken fear that the royal line would fade into obscurity. Yuvanashva's queens, adorned in silks that shimmered like twilight skies, shared his sorrow but could offer no solace. Determined to find a solution, the king turned to the great sages for divine intervention.

In time, a conclave of *rishis*, their ashen robes billowing like storm clouds, arrived in Yuvanashva's court. They performed a powerful yajna, invoking the divine energies to bless the queens with progeny. Amidst the sacred fires and the chanting of *mantras*, the sages prepared a potion imbued with the essence of fertility—its golden liquid glowing faintly as if kissed by the sun itself. It was to be consumed by the queens, ensuring the birth of a child who would be both noble and virtuous.

But fate, with its capricious nature, intervened.

One night, whilst the kingdom lay under the spell of a moonlit tranquillity, Yuvanashva found himself wandering the grounds of the yajna. The flames of the sacrificial altar still flickered in the distance, casting a warm, ethereal glow. Thirst gripped him suddenly—an all-consuming need that seemed to rise from the depths of his being. Drawn by instinct, he stumbled upon the golden vessel holding the sacred potion. Mistaking it for water, he drank deeply, the cool liquid sliding down his throat like a river of light.

The sages, upon discovering what had transpired, were struck with awe and dread. 'O king!' they exclaimed, their voices trembling, 'the potion was not meant for you! It was crafted to bless your queens with a child. Yet what is done cannot be undone. The divine powers will now manifest within you.'

And so it came to pass that Yuvanashva, a man, bore within him the seed of life.

The news spread like wildfire, stirring disbelief and wonder across the land. The king, though startled by the turn of events, accepted his fate with dignity, embodying the dharma of one who surrenders to the will of the gods.

Months passed, and the king's body transformed in ways that dumbfounded human understanding. The sages tended to him, their chants weaving a protective cocoon around the miraculous event. Yuvanashva, however, grappled with profound emotional turmoil. He feared judgement and ridicule, yet he also felt a deep sense of awe and responsibility. The king often found himself questioning the gods' will. Would he be seen as a king who upheld dharma or as one who disrupted the natural order?

When the time came, the gods themselves intervened. From Yuvanashva's side emerged a radiant child, a boy whose very cries seemed to echo with divine blessings. The earth rejoiced; rivers swelled with joy, and the heavens rained flowers upon the kingdom.

Yet, amidst the jubilations, Yuvanashva found himself wrestling with an extraordinary situation. The child, born of his own body, now sought sustenance. 'Who will nurse and nourish the child?' the king wondered, his voice laden with a mixture of panic, awe, and worry.

It was then that *Indra*, king of the gods, descended in a radiant blaze, his golden armour shimmering like the midday sun. 'Fear not, O Yuvanashva,' he proclaimed, his voice carrying the weight of celestial authority. 'I shall sustain him.' With that, Indra placed his forefinger into the crying infant's mouth.

And when the wielder of the thunderbolt uttered,

'*Mama dhata*'—'He will suck me'—the denizens of heaven came together to name the child *Mandhata*. The boy, having tasted the divine forefinger of Indra, was instantly endowed with great strength.

From that moment forth, the child was nourished by the grace of the gods, growing in strength and wisdom under their divine protection.

Mandhata would go on to become one of the greatest rulers to ever walk the earth, his mighty deeds enshrined forever in the hymns of sages and in the hearts of his people.

As for Yuvanashva, he continued to reign with unmatched wisdom, his miraculous experience having bestowed upon him a profound understanding of life's deepest mysteries.

The First Bittersweet Romance

From The Mahābhārata

In a kingdom where the rivers sang to the skies and the winds carried the scent of blooming flowers, King *Pururavas* reigned—a man of unmatched beauty and grace, destined to be remembered in the stories of mortals and gods. He ruled his land with a heart that beat for his people, his courage unyielding and his wisdom profound. Yet, despite all his splendour, there was a longing within him, a yearning for a love that transcended the boundaries of time and realm.

One day, amidst the celestial realms, *Urvashi*—the *Apsarā* (celestial nymph) of unparalleled beauty and grace—performed a dance in the court of *Indra*, the king of the gods. But her steps faltered, her mind lost in thoughts of Pururavas, whose fame as a mortal with divine qualities had reached the heavens. The lapse did not go unnoticed. Indra, angered, cursed Urvashi to live among mortals until her bond with one of them brought her heartbreak.

Banished from the celestial abode, Urvashi descended to Earth, her feet touching mortal soil for the first time. The forest where she appeared was dense and alive, with sunlight filtering through the leaves like liquid gold. As she wandered, the whispering wind carried her to Pururavas' court, where she saw him for the first time—a man who looked as though he had been sculpted by the gods themselves.

Their eyes met, and time seemed to hold its breath. For Pururavas, she was a vision of ethereal beauty, her very presence making the world around him fade into insignificance. For Urvashi, he was a blend of mortal strength and divine charm, a being who stirred her heart in ways she had never known.

Pururavas:

'O goddess fair, whose form doth shine,
Like moonlit rays in twilight's prime,
What art thou, in mortal guise?
Thine eyes sparkling like starlit skies.
O wondrous beauty, gentle and bright,
A vision to behold in the silver light!'

'I am Urvashi,' she said, her voice soft as the first drizzle of rain, 'cast from the heavens to walk among mortals. I have heard of your valour and handsomeness, O king, and I seek your protection.'

Pururavas knelt before her, as if before a goddess. 'Lady, you need no protection from the likes of me. But if it is in my power to shelter you, I will do so with all my heart.'

Thus began their tale of love, a bond that seemed to defy the boundaries of their worlds. Yet, even in her affection, Urvashi set a condition. 'My king, there is but one vow I ask of you. Never let me see you naked, for the sanctity of our bond rests upon this promise.'

Pururavas agreed, his heart too full of love to question her terms. Together, they created a paradise on Earth, their love the envy of all who beheld them. Urvashi brought an otherworldly joy to his life, her laughter ringing like bells and her touch as light as the breeze. Pururavas, in turn, gave her a sense of belonging she had never known among the gods.

Urvashi:

'Sweet love, thy touch is heaven's grace,

I find no sorrow in thy face.

In every breath, in every sigh,

We touch the earth, we kiss the sky.

No mortal dream, no fleeting hour,

Shall dim the light of this love's power.'

Pururavas:

'O Urvashi, my heart's delight,

In thee, all joy doth take its flight.

Let time stand still, let fate delay,

For in thy arms, I wish to stay.

The world may change, the stars may fall,

But in thy love, I need no more.'

Years passed like fleeting shadows, and their love remained steadfast. Yet, the *gandharvas*, celestial beings who had once shared Urvashi's laughter, grew restless in her absence. Unable to bear her exile among mortals, they devised a plan to separate her from Pururavas.

One moonlit night, as the lovers rested in their chambers, the gandharvas stole into the palace's royal paddocks and carried away the lambs Urvashi cherished dearly. Their plaintive cries woke her, and she turned to Pururavas, her voice trembling. 'My king, the lambs! They are my companions, my solace in this mortal world. Save them, I beg you.'

Pururavas, bound by his love for her, rushed to their rescue. Unthinking, he ran into the night unclothed, intent on confronting the thieves. At that moment, the gandharvas unleashed a flash of divine light, illuminating the king in his vulnerable state. Urvashi, witnessing this, was bound by the curse that had tied her to Earth. The condition of their union was broken.

The morning found Urvashi standing by the gates of the palace, her form shimmering with the light of her celestial nature. Tears streamed down her face as she prepared to leave. Pururavas, realising his mistake, fell to his knees before her.

'Do not go,' he pleaded, his voice breaking. 'I cannot bear a life without you.'

Urvashi looked at him, her own heart heavy with sorrow. 'My king, our love was destined to be fleeting. The gods have bound me to the heavens once more. But know this—my love for you is eternal.'

With a final, aching gaze, she ascended to the heavens, leaving Pururavas behind. The palace, once filled with their laughter and love, now seemed a hollow shell.

Pururavas's life after Urvashi's departure was a shadow of its former self. His once-vibrant court, filled with joy and laughter, became a hollow place of memories and longing. The king wandered through forests and mountains, calling out her name, his voice echoing in the wilderness. His heart ached with an emptiness only her presence could fill. His once-brilliant eyes were clouded with grief, his voice tinged with longing. Even the earth seemed to mourn with him, the flowers drooping and the rivers murmuring in sympathy.

Pururavas:

'Alas! The gods are cruel to man,
And love is, but a fleeting span.
What joy is there in life's bright gleam,
If love is lost, a broken dream?
I've walked the earth, I've searched the skies,
Yet haven't found her sparkling eyes.

How shall I live, and to what end,

When all I sought was but to mend

A love now lost, a bond now torn,

That left me broken, shorn, and worn?'

Urvashi, too, felt the pangs of separation. Though back in Indra's court, her heart remained tethered to Pururavas. Their love, forged in the meeting of earthbound and celestial, had transcended the barriers of their realms, leaving them forever yearning for what could have been.

Urvashi:

In heaven's halls I roam, yet dream of thee,

Thy face, thy voice, thy touch, are all I see.

Did gods decree our love to burn so bright,

And snuff it out in shadows of the night?

One fleeting hour, a breath, a starry kiss,

And now, alas, there is but emptiness.

The heavens call, and surely I must heed,

Yet 'tis thy name my soul shall ever need.

To thee, my heart, and to thy earthly shore,

I would return—if only fate allowed me more.

One day, deep in the forest, Pururavas encountered the gandharvas who had orchestrated their separation. 'Why did you take her from me?' he cried out, his voice trembling with a mix of anger and despair.

Gandharvas:

'Thou seekest what can't be attained,
A dream, a wish, a joy unfeigned.
Return, O king, arrest your plight,
For she doth dwell in realms of light,
No mortal man, no flesh, no thought,
Doth enter godly worlds unsought.'

Pururavas:

'Then let me die, if I must part
From that which once did fill my heart.
For life without her is unjust,
A fleeting shadow, bound to dust.'

The gandharvas, moved by his devotion, relented. 'Your love is true, O king. We cannot undo what has been done, but we can grant you a boon. For a single night each year, Urvashi may descend to Earth and be with you.'

Though the gift was a mere shadow of what he had lost, Pururavas accepted it with gratitude. Each year, on that fateful night, he and Urvashi would reunite, their love burning as brightly as ever. Yet, as dawn broke, she would return to the heavens, leaving him to face the emptiness of his mortal life once more.

The tale of Pururavas and Urvashi is haunting in its lament of love's impermanence and the bittersweet beauty of fleeting connections. It is said that the rivers of Pururavas' kingdom still echo his calls for Urvashi, and the moonlight carries whispers of their eternal love—a love that, though brief, transcended the boundaries of mortality and divinity.

The gods decreed their love was to be brief,
One night each year, free from all worldly ties,
A fleeting gift, cruel yet bittersweet,
Whispered softly by winds and starry skies.
They met again, in love's sweetened embrace,
Finding solace for just a single night.
The world around them faded, time stood still,
The heavens seemed to dim out every light.
During that fleeting time, their hearts were whole,
Bound by longing, in love's eternal state.
In pangs of an embrace that would be torn,
As dawn approached, they felt the tug of fate.
Yet in their hearts, their love remained complete,
No bond of time could ever make them turn.
Their longing, through endless days, bittersweet,
A year apart, their promised day they yearn.

Navagunjara: The Many Within the One

From The Sarala Mahābhārata

In the quiet wilderness, far from the echo of cities and palaces, *Arjuna* walked alone. His exile had begun with a vow broken for a cause he could not ignore. A *Brahmana* had come to him, frantic, pleading for help—his cattle stolen by thieves. Arjuna's bow, the divine *Gandiva*, was locked away in *Draupadi*'s chamber where she was with another brother. The law was sacred: none should enter in such a moment. But duty, the cry of dharma, drowned every hesitation. He stepped across the threshold, took Gandiva in hand, and with it sealed his punishment. Twelve years of solitude would now be his companion.

"What is dharma," he had asked himself, "if not to protect those in need? Yet every choice carves its own sorrow."

As he walked deeper into the wild, memory swept over him

like a sudden wind. He remembered how, years ago, the Gandiva had come to him in a moment of divine encounter. *Agni*, the fire-god, had once approached him disguised as a Brahmana, his hunger unbearable. He had pleaded for help to consume the *Khandava* forest, but Indra, Arjuna's own father, had thwarted him with storms. Agni, moved by Arjuna's resolve, summoned Varuna, who gifted him the Gandiva, two inexhaustible quivers, and a divine chariot.

With Krishna by his side, Arjuna had loosed a storm of arrows, shielding Agni's flames from the gods. The forest blazed, trees collapsing in fire, animals scattering in panic. Arjuna remembered the smoke curling like serpents into the sky, the air thick with the clash of fire and thunder. It was there that he had earned the bow that would now shape his destiny.

Time passed. The forests wrapped themselves around him like old, wordless storytellers. Trees whispered in the wind. Rivers offered him no reflection, only motion. In that vast silence, Arjuna wrestled with the weight of choice. The faces of his brothers and Draupadi came and went like drifting clouds. He missed *Krishna* most—his laughter, his insight, his unsettling truths.

Far away, Krishna searched for him. He travelled from one sacred grove to another, questioning sages, listening to winds, speaking to the silence itself. "Where is Arjuna?" he asked. But no one knew. No one could know. Arjuna had disappeared into the folds of his own seeking. And even Krishna, knower of time and thought, did not yet find him.

Eventually, Arjuna reached a solitary hill, high and shrouded in drifting mist. The forest thinned as he climbed, the path narrowing to nothing but stone and silence. At the summit, he sat down to meditate. Fog clung to the rocks and wrapped around his body like a shawl. The wind fell quiet. Even the birds did not call.

Then, all of a sudden, the earth trembled.

From the horizon rose a creature unlike anything Arjuna had ever seen. It moved with calm yet undeniable power. Its head was that of a rooster, sharp-eyed and majestic. A peacock's long neck curved with regal pride, feathers shimmering like a ripple of stars. A bull's hump rested on its back, steady and grounded. The waist of a lion rippled with strength, its tail that of a serpent, coiling and uncoiling with slow intent. Three legs carried it forward: one like an elephant's, one like a tiger's, one like a deer's. The fourth limb was a human arm, raised high, holding a pink lotus that pulsed with quiet light.

Arjuna's heart pounded. He reached for the Gandiva, pulling back the string, eyes narrowed.

But the creature did not attack. It stood still, its gaze unwavering. The lotus in its hand offered no threat—only presence.

Then a voice spoke, not through lips, but in Arjuna's mind.

"Behold! I am Navagunjara!

The forms of the supreme are countless.

What you have seen, heard, or imagined,

is but a drop in the infinite ocean.

Do you not recognise me, O Partha?"

The air felt thick with truth. Arjuna's hand trembled. He lowered the Gandiva.

A wave of shock swept through him. His breath caught in his throat, his eyes wide in disbelief. The vision before him was neither beast nor deity—it was something far greater, something beyond the grasp of thought. Awe took hold of him, rooting him to the earth. His heart thundered not from fear, but from the weight of understanding breaking through. This creature, terrifying and divine, was revealing to him something essential, something that language could never fully hold.

The creature remained silent. Its very stillness was a lesson. The composite form, strange and unsettling, spoke not of fear but of the vastness of reality. It was beauty and terror, unity and contradiction.

Arjuna bowed. Not because he understood—but because he realised how much he did not.

The creature shimmered, began to dissolve, and from its form emerged *Krishna*.

"Arjuna," he said, stepping forward, "the world is not made of simple things. You look for the divine in forms you can name—in friends, in fathers, in avatars. But the truth is not bound by form, or name, or mind."

Arjuna stood dumbfounded. He found his eyes closing on their own accord.

Krishna continued, "What frightens you today may teach you tomorrow. What seems strange may be closer to the divine than what you cherish. Surrender your fear. Surrender your pride. The dance of creation is wild and precise. It does not need your understanding—it asks for your openness."

Arjuna listened, every word lodging deeper than arrows ever could.

"When you see the infinite in the finite, the known in the unknown," Krishna said, "you will no longer be alone."

The forest returned to life. The wind stirred the trees. The birds sang again.

Arjuna slowly opened his eyes.

The memory of the creature lingered—not as fear, but as invitation. His exile was not a punishment. It was a journey into something larger than kingship or war. It was a path to truth, clothed in uncertainty.

Later, Krishna found him. Their embrace needed no words.

And *Navagunjara* remained within him—a vision, a reminder, a guide.

"The forms of the supreme truth are countless.

What we have heard, seen or imagined is just a drop."

Afterword

Dear Reader,

As you close the final chapter of *Epic Kathā: Stories from the Vedas, Puranas, Upanishads, Ramayana, Mahabharata and Folklore*, you stand at the edge of a vast and shimmering ocean—the ocean of knowledge contained within the stories of Hindu scriptures. What you hold in your hands is but a drop from that endless expanse, a glimpse of the treasures that lie within the Vedas, Upanishads, Purānas, and epics.

Hinduism is a tradition that has never confined itself to a single path or perspective. Instead, it celebrates diversity, embracing countless ways of understanding life, the universe, and the divine. Stories play a central role in this tradition, serving as bridges between the ordinary and the extraordinary, the mortal and the divine.

In these stories, the gods and sages are not distant, unattainable figures but mirrors of human nature, embodying our strengths, weaknesses, and potential. When Indra slays Vritra and frees the rivers, we see not only the might of a deity but also a reflection of our own struggles to overcome obstacles and restore flow to our lives. When Nachiketā seeks the ultimate truth from Yama, we are reminded of our own quest for answers to the eternal mysteries of life and death.

This book has sought to bring these stories closer to you, dear reader. It has illuminated their layers of meaning, weaving them into a tapestry of wisdom that is as relevant today as it was thousands of years ago. The tales you have encountered are not just relics from the past but living lessons, waiting to inspire and guide you.

One of the most profound aspects of Hindu storytelling is its ability to hold space for contradictions and paradoxes. Consider the hymn of creation from the Rig Veda, which questions its own narrative and leaves the origin of the universe shrouded in mystery. This openness to uncertainty is a hallmark of Hindu thought, inviting us to sit with questions rather than rush to answers.

The wisdom of these stories lies not in their conclusions but in their capacity to provoke contemplation. The tale of Svetaketū and the banyan seed, for instance, challenges us to see the infinite in the finite, to recognise the unseen essence that underlies all existence. It is a call to look beyond appearances and seek the deeper truths that connect us to the cosmos.

As you reflect on these tales, I invite you to carry their lessons into your life. The stories of Hindu scriptures are not meant to remain on the page; they are meant to be lived, to be experienced in the choices we make, the relationships we nurture, and the paths we walk. They remind us of the interconnectedness of all things, urging us to live with humility, compassion, and awareness.

The beauty of storytelling is its ability to grow with us. Each time we return to these tales, we find new insights, new meanings, and new connections. They evolve as we evolve, offering guidance and inspiration at every stage of our journey.

In a world often dominated by noise and haste, these ancient stories invite us to pause, listen, and reflect. They are a reminder of the timeless truths that underpin our existence, truths that can be glimpsed in a humble seed, a flowing river, or a quiet moment of meditation.

Let this book be the beginning of a deeper exploration. Beyond these pages lies an entire universe of narratives waiting to be discovered. Whether you delve into the Purānas, explore the philosophical discourses of the Upanishads, or immerse yourself in the epics, you will find stories that resonate with your own experiences and aspirations.

Remember, dear reader, that the ocean of knowledge is vast, but each drop contains the essence of the whole. In the same way, these stories, though few in number, hold within them the wisdom of the infinite. They are gifts from the sages and seers who sought to understand the mysteries of existence and share their insights with the world.

As you journey forward, may the light of these stories guide you. May they inspire you to seek, to question, and to grow. And may you always carry with you the knowledge—that you too, are a part of this eternal story—a story that is still unfolding, a story in which you are both the teller and the told.

With gratitude and reverence,

Deepam Chatterjee

Bhāratvarsha

Acknowledgements

As I present *Epic Kathā: Stories from the Vedas, Puranas, Upanishads, Ramayana, Mahabharata and Folklore* to you, my heart is brimming with gratitude for all those who have been a part of this journey.

First and foremost, I express my deepest thanks to my publisher, Sohin Lakhani, for believing in this book and for his unwavering support and encouragement. His enthusiasm for these timeless stories has been an inspiration to me every step of the way. To my editor, Aruna Joshi, I am deeply grateful for her keen eye, thoughtful suggestions, and tireless efforts in shaping this manuscript into its best form. I must also thank the immensely talented artist Onkar Fondekar, whose illustrations have brought these stories to life.

My parents Varun and Manjushree kindled my love for storytelling. The countless magical evenings we have spent together, with them listening to my tales, will remain etched in my memory forever. They have laid the foundation for my lifelong fascination with the wisdom of stories.

I am profoundly thankful to the listeners and readers who have embraced my stories over the years. Your encouragement has been the guiding light that has kept my passion alive and this dream thriving.

Finally, my deepest gratitude is reserved for the great teachers and ancient masters who, through their wisdom and insight, have shared the eternal truths hidden within these simple yet profound stories. Their timeless teachings are the heart of this book, and it is an honour to carry forward their legacy in my humble way.

This book is a labour of love, an offering to all who seek wisdom, connection, and inspiration in stories of yore. Thank you for being part of this journey.

Glossary

Note: These Sanskrit terms have evolved over millennia of Indian philosophical and religious thought, often containing multiple layers of meaning depending on context and tradition.

A

Ādi Shakti - The primordial divine feminine energy; the original creative power from which all existence emerges

Agni Vidyā - Sacred knowledge of fire sacrifice; ritual teachings about fire worship

Amrita - The nectar of immortality obtained from the churning of the cosmic ocean

Ānanda - Bliss; eternal joy; divine happiness that comes from union with Brahman

Andajas - Those born of eggs (one of the four types of creation)

Anna - Food; nourishment; sustenance that supports all life

Anusuyā - Wife of Sage Atri, known for her virtue

Apasmāra - The demon representing ignorance, delusion, and spiritual darkness

Apas - Water; the primordial element of water in creation

Apsarā - Celestial nymph or divine maiden who dances in the courts of the gods

Āshram - A hermitage or spiritual retreat; the dwelling place of a sage or ascetic

Ātman - The self; the individual soul; the true essence of a person that is eternal

Aum - The sacred primordial sound; the cosmic vibration that underlies all creation

B

Bhāratvarsha - Ancient name for the Indian subcontinent; land of Bharata

Bhikshātana - Shiva in his form as a wandering mendicant or beggar ascetic

Brahmaloka - The celestial abode of Lord Brahmā

Brahman - The ultimate reality; the supreme, unchanging truth that pervades everything; universal consciousness

C

Chakshu - Eye; the organ of sight; vision

Chatur-Yugas - The four cosmic ages (Satya, Tretā, Dvapara, Kāli Yuga)

Chhāyā - Shadow; also the name of the shadow-wife created by Sanjna

D

Damaru - The small hourglass-shaped drum carried by Shiva, representing the cosmic sound of creation

Dānava - A class of demons, descendants of Danu

Dharma - Righteous duty, moral law, or the cosmic principle of order and justice; the natural order that maintains harmony in the universe

Dhruva-tāra - The pole star, named after Prince Dhruva

Drishtadyumna - Name meaning "one with a bright splendor"; Draupadi's twin brother born from the sacrificial fire

G

Gandharvas - Celestial musicians and singers who serve in the courts of the gods

Ghee - Clarified butter used in religious rituals and cooking

Gurukula - Traditional residential school where students live with and learn from a teacher

H

Hāhā and Hūhū - Two celestial Gandharva musicians

Hala - Balarama's divine plough weapon

Halāhala - The deadly poison that emerged during the churning of the cosmic ocean

I

Ilā - The feminine form/name of Prince Sudyumna when transformed by divine curse

J

Jarayujas - Those born of wombs (one of the four types of creation)

K

Kailāsa - Mount Kailāsh, Shiva's abode

Kapāla - A skull used as a begging bowl, often carried by ascetics

Kusa/Kusha - Sacred grass used in Hindu rituals and ceremonies

L

Leelā - Divine play or cosmic sport; the playful activities of the divine

Linga - The symbolic representation of Shiva, neither wholly form nor formless

M

Mahādeva - "Great God," an epithet for Shiva

Mahāmāya - The great divine illusion; the cosmic power that creates the appearance of the material world

Mahāyogi - "Great Yogi," referring to Shiva as the supreme ascetic

Mama dhata - "He will suck me" - Indra's words when he placed his finger in baby Mandhata's mouth

Manas - Mind; the thinking faculty; consciousness that processes thoughts and emotions

Mantras - Sacred sounds, words, or phrases repeated in prayer or meditation

N

Nachiketa Agni - The sacred fire named after Nachiketā; a specific ritual fire sacrifice

Nāsadiya Sūkta - "The Hymn of Creation" from the Rig

Veda; a philosophical hymn about the origin of the universe

Natarāja - Shiva as the "Lord of Dance," representing the cosmic dancer

Neelkanth - "Blue-throated," the name given to Shiva after drinking the poison

P

Parameshwara - Supreme Lord, another name for Shiva

Pāshupatāstra - A divine weapon of immense destructive power, associated with Lord Shiva

Prasād - Blessed food that has been offered to a deity and then distributed to devotees as a divine blessing

Pralayāgni - The fire of dissolution or cosmic destruction

Prāna - Life-force; vital breath; the energy that animates all living beings

Purusha Sūkta - "The Hymn of the Cosmic Being" from the Rig Veda; describes the sacrifice of the cosmic man

R

Rajas - One of the three fundamental qualities of nature; the energy of activity, passion, and creation

Rishis - Sages or seers; ancient wise men who received divine knowledge and have attained spiritual knowledge

Rudrāksha - Sacred seeds worn by Shiva's devotees

S

Sāl - A type of large deciduous tree native to the Indian subcontinent, often found in forests and considered sacred

Samudra - Ocean

Samudra Manthan - The churning of the cosmic ocean by gods and demons

Samsāra - The endless cycle of birth, death, and rebirth that souls go through until they achieve liberation

Saptarishis - The seven great sages

Sat - True Being; existence; reality; the fundamental principle of creation

Sattva - One of the three fundamental qualities of nature; the energy of balance, harmony, and purity

Setu - Bridge or causeway; specifically refers to the bridge built by Rāma's army to cross the ocean to Lanka

Shakti - Divine feminine power; the dynamic energy that drives all creation and transformation

Shankha - Conch shell, Vishnu's weapon

Sharavana - Name of the enchanted forest sacred to Goddess Pārvati where only women could enter safely

Shāstras - Sacred texts; religious scriptures; authoritative spiritual writings

Shrotra - Ear; the organ of hearing; the faculty of listening

Soma Rasa - The divine nectar or drink of the gods; provides immortality and strength

Sudarshana Chakra - Vishnu's discus weapon

Sūryavamsa - The Solar Dynasty, a legendary lineage of kings

Svāhā - Goddess of sacrificial chants; also an exclamation meaning "so be it"

Svedajas - Those born of sweat (one of the four types of creation)

T

Tamas - One of the three fundamental qualities of nature; the energy of inertia, destruction, and transformation

Tāndava - The cosmic dance of creation and destruction, particularly associated with Lord Shiva; Shiva's cosmic dance of creation, preservation, and destruction

Tapasyā - Intense spiritual austerity, penance, or meditation performed to gain divine favor, spiritual power, or enlightenment

Tat Tvam Asi - "That thou art"; a profound statement meaning "you are that ultimate reality"

Tejas - Fire; the element of fire; divine radiance or brilliance

Tretā Yuga - The second cosmic age

Trishūl - Shiva's trident weapon

Tulsi - Sacred basil plant, dear to Vishnu

U

Udbhijas - Those born of germination (one of the four types of creation)

V

Vaikuntha - Vishnu's celestial abode

Vajra - Indra's thunderbolt weapon; represents indestructible truth and spiritual power

Vajrayudha - Indra's thunderbolt weapon, made from sage Dadheechi's spine

Vānaras - Monkey-like beings or forest dwellers; the monkey warriors who served in Rāma's army, including Hanumān and Sugriva

Varnas - The four traditional social divisions in Hindu society (Brahmins, Kshatriyas, Vaishyas, Shudras)

Vibhūti - Sacred ash worn by devotees of Shiva, symbolizing the destruction of ego and illusion

Vijnāna - Intelligence; discriminating wisdom; the faculty that discerns truth from falsehood

Vrata - A religious vow or observance, often involving fasting, specific rituals, or spiritual practices undertaken for a set period

Y

Yajna - Sacred fire ritual or sacrifice; ceremony of offering to the gods; performed to honor the gods, seek their blessings, or maintain cosmic harmony

Yajnaseni - "Daughter of the yajna" - another name for Draupadi, referring to her birth from the sacrificial fire

Yaksha - A class of nature spirits or demigods, often guardians of treasures or sacred places

Yuga - Cosmic age or epoch

About the Author

Deepam Chatterjee is a Happiness Coach and Corporate Speaker on 'Healthy Mind-Body-Spirit'. A former Army Captain and NDA alumnus, he writes on Hindu thought, spirituality, mysticism, and wellness, with regular columns in The Telegraph and The Daily Guardian. A keen chronicler of lost myths and oral traditions, he blends ancient Indian wisdom with modern living. After retiring from the Army, he explored filmmaking and trained under spiritual masters like Sri Sri Ravi Shankar and the Dalai Lama, shaping his journey of inner growth.